Call Me Myra

By
David R. Cummings

PublishAmerica
Baltimore

© 2004 by David R. Cummings
All rights reserved. No part of this book may be reproduced, stored in a retrieval system or transmitted in any form or by any means without the prior written permission of the publishers, except by a reviewer who may quote brief passages in a review to be printed in a newspaper, magazine or journal.

First printing

ISBN: 1-4137-1406-4
PUBLISHED BY PUBLISHAMERICA, LLLP
www.publishamerica.com
Baltimore

Printed in the United States of America

To my loving friends that stood by me through many troublesome years and encouraged me to go on.

*Many people have read my works and offered their
kind opinions, both good and bad, but only one put
forth a helping hand. This act of friendship was
from the helpful heart of
Barbara Guilland.
And will not soon be forgotten.*

Chapter 1

The old man lay bleeding, his feet in the stream. Clutched tightly in his hand, a lock of brown hair waved slowly in the passing current. His face was swollen and distorted. There seemed to be blood everywhere. Two fishermen in their twenties stood over him and spoke in horrified whispers.

"Holy smoke, Dan, what do you think we should do?" the younger of the two whispered.

"Don't know," Dan Wallace answered. "But I think the first thing is to drag him out of the water."

Pulling the old man onto the bank, they knelt beside him. He opened his eyes and tried to speak. Dan bent close to him and he heard a raspy whisper, "Myra, Myra, Myra." The old man let out a long breath that seemed to Dan like a sigh of sadness and lay very still; his life was gone.

Lester Dunn squeaked:

"What should we do now, Dan? Is he dead?"

"I think so. How the hell do I know?"

Dan snapped, "Look, Les, you go back to the pickup and see if you can raise someone on the CB. I'll go back to the shack we saw by that waterfall to see if maybe that's where he lived. You take the fishing gear with you and if you can't raise anyone on the CB, drive the truck down to that little road where the milk can is. I think that's the driveway to the shack."

Dan started toward the cabin with long hurried strides and thought *that darned Les sounded like a moose crashing through the woods.* He hoped he didn't break his fool neck.

The cabin had three rooms and a large porch. Dan peered through a tattered old screen door. He knocked and called hello twice, then stepped inside. There was a fire going in the old wood stove and the table was set for two. He called hello again and stepped into the bedroom. The bed was made and Dan noticed how clean and neat everything looked. The sound of his truck coming up the drive took away the creepy feeling he had and he stepped back onto the porch.

Les came to a dusty stop by the corner of the shack, and yelled.

"Is there anyone home?"

"No, there isn't, Les. Did you get someone on the CB?"

"Yeah, I raised the guy in the general store at Travis Corners, and he's calling the cops. He knows where this place is, and he'll tell the cops how to get here."

Sheriff Theodore "Ted" Tate was having a good day. His brother Terry had called and was coming for a visit. This meant he would get in some fishing and have a chance to get even with Terry on the chessboard. Darlene got on well with Terry's wife Vicki and he was really looking forward to Saturday. He had been parked by an old barn on Hi-way 3K for over an hour and not one speeder. Must be the weather, he thought. He slipped the Ford into gear and eased out on the road just as the very excited voice of his office girl and all-round gal Friday crackled on the radio.

"Sheriff Tate, you'd better get out to the store at Travis Corners; they found a body!"

"Margaret, did you get any more information?"

"No, Sheriff, just that some boys from Logan found a body and it sounds like it could be that old prospector fellow that moved into the cabin out on the Downs place."

"Okay, Margaret, you call what's his name at the Travis Corners store and tell him I'm going directly to the cabin since I'm closer to there by several miles and we'll let him know what we find."

"All right, Sheriff – you remember I was going home early today?"

"Yes, Margaret, I know, but would you stick around till we make some sense out of things and Paul comes in?"

"Is Paul coming in early?"

"Yes, Margaret, when you asked to get off early, I had him come in."

"Where are you now, Sheriff?"

"I'm at the Tom Creek Bridge and I'll be at the cabin in about three or four minutes."

"Okay, Sheriff, keep us posted!"

"Yes. Margaret."

Tate eased the patrol car into the clearing below the cabin and saw two young men standing by a new metallic blue pickup. It was one of those city pickups with all the gewgaws in the world on it. He wondered what they were doing in country like this with a rig like that. He clicked the mike and said, "Margaret, I'm there now. Run a check on a Chevy pickup, license YAD 244 – pronto."

He turned his attention to the two men in front of his car.

"I'm Sheriff Tate; I understand you fellas found a body?"

Dan spoke first. "We sure did. It's an old man. He was lying almost in the creek and he's all beat up and covered with blood."

The radio squawked, "No wants or warrants on that license, Sheriff."

"Okay, Margaret, thanks."

"Boys, how far is the body?"

Dan pointed and said, "About 200 yards."

"Could I get you fellas' names?"

"I'm Dan Wallace and this here is Les Dunn. We're from Logan."

Tate knelt by the lifeless form and started making mental notes.

The man was about sixty or older, slight build, clean-shaven and dressed in clean but well-worn clothes. His face was a mess, swollen and twisted from an obvious beating. The upper part of his body was drenched in blood and the first signs of rigor mortis had set in.

"Was he alive when you found him?" Tate queried.

Les squeaked, "Yeah, he was out in the creek."

"Did you pull him out of the water while he was still alive?"

"Yeah, Dan and I did, yeah."

"Then I gather from what you have told me that he has been dead about an hour. Is that right?"

"Yeah, about an hour. That's right, yeah."

Tate looked down at the still form and wondered about the life that had so recently lived there. He then noticed the clenched fist and the lock of brown hair. This job must be getting to me he thought. It's only 2:15 on Wednesday and I'm already beat. Tate looked around the area and saw no reason to feel anyone would disturb any thing that could amount to evidence. He got to his feet and brushed the sand off his knees. Dan and Les stood close to each other, looking like a couple of statues.

"You guys come with me. We'll go back and call for an ambulance, get some information in case we need you, and then you can go home."

It was 3:05 when a tired sheriff sent the two boys from Logan on their way. He had called for the ambulance and figured it would be there in about twenty minutes. He had some time to relax, and maybe look around a little. The kitchen was as clean as a pin and the table was set for two. The stove was still warm, but there was nothing on the top except a whistling teakettle. He looked in the bath room and there was nothing unusual there, just men's stuff. The bed in the bedroom was made with hospital corners and there wasn't a wrinkle in the spread. Most men don't make beds that way, Tate thought. He looked in the closet and the dresser and found nothing; the place was almost sanitary. He stood looking out the window and wondered what could have gone on here that would lead to such a violent death of the old man.

As he turned to go, he noticed the bedspread on the backside was crooked like someone had put something under the bed. He bent over to look and found one of the floorboards near the head of the bed was pried up and was on top of the other flooring. He moved the board and found it covered a box-like hole, about six inches by twelve, and ten inches deep. Must be where the old boy kept his goodies, he thought. The hole was empty and the thought of robbery crossed his mind. The corner was dark and visibility was not the best, so Tate had not seen it, but when he stood up, there was blood on his hand and shirtsleeve, where he had rubbed against the wall. He turned on a little pocket flashlight he carried and saw the entire corner was smeared with partly dried blood. When he walked through the kitchen, he tore off three paper towels from a roll on the sink counter and wiping his hands, went out on the porch. There was an old swing at one end of the porch and he sat down, trying to piece things together. He heard the sound of a car coming up the drive and saw the flashing lights through the trees. The ambulance pulled into the clearing, followed closely by a patrol car driven by Paul Bench, Tate's young deputy.

"Good boy," Tate said, "I can sure use you. The body is about two hundred yards down stream in a little clearing. Take these two ambulance guys and go get him. Take a body bag and don't disturb anything you don't have to."

Paul said, "You look like hell, sheriff. Why don't you take it easy for a while? The boys and I can handle it. Okay?"

"Yeah, sure, Paul, just don't screw up anything in the way of evidence."

The three men headed out on their mission and Tate was glad to have been relieved of the task. He was standing by the patrol car when he noticed a little shed like a pump house, only smaller, that he hadn't seen before. It was back in the trees a little ways and about the same color as the woods around it; he walked over. The structure was an old light plant that had been used before the Power Company came through with service. Other than parts of an old generator, the shed was empty. He turned to leave when he saw it. It was a pick-handle lying in the ferns about ten feet from the shed and covered with blood. He used the paper towel he was wiping his hands on and picking it up by the wedge end carried it back and placed it in the trunk of his car.

It was almost five o'clock when his deputy returned with the body and they were ready to go.

"Paul, you take charge of getting the body back to the Coroner's office. Make sure you get it logged in properly and write up your report, so I can have it by morning. Okay, Paul?"

"Sure thing, sheriff, don't you worry about a thing; I'll do a good job. Why don't you go home and get a good night's sleep? I'll see you in the morning."

"Thanks, Paul. Good night."

It was 6:05 when he passed Travis Corners and Tate realized he had not eaten all day. Oh well, maybe Darlene would fix him a sandwich when he got home. It had been a long day.

Chapter 2

Al Blessing felt like a million. He had completed the largest sale of his career. His boss had spoken about a promotion and given him the rest of the week off. He was on his way home to Donna. He smiled—home to Donna. It seemed funny that after all these years he would still feel a rush when he even thought about Donna. The afternoon was warm, and with his sleeves rolled up and the window rolled down he felt great.

He slowed the Chevy wagon for a tight curve and then slammed on the brakes. He pulled almost off the road to avoid a woman who had stumbled out of nowhere and almost fell into the road in front of him. The car came to a stop on the far shoulder and Al was out of the seat and running back to her before his heartbeats caught up with him. He knew he hadn't struck her, but she was covered with blood and sobbing hysterically.

"Good lord, girl, what happened?"

When she spoke between the tears, all Al could understand was, "He… He… I…"

"Did some man do this to you?"

"Hurrrt me, I…" she gurgled.

She slumped in his grasp and almost bumped her head on the pavement. She wasn't very heavy, but as limp as she was, she was hard to carry. He finally got her into the car and headed for the little town up the road about six miles. Once on the road, he looked over at her. She was a pretty woman and he wondered how could some man do this to a nice little girl like her. She had probably been raped and he thought how embarrassed she would be when the law, or somebody, started to ask questions. She stirred and tried to sit up.

"No, no, don't move. We'll be at the hospital in a few minutes and they'll take care of you."

Her eyes got wide and a strange bubble formed on her swollen lips as she yelled.

"NO, NO, UGH, CAN'T TELL THEM."

"What do you mean you can't tell them? Don't you want to get the guy that did this to you?"

She shook her head wildly, and said,

"NO, CAN'T TELL – NO HOSPITAL."

"If you don't want to go to the hospital, where do you want to go?"

She whispered, "Take me home."

Again, she fell unconscious against the car door. *Home is a good idea* Al thought. Donna could help. He pushed the Chevy a little faster; home and Donna were only twenty minutes away.

Donna Blessing saw their car jerk to a stop in the drive by the back door; then she saw her husband get out and run around to the passenger side. She stepped onto the porch and caught sight of the figure of a woman slumped in the front seat.

"Al, honey, what's going on? What's?"

She stopped short when she saw the bloody right side of the woman's head.

"Good lord, Al, did you have an accident?"

"No, dear, I found her alongside of the road. She's been beaten and I think raped; help me get her in the house."

"What? Oh, Al, don't you think we should get her to a doctor?"

"Not now, Donna; help me."

Donna gave a small whistle when she entered the kitchen and sat by her husband.

"Well, she's all cleaned up and sleeping like a baby. What now?"

Al hunched his shoulders.

"I guess we should find out who she is. I found this wallet in her jacket pocket. Do you think it would be okay if we opened it?"

"Well sure, Al. If we are going to play General Hospital, I think we should know who the patient is."

"Women sure do carry a lot in their billfolds. Look here, there's so much stuff in it that it won't close. Look at this thing. It's as big as a ...WHOA! Look at all this money!"

"My God, Al, how much is there?"

"I don't know—three, five, six, seven, eight, nine, twelve ... Gees, Donna, there's SIXTEEN THOUSAND DOLLARS!"

Donna stared at the bills, "Well, if she didn't want to go to the hospital, it wasn't because she didn't have the money. Is there any I. D?"

Al opened a little compartment and took out a few plastic cards.

"Let's see now—Master card, Visa, J.C. Penney's and a Washington State driver's license. Her name is Myra A. Dillon, and she lives in a place called Puyallup."

"Where the heck is Puyallup?"

"I don't know Donna; never heard of it before."

"The picture doesn't look much like her. Look, Al, this license has been expired for six years."

They both sat still for the longest time. The kitchen was getting dark and Al finally spoke.

"What a day! It's 8:30 already! What a day!"

"I'll bet it has been darlin'. Is my Good Samaritan hungry?"

There was a sound of movement in the next room.

"She's awake!"

Donna scooped up the wallet and the bills, stuffed them in a plastic container from the kitchen counter, and jammed it in the back of the freezer compartment of the refrigerator.

"There, that will keep things cool, till we find out what's going on."

She smiled at her little joke and followed Al into the spare room.

Al knocked on the half-open door and went gingerly into the room. The patient was sitting up in the bed, the spread was pulled smooth, and she was combing her hair. Donna had dressed her in an old flannel nightgown and cleaned her all up. She had a small bandage on her ear and looked like she was trying to cover up the raw spot on her head by combing hair over it.

"Hi, I'm Myra Dillon."

Al thought she sounded darned cheerful for someone who had been through so much.

"We're Donna and Al Blessing," Al whispered.

"Yes, I know. Your wife told me. I think I will never be able to repay you for all your kindness and letting me spend the night."

"Don't think a thing about it, honey." Donna cooed, "We were glad we were able to help."

Al stood by the end of the bed and asked,

"Can you tell us what happened? Who hurt you this way? Were you raped?"

She suddenly slumped in the bed and looked very tired. Al was reminded of seeing those funny Chinese noodles go soft when you put them in hot water.

"Please, Mister Blessing, could we talk about that in the morning? I'm really too tired right now."

"Okay," Donna cooed again. "We'll talk later. Come on, Al. Let this girl get some rest. Good night, dear!"

They closed the door and went to their own room.

"Al, did you see her change when you questioned her? I think she's up to something. Let's not mention her wallet and the money until she does."

"Oh, Donna, I think you are having much to do about nothing."

"Well, I don't, Al. There's something very strange about this woman and I don't trust her. Did you see the way she changed when you wanted to know what happened? Very strange."

"Donna, do you want to watch the eleven o'clock news?"

"Not tonight, Al. Let's go to bed. It's been a long day."

Chapter 3

The morning had not gone well for Sheriff Tate. Margaret and Paul had had a tiff in the office about who was going to work on Saturday and he had spilled coffee on his new patrol jacket. As he walked down the hall he thought *I don't care who works on Saturday. All I know is things are not looking good for fishing and chess.*

He stood in front of a glass door with a sign that read

E.W. Russell
Minton County Coroner
ENTER

Ertis Wayne Russell and Theodore Tate had been friends since the third grade. E.W. had gone away to collage and medical school, at the same time that Ted went into the army. Ted spent four years in the army as a military policeman, and E.W. went to work in a forensic lab for the Dallas police department. Ted came home in four years, and ran for sheriff. He had been sheriff for close to twenty years when, much to his surprise, E.W. requested his help in running for the office of county coroner. Tate responded and worked many long hours on his old friend's election committee. Of course he got the job and soon settled down to life in a small community. Over the years they had worked well together, and both men were at ease with themselves and each other.

Tate went through the inner doors, and came up behind his old friend. E.W. was about six feet tall and a bit on the heavy side. His hands were large and square with short stubby fingers. It was strange to watch him work because he was so nimble. His actions were deft and no movement was wasted. He was as skilled with a scalpel as he was at the piano, and Tate was always amazed to see the talent in those powerful hands.

E.W. spoke without turning. "By doggies, you sure turned up a good one this time, Teddy."

"Did you find something interesting?"

"You bet I did. This old boy really went through the mill before he cashed in. He has three broken ribs, a broken collarbone, and a fractured skull. Except for where you found him, and some other stuff, he looks like he was run over by a truck."

"What other stuff?"

"Well, for instance, he's covered with blood that's not his own. He has female skin with makeup on it under his fingernails, and then there's that hair in his left hand. That's not all, though. I had to pry his hand open to remove the hair, and I found an earring stud stuck into the palm. The stud must have been torn from whoever with great force because there is human tissue still on it. Whoever that stud came from must have a heckuva sore ear; to say nothing of a scalped spot where all that hair came from. I think the victim must have grabbed for her, got a hand full of hair and an earring, and wouldn't let go."

Tate moved around the table and studied E.W.'s face for a long time. He knew this man well and had never seen him this excited.

Finally he said, "What else can you tell, from what you found?"

"Well, judging from the condition of the old man, he was under attack when he grabbed the hair. This would mean he was probably facing his assailant. If this is true, the hair and the earring probably came from the female's right side. The old boy wasn't very big, but he was as strong as a cat, and it probably took a good-sized woman to inflict those kinds of wounds. The hair is natural and brown with very little sign of hair treatment burn and the like. The skin under his nails was very fair, and I would guess she had blue eyes. Putting this all together, I would also say she was fairly young – less than forty. I'll know more when some of the lab work is done, but that's at least a start."

"Oh, one more thing. Most or all of the wounds were from the same or similar weapon. I think he was struck in the head first, probably from behind, and then systematically struck, very hard, thirty to forty times. The blow on the head should have killed him instantly, but I don't think it did. Most of the fight took place after the original blow. I think the hair and ear pulling took place, and then he went down. After he was on his back, and probably unconscious, most of the blows were struck. I think this because all of the blows were about the same angle, and all in the front. However it was done, it was a vicious beating, and done by a real nut who probably thought the old guy was already dead."

"Ertis, do you feel this could be anything but murder?"

"No chance."

Tate rubbed his neck and thought there goes the weekend.

Tate was back at the office by noon. Margaret was sitting at her desk eating her lunch.

Tate said, "Margaret, I want you to call the district attorney's office and get me an appointment as soon as you can."

"No problem, sheriff. He just called and wants to see you at one o'clock sharp. He has heard all about the murder and needs to talk with you."

"How did he find out so soon?"

"Don't know, sheriff, probably from the coroner's office."

News sure travels fast around here, Tate thought. I wonder how much of the story he's got wrong already?

It was 12:59 when Tate walked through the door of the Minton County District Attorney. David Cline was a newcomer as far as Tate was concerned. Everyone said what a great prosecutor he was, but Tate felt he was too young to be anything but wet behind the ears.

A very stiff woman secretary that Tate thought he recognized, saw him come through the door and, with a wave of her hand, guided him into the inner sanctum.

Cline was a small, slim man, about five feet six. He greeted Tate with a firm hand and offered him a chair.

"I'm told we have a murder on our hands, sheriff. You want to tell me about it?"

Tate pulled his notes from his shirt pocket and gave a complete rundown of everything he had, including the pick handle and the hidden cache under the bed.

When he finished, Cline said, "It looks to me like you have a lot of work to do yet. Do you know who the victim was?"

"No, not yet. There was nothing on the body, and I couldn't find anything in the house—no letters, no nothing. I've got the lab boys working on his prints and stuff; we should know soon."

"So what we have here, sheriff, is a crime of murder against a party unknown, committed by a person or persons unknown. Right?"

"Right."

Cline laughed out loud. "Up to now, Sheriff Tate, we haven't gotten to know each other well, but I think before this is over, we will know each other like kin folk."

"Right."

"As soon as you can, I would like a written report on everything you've told me and keep me up to date on all the new developments. Thanks for your time, sheriff. I'll be in touch."

"Right."

Tate walked slowly back to his office and thought *I guess he's not so bad, a little pushy though.* He thought about the long afternoon ahead with Margaret, getting the notes typed. The picture of fishing and chess seemed to be fading.

Chapter 4

What was that? Donna woke with a start. She heard a noise from the kitchen and sat up in bed. Al was sleeping soundly and as usual was snoring a little. She heard the noise again and then it came to her; that girl is up! She stepped into her slippers and pulled on a robe. Halfway down the hall, she could see Myra at the kitchen sink, doing a few dishes that were left from the night before.

At the kitchen door she asked, "Myra, what are you doing?"

"Oh, good morning, Donna; I'm just getting breakfast and cleaning up a little. It's such a beautiful day."

Donna thought, *boy, what a change. You'd have thought she was going to die yesterday and now look at her.*

"You don't need to do that, dear. You should be resting."

"It's no trouble at all. How else can I repay you two for your kindness? Besides I love cooking and cleaning. What does Al like for breakfast?"

Donna laughed and said, "He likes a big one!"

"Most men do if they don't have to fix it themselves. What time does he get up?"

"He's up now. I just heard him go into the bathroom. Do you want some help?"

"No, I've found everything I need except almond extract. I like to add it to French toast batter. It makes it taste so good."

"Donna, when Al comes out, see if you can get him not to talk about what happened yesterday. I know I owe you both an explanation, but not just yet, okay? I'll tell you all about everything, but not just yet – and not to Al at all. You can tell him later, after I'm gone."

"Okay, honey, whatever you say."

Al came into the kitchen dressed in clean jeans and a sweatshirt that he got for Christmas but had never worn. He was clean-shaven and smelled of that expensive after-shave Donna had given him for their anniversary.

Donna wondered if it was his job going so well or if it was Myra that made him be so perky.

Al ate with gusto and this seemed to delight Myra. She filled his plate three times but only offered Donna one piece of French toast and had nothing for herself.

Al was more talkative than Donna had ever seen him, and before the meal was over, he had told Myra his entire life story, especially the successful parts. It made Myra beam and Donna sick.

When Al had finished eating, Myra cleared the table and did the dishes in a wink. Donna had to admit this girl was one fine housekeeper.

The phone rang. It was one of the people from Al's office, and he needed something from the little office in the den. Donna followed him to the den and closed the door.

When he was through on the phone, Donna said, "What's going on, Al? Why are you acting this way?"

"What way, Donna?"

"Well, like you were on the make for this girl."

"Oh, for Pete's sake, baby, I don't give a hoot for this girl. She's had a bad time, and I'm just trying to be nice to her. It's you I love, always have, always will. I wouldn't jeopardize what we have for anything."

"Okay, Al, but slow down a little will ya – it's turning me green."

When they came out of the den, Myra had made both beds and was just plugging in the vacuum to do the front room.

Donna gasped, "What are you doing, Myra? You should be taking it easy, not working like a chore woman."

"Gee, Donna, don't you see? This will get me well sooner than anything in the world. Scrubbing and cleaning are the best therapy I can think of. Whenever I'm troubled, or worried, I start cleaning, and I can work my way through anything. I had almost seven years of training from the best teacher in the world, and it really works."

Donna said, "Who was your teacher, dear? I'd like to take a few lessons."

Before there was an answer, Myra turned on the vacuum, and the noise drowned out any further conversation.

"What should we do, Al?"

"Well, we could go out and mow the yard. It really needs it, and it's clear we are not needed in here."

It usually took two hours to do the yard, but with both of them working they finished in little over an hour. They put the tools away and washed off their shoes, leaving them to dry on the back porch.

When they entered the house, Myra was just putting away the silver polish after having cleaned the silver tea set in the dining room.

They met in the kitchen and Myra said,

"I hope you don't mind, but it's 11:30 and time for my nap. I rest every day at this time, and if I don't get my nap, I don't feel good. I usually rest for two hours, and since I didn't get my nap yesterday, I really need one today."

"You go right ahead, dear. Al and I have some things to do too. I want to grocery shop, and Al has some work to get done for his business. We'll be very quiet so you can have a good rest. Sweet dreams."

Myra went into the bedroom and closed the door. Al and Donna just stood and stared at each other.

Finally Donna spoke. "Now there's a weird one! Have you ever seen anything like that in your life?"

"No, Donna, not even close."

"Well, honey, why don't you get started on your book work, and I'm going to jump in the shower before I go shopping. I should be home by two o'clock. If you're finished by that time, maybe we can have a talk with Miss Strange One."

"Miss Strange One is right. Do you think we should ask her to leave?"

"We'll see."

Donna finished her shower and called goodbye as she went out the door on her shopping trip. Al heard the car back out of the drive, and the house became very quiet.

He worked for little more than half an hour and suddenly had the feeling that someone was looking at him. He turned and there was Myra. She was standing in the doorway dressed in his old bathrobe. The robe was open down the front, and she had nothing on under it.

Trying not to show his amazement, Al said, "All finished with your nap?"

She smiled and crossed the room, and pulling the robe apart, she straddled his lap, pushing her breasts against his face, as she hugged him around the neck.

Then she purred. "I'm sure we can find something better to do than nap – aren't you?"

Al sat frozen. He didn't even move. What was she up to?

Finally he said, "What do you want?"

"What do I want? I think you're sexy. Do you think I'm sexy?"

"I think you are a very troubled girl, and you have to stop this, NOW!"

He stood and she slid to the floor at his feet. She looked up, and Al had never seen anything like it in his life. She had a look of a wild thing, wild and angry. She snarled like a cat,

"Damn you, where's my money?"

Al remembered Donna saying, "Let's not tell her about the money until she asks." He thought, *what should I do? Where was Donna?*

He answered, "What money?"

"Don't you lie to me, you thievin' bastard. You've got my money, and I want it now."

"I don't know what you're talking about!"

She got to her feet and ran out of the room like a crazy woman. She returned a moment later just as Al picked up the phone to call the police. Al heard her heavy breathing and turned before he finished dialing the phone to stare point blank into the business end of a Colt 45. He knew what the gun was because he had brought it home when he got out of the army. He also knew it was loaded. He hung the phone up and choked.

"Be careful with that thing; it's very dangerous."

"Not for me, you bastard. You tell me where my money is, or I'll blow you to hell."

"I told you, I don't know what you are talking about."

She crossed the room and picked up an old zipper front windbreaker from a chair by his desk, and commanded,

"Here, put this on, and zip it up half way."

"What are you going to do?"

"Never mind, just do what I say or I'll shoot you dead. I've got nothing to lose, so don't push me, or I'll turn you into dog meat. When you get it on, sit in that chair."

He put on the jacket, and sat in the chair. She went behind him, and with the gun in his ear, she used her free hand to pull the collar of the jacket out and down over his shoulders so that it made a very effective straitjacket. He wondered where she had learned that little trick. He turned to look at her, just in time to see her hand go up but not soon enough to duck. The gun in her hand came down, and struck him just above the left ear. A big, dark hole swallowed him.

Donna parked the car by the back door, and with her arms full of groceries, went into the kitchen. As she came through the door, she called out.

"Yoo-hoo, Al, where are you? Al, Myra, where are you? Come on you two; where are you?"

She went down the hall and into the den. Al was on the floor with a small line of blood running down his cheek, and over his neck. Donna went to her knees, and cradled Al's head in her arms.

"Oh, baby, what happened? Oh, Al, Oh, AL."

She looked up just in time to see the gun strike her in the face. She felt a pain in her jaw, and the sharp fiery pain of a tooth breaking. She fell to the floor, and when she tried to get up, the gun came down again. She too, went into that big dark hole.

When Al woke, it was dark. He could hear the eleven o'clock news on the TV. The office was a mess, everything out of the drawers and on the floor. He had a splitting headache, and he couldn't see out of his left eye. He tried to roll over and found he was on the floor next to Donna. He tried to sit up, but the pain in his head made him dizzy, and he fell back to the floor. The big black hole opened again, and once more he fell in.

Chapter 5

Sheriff Tate had had a restless night and needed to get his teeth into something. He was up at 5:00, shaved and showered by 5:30, and by 6:00, on his way to Travis Corners. He stopped at McDonalds for a cup of coffee, and arrived at the Travis Corners store just as Gill Condon was turning the open/closed sign over in the front window.

Gill held the door wide, and said, "Mornin', sheriff, what brings you out so early?"

"Nothing much, Gill, just wanted to ask you a few questions about that old fella we found Wednesday. Did you know him?"

"Sure did, Sheriff; his name was John Martin."

"Do you know anything else?"

"Not much. He lived in that old shack, and came by once or twice a week for supplies. I heard him talk to the mailman one day about panning gold in the creek. Don't know as he ever found any though."

"Did he live alone?"

"Yeah. Well, anyway, he did until about a month ago."

"Oh?"

"Uh-huh. About a month ago, he started coming by with a young woman in the car. Never did get to meet her though. She always stayed out in the car."

"I didn't know he owned a car, Gill. What kind of a car did he drive?"

"It's that old Chevy sittin' out back. He had a problem startin' it and asked if he could leave it out there till he could get someone to fix it."

"When was that, Gill?"

"Oh, last Tuesday I think. Yeah, just the day before he died."

"Anything else you can think of?"

"Well, he paid by check a lot. Checks were drawn on Liberty Trust and Savings here in town."

"Thanks, Gill, if I need anything more, I'll be back."

"Any time, Sheriff!"

Tate drove around to where the old Chevy was parked. The doors were locked, and he could see nothing through the windows that had any meaning. He made a note of the license so he could get a warrant and have the car impounded. He was driving past the front of the store towards the highway when he saw Gill trying to wave him down. He stopped and rolled down the window.

"What's up, Gill?"

"Hey, Sheriff; my wife just told me something about that girl that was living out there with old John."

"What's that?"

"Well, yesterday we got a reject on a credit card purchase she made here a week ago. The bank kicked it back because it was out of date. That darn wife of mine, she never looks. It's only for eight dollars—no big deal. Her name is Myra Dillon."

"Do you know what she bought?"

"Yeah, it's right here on the slip. She bought some groceries. I can't tell what. It just says groceries and a pickax handle."

"Can I get the information from that receipt?"

"Oh, sure, Sheriff. Here, you can have this extra copy; then you'll have everything."

"Thanks again, Gill, you've been a great help. I'll be in touch."

It was 8:15 when Tate headed for town. Lots of work to do now he thought.

Gill stood watching the patrol car make a dusty retreat and felt his wife standing beside him.

"Why did you give him that receipt? It might be the only thing we need to collect our money!"

"Shut up, damn it. If you had been more careful when you made the sale, we wouldn't have the problem now. The sheriff is a good old boy and if he runs that dame down he'll let us know. I've known him for years and he's a man who can be trusted."

"Well, maybe so, but I've never had a lot of faith in the guy. He dresses more like a cowboy than a sheriff. He always wears that big hat and those cowboy boots."

"Yeah, I guess it's a left over from his youth. He comes from Texas you know? His father was a sheriff in Texas back in the early cattle days and was pretty famous I heard.

He parked the patrol car in the Liberty Trust and Savings lot, at seven minutes past nine. It was Friday, and the bank opened early. He saw Peggy Danforth at a desk in the back of the bank, and motioned that he wanted to talk. She waved him back. Peggy was an old friend. He went to high school with her, and she was a bridesmaid for Darlene when they got married.

"Hi, Ted, how ya doin? How's Darlene?"

"We're all fine Peg, and you?"

"Oh, I'm just fine, but with Roy gone now, it's kinda lonesome. Hey, big fella, what can I do for you?"

"Peg, I'm checking on the affairs of a deceased person by the name of John Martin. I think he's one of your depositors."

"Oh, my, did old John pass away? What happened?"

"Some boys from Logan found him out by his cabin on Wednesday. What can you tell me about him?"

"Let's pull him up on the computer. Yes, there he is. Just what do you want to know, Ted."

"Anything you can tell me, Peg. All I know about him now is his name and that he's dead."

"Well, let's see. He's single and shows no next of kin. He's sixty-eight years old, and he's retired. His income seems to all be from Social Security, and he has had an account with us for three years. Hold it; this is strange. He withdrew all but fifty dollars from his account last Tuesday. $16,051.32 – Wow!

"Thanks, Peg, that's all I need for now. I'll get back to you, okay?"

Tate sat in his car, and went over the morning. What a mess. Got to find out who this Myra Dillon is. All I know now is that she uses a bad credit card. Bad credit card! I'll bet Sandy over at the credit union could help.

He slid the Ford into gear and headed across town. The credit union was only three blocks from his office. Darlene and he had been one of the first members of the credit union, and Darlene had served two terms on the board of directors. Sandy greeted him as he came up to the counter.

"Hi, Sheriff! Haven't seen you for a while. How are you? How's Darlene?"

"We're all just fine, Sandy. May I see you in private? I need some information."

"Sure thing, Sheriff, come in my office."

Sandy sat with quiet attention while Tate told her of Myra Dillon, and the out-of-date credit card.

"What I want to know, Sandy, is can you find out any thing about this woman through her credit record that might help me?"

"Well, let's see."

She spun her chair around and put something in the computer. She paused a moment, then entered some information from the credit card rejection slip Tate had given her. There was another pause and striking another key, she started a printer.

"I think we have what we are looking for, sheriff. Let's see."

She tore the printout from the machine and handed it to him. The record had all the usual things—date of birth, next of kin, date of last entry, and the number of the bank where the card originated. It showed the last transaction date over seven years ago, and that there was an outstanding balance of $451.22 that had been charged off for over two years. The next of kin was a spouse named Oliver (deceased).

"Can you tell from this bank number what bank it is?"

"Sure, I think so."

Sandy picked up a small book and said,

"It's the National Bank of Commerce, in Tacoma, Washington."

"Is there anything they might be able to tell us?"

"Don't know; it's been a long time. Let me see. I knew the credit manager of that branch at one time, and if she's still there, we might get lucky."

She dialed the phone, hung up, and dialed again. She spoke at length to someone named Sue. She took many notes and finally hung up.

"Wow, Sheriff, can you pick'em. My old friend Sue is still with the same bank even though it's changed names. She remembered the account well. There was a big scandal about Myra and her husband Oliver. It seems Myra murdered good old Ollie because he found she was skimming off the house money a few dollars a week and took it away from her. He wouldn't give it back and it made her so mad, she shot him. The last Sue could remember about the deal was that Myra got sent to the local nut house up in Snohomish County and was probably still there."

Tate thought, *I wish she was.* He thanked Sandy for her help and headed for the office.

He walked through the door to find Margaret and Paul in a tangle over who was going to have Saturday off.

Sheriff Tate snapped, "If you two can't find something better to do than squabble over your days off, I'll give you both some time off without pay, and you can fight on your own time."

Paul turned white and disappeared into the jail area, and Margaret went back to her filing.

Tate growled, "Margaret, get the sheriff of Snohomish County, Washington, on the line. I want to talk to him, PRONTO."

Tate sat going over his notes when the phone rang. It was the Snohomish County sheriff. Tate filled him in on some of the facts about Myra, and asked if he could find out why Myra was out of the hospital. The sheriff said he would check, and so that Tate could have the complete record, he would FAX the file ASAP. Tate thanked him, and hung up. He laid his head back and heaved a big sigh. Tate dialed the phone, and Darlene answered on the first ring.

"I need a break, honey. If I came home, would you fix me a cup of soup and a sandwich?"

"You bet I will, Teddy. Are you coming now?"

"Yes, give me twenty minutes."

"Margaret, I'm going home for a while. When that stuff comes in from Snohomish County on the FAX, call me at home."

"Okay, Sheriff."

Chapter 6

Donna felt the pain in her jaw and wanted to cry. She could hardly breathe and she couldn't move. It slowly came to her that she was tied hand and foot. It was light out, and she could hear a radio or a TV playing in the distance. She arched her back and could make out the form of Al, lying on the floor a few feet away. What was going on? The memory of the past night started to return, and she felt sick. Was Al dead? Where was Myra? Is this a dream? She closed her eyes and tried to work her tongue under the tape over her mouth. She felt someone was close and opened her eyes to look into Myra's face only a few inches away.

"Well, I see you're finally awake. Are you ready to tell me where my money is?"

"Myra yanked the tape from Donna's face, and Donna screamed with pain. She tried to speak but couldn't move her jaw. She knew it was broken."

Donna finally got the word "Al" out, and Myra slapped her face. The pain was awful.

"I guess you're going to be as stupid as that old man of yours. He's just like Oliver, too stupid to know he has to give me my money."

Al rolled over and tried to sit up.

"Never mind, you jerk. You aren't going anywhere with that duct tape on you. Are you ready to talk yet?"

She reached over and pulled the tape from his mouth.

"My God, Myra, what are you trying to do, kill us? What have we ever done to you?"

"Plenty, you bastard. Why won't you give me my money? Tell me where it is."

Al tried to think. He reasoned that if he told her, he was dead. He looked at Donna and saw just the slightest shake of her head. My God, was she telling him not to give in?

"I don't know where any money is or what you are talking about."

Myra screamed. "Damn you. Don't give me that. I know you're lying. I had it in my pocket when you picked me up. I had to take it away from that nasty old man, and he hurt me. It's mine. Everyone tries to take my money. They wouldn't let me have any money at the facility. All they did was make me work and clean, work and clean."

"I don't know about your money, but if you will untie me, I'll write you a check for $50.00 if that will help."

"You're just like that old man John. All he wanted to give me was pennies. It took me weeks to get him to get the money out of the bank, and then he tried to hide it. I fooled him though. I found where he put it and now it's mine. If you don't give me my money, I'm going to hit you like I did him, only you won't be able to hurt me back. Are you going to give me my money?"

Al looked at Donna out of the corner of his good eye, and clearly saw her shake her head—NO!

"I can't give you what I don't have, Myra!"

She stood and screamed. "I'll see you in hell before I let you keep my money."

She kicked him full in the face, the black hole opened again, and he fell in.

When he woke, he could see Donna sitting up against the wall. Her face was swollen and blood had dried all down her chin and the front of her dress. They were alone in the room, and he could hear Myra banging things around in the other end of the house. It sounded like she was in the kitchen or the utility room.

"Can you speak, Donna?" She shook her head.

"What should we do?"

She shrugged her shoulders. Al was trying to think when he looked up and saw Myra standing in the doorway with a knife in her hand. She looked wild!

"Have you had enough yet? Are you going to tell me where you put my money? If you don't tell me, I'll cut you."

Al really didn't have time to answer. She came at him with the knife, and he put up his hands to protect his face. The knife sliced through the windbreaker, his sweatshirt, and deep into his arm. He knew the cut was bad, but it just didn't hurt that much.

"Go to hell, you crazy bitch, I wouldn't tell you now if I knew."

Something hit him again, and everything got black.

When he came to, it was starting to get dark out and it took a few minutes to get used to the dim light. Finally he could see Donna lying by the door, She was on her back, and the front of her dress was cut, or torn away. He could see her breasts and stomach. There were small X's cut everywhere, and each one had been bleeding. At first, he thought she was dead, but soon he could see she was breathing.

He called out, "Donna, are you all right? "

He tried to move closer. His arm felt like it was on fire. With great effort, he rolled over and found the telephone on the floor in front of his face. He worked the receiver off with his nose, and managed to push the buttons and dial. A woman's voice said it was 911, and could she help. Al gathered all his strength, and said, "I'm Al Blessing. Myra Dillon has me."

He heard a noise, and looked up to see Myra at his feet, with the .45 in her hand. She hung up the phone and then just stood there, cocking and uncocking the gun. Myra went behind his desk, and pulled the phone wire out of the wall. She looked down at him and hissed.

"You won't get away with this you know. I'll get my money. You just see if I don't."

She left the room again and was gone for what seemed like hours to Al. The house was completely dark now, except for a light in the hall that silhouetted Myra in the doorway. He couldn't see her face; she stood there rocking back and forth like a little kid that had to go to the bathroom. In the distance he heard sirens; they came closer and closer. Myra cursed and ran down the hall.

Chapter 7

It was nearly 4:30, when Tate parked his car in front of the courthouse. He felt much better. He had discussed the entire case with Darlene, and she had listened without interruption. She had a way of saying very little and helping a lot. He strode into the office and Margaret said,

"The District Attorney is here, and that stuff you wanted from Washington is here. That gal must be something else. It took 22 pages on the FAX machine."

David Cline was seated in his office. He was just finishing the last page of the file on Myra as Tate closed the door and sat down.

"This woman, Myra Dillon, is a real dilly. She shot her husband over some house money, and her attorney got her off on an insanity plea. She was sentenced to seven years in a mental institution and was released two months ago with time off for good behavior. While she was in the mental facility, she was a model inmate, never did anything wrong. After the second week of missing her parole check-in, they issued a warrant for her arrest, and they have no idea where she went. Her parole officer thought she could be in Oregon."

The door opened and Margaret came in with the daily work sheet from the 911 calls.

"Okay, Margaret, have a good night, and thanks for staying."

"Sure thing, Sheriff!"

As she turned to go, Tate said to Cline.

"Who would know where a nut like Myra Dillon would go, especially with as much money as we think she has."

Margaret stopped half way out the door, and said, "Myra Dillon?"

"Margaret, do you know something about her?"

"Yes – Well, I don't know for sure, but just a little while ago I got a call on 911; all the man said was, this is Al Blessing and Myra Dillon has me. The phone went dead, and I thought it was a crank call; it's all there in the report."

Tate came out from behind his desk like a shot. "Margaret, see if there is an Al Blessing in the phone book." He grabbed the intercom to the jail and said, "Paul, Get up here PRONTO. Margaret, did you find a number for that Blessing guy?"

"Yes, Sheriff, it's right here."

"Where does he live?"

"2628 Rosewood."

Paul came into the room.

"Did you get that address, Paul? Do you know where it is?"

"Yes!"

"Margaret, call that number, and if you get someone, keep them on the line as long as you can."

"I already tried it, Sheriff, the line is busy."

Margaret, call the city boys, and give them the address. I want the city police in on this since the address is inside the city limits. Tell them we have a dangerous fugitive and we want back up."

"Come on, Paul, let's roll."

As they turned the corner onto Rosewood, Tate could see the lights of the two city cars, coming from the other direction. They met, almost head on, in front of 2628. Tate stepped from the car. The house was dark, except for a single light in the center of the house that gave the place an eerie look. He waved the two city boys back and approached the back door, which seemed to be standing open. The kitchen was dark except for a small light in the hallway, casting a shadowy gleam on the refrigerator. Tate stepped inside and stood in the shadows for over a minute. There was no sound at all, and Tate about jumped out of his skin when Paul appeared at his elbow.

"I don't think there's any one here. Do you, Sheriff?"

"I don't hear anything, Paul. Use your light."

Paul swept his flashlight back and forth. The place was a mess, everything on the floor; all the drawers empty, and the contents of the cupboards broken and under foot. The refrigerator stood open, and Tate noted that even the little light inside was broken. The freezer had been emptied, and a part carton of ice cream was starting to melt and run down the front of the sink cabinet. They started down the hall toward the front room, and as they passed the den, Paul's light shown on a man's feet, bound in duct tape.

Tate whispered, "In here!"

Both men crouched and went into a defensive stance. Paul swept the room with his light, and they saw a man and a woman bound on the floor with blood and trash everywhere. Paul said, "Gees, what a mess. Are they alive?"

"Don't know. You check the rest of the house, and I'll take care of things here. Get those city boys in here."

"Okay, I'll call for an ambulance too. These people are hurt bad. What do you think, Sheriff, are they still alive?"

"Yes, I'm sure they are. When you're on the radio, get some more back up in here and call for an evidence team. Okay?"

"You bet. I'll be right back."

Tate stood and turned on the room light. The place looked like a slaughterhouse. He bent to cover the woman. Her clothes were torn away from the waist up, and she had small cuts on her breasts and stomach. The blood had dried and she looked like she was in a dark red cast. He covered her as well as he could, and when he looked at her face, saw that she was looking at him. Her face was a mess, her lower jaw twisted to one side.

Tate said, "Don't move, ma'am; we have help on the way. Can you speak?"

She made a gurgling sound and shook her head. Tate turned his attention to the man. He was lying on his face, and Tate turned him over. What he saw almost made the old veteran sheriff sick. The left side of the man's face was so beaten, it had almost lost its shape, and his left eye was beyond recognition. Tate could tell the man was awake but had said nothing.

"Are you Blessing?"

The man grunted.

"Don't worry, Mr. Blessing, we will take care of you now and help is on the way. Your wife is hurt, but I'm sure she'll be all right."

"Al Blessing slumped back and Tate stood. In the doorway stood his deputy and two wide-eyed policemen. Their name tags said C. HARRISON and J. BELL. In the next few minutes, Tate left the three younger men in the den and made a quick check of the house. Every stick of upholstered furniture was ripped or cut open, and every room in the house was trashed. Tate was coming out of the master bedroom when he heard the back-up units and the ambulance pull up. He stepped onto the back porch and waved the ambulance drivers to the front door.

The badge in front of Tate's face said Deputy Chief, and it was on the breast pocket of Julius Harts. He was a giant of a man, and Tate had known him since he was the local high school football hero. Harts and Tate's son Bob had been in the same grade in school. It always surprised Tate that both boys were now men. Jewels, (as everyone called him) and Bob had both gone into law enforcement. Jewels was, to Tate's amazement, promoted to deputy chief before his twenty-fifth birthday, and Bob had just been assigned to the Portland, Oregon, district office of the F. B. I.

"I'll take over now, Sheriff. As soon as we get things tied down, I'll want some time with you, to fill me in on what took place here."

"Sure thing, Jewels. I'm going out in the front yard. When you get ready, I'll give you everything we have."

Tate went out the front door and stood on the front porch just as the ambulance attendants were taking Al Blessing out. As the stretcher passed, Blessing said to Tate, "The money, did she get the money?"

"What money?"

"The sixteen thousand, did she get it? It was in the refrigerator. Did she get it?"

"Yes, I think so."

"Damn!"

Tate saw Paul standing next to the patrol car looking like a lost soul. He crossed the yard and said, "Paul, get on the radio and have one of the night shift come and pick you up. I have to stay here and fill in Chief Harts. I'll need the car."

"Okay, Sheriff. I have the duty tomorrow, so I'll be able to have my report on your desk on Monday."

"Good job, Paul. I'll see you on Monday."

Paul's ride arrived, and Tate stood watching their lights disappear, when he saw Chief Harts coming towards him across the yard.

It was after 11PM when Tate turned up his street, saw the lights were on in his house and Terry's car in front. Tate thought *I've got to get my mind off this mess for a few hours or the fishing and chess won't be worth a damn.*

Chapter 8

Myra went into the darkness behind the house. She could hear the sirens coming closer. They seemed to be coming from everywhere at once. It took less than a minute to pick her way through what seemed to be a maze of clotheslines and children's toys and emerge onto the next street. She walked slowly in the direction of some bright lights and thought about the Blessings. *I should have shot them* she cursed. *Those thievin' no-goods tried to take my money, and they deserve everything they got.*

The lights of a theater marquee nearly blinded her, and she stood for a moment trying to get her bearings. Her hands felt cold, and she realized she was still holding the plastic freezer container that held her wallet and her money. The lid came off hard, and when it did, she dropped it in a nearby garbage can. She counted the bills as she put them back in the inner pocket of the wallet.

Old John had bought her a jeans jacket with large zipper pockets, and she carefully stowed the wallet in the left pocket. She slipped her hand into the warm slash pockets, and felt some coins and paper. She removed the money, and held it up to the light. There was $11.46 in bills and change. She smiled, and thought, I won't have to spend my money, thanks to good old Al. She had found the money in his desk drawer, and felt she was being partly paid for all the trouble she had been put to. A bus marked CITY CENTER came by, and Myra stepped to the bus stop. The bus came to a noisy stop, and Myra climbed aboard. The city lights passed slowly by and Myra watched them through her reflection in the window. *What should I do now* she wondered. *I can't stay in this town, and if I go back to Seattle or Portland, somebody might recognize me.* She stood, and walked forward to the front of the bus, and asked the driver,

"Can you tell me where the bus station is?"

"Yes, ma'am, it's about a mile ahead. I'll let you know when we get there."

Yes, that's what she would do. Go someplace where she had never been before and get a clean start. That's what I tried to do when I found Oliver. Maybe it will work this time.

Living with Oliver had been her way out at the time and she had to get away from poverty. She had grown up with her folks, a brother, and a sister. Her mom and dad treated her okay, but the family was dirt poor in Myra's eyes, and she couldn't stand the farm another day. School was the only bright spot in her life, and when her father announced there was no money for her to go on to college, she was crushed. Oliver had been her safe harbor; he had been educated and had a good job. He encouraged her to read, found her a job, and helped instill an appreciation of music and art she had not known before.

The bus driver called to her, "Here's your stop, lady. The bus station is two blocks that way."

"Thank you very much. You are very kind."

"Yes ma'am. Have a good night."

The station was nearly empty and Myra looked at the schedule board but couldn't see any place that suited her.

She suddenly felt very hungry and realized she had not eaten all day. The lunch counter had only one other customer, and Myra ordered a hamburger and fries with a chocolate shake. While she ate her meal, she studied the dozen or so people in the terminal. Just as her bill came, a new person entered the station and stood reading the schedule board. He was dressed in slacks and a sport jacket that Myra could tell were very expensive. Myra thought how good-looking he was, and then wondered where he was going. He picked up a large suitcase and went to the ticket window. Myra paid her bill and slid to the end of the counter where she dug out her wallet and removed a bill. She crossed the room and managed to bump into the handsome man just as he turned away from the ticket window.

"Pardon me, miss, are you all right?"

She smiled but didn't answer. The young man checked his suitcase and headed for the men's room. Myra waited till he was out of sight and turned to the clerk.

"Give me a ticket to the same place as the man that was just here is going."

"Yes ma'am. Will that be one way, or round trip?"

"One way."

"Okay, that'll be one way to Twin Falls, Idaho. Forty- seven, sixty-seven. Forty-seven sixty-seven out of a hundred. Here's your change and have a nice trip. Your coach is ready to board now."

The young man had not come out of the restroom yet when Myra got on the bus. Most of the seats were taken by through passengers, and she had to go nearly to the back of the bus to find an empty seat next to a window. She was watching a bus navigate into the next spot when she saw him board. He worked his way back to her seat, and she caught his eye with the sweetest smile she could muster.

He smiled back and said, "May I join you?"

"Yes, please do."

His smile was bright, and his teeth were even and white. Myra noticed his hands were clean and well kept. He removed his jacket, stowed it in the upper rack and as he sat down, she could smell the clean scent of him.

He smiled again and said, "There now, that's better. My name is Dave Miller, and I'm going to Twin Falls."

"Hi, Dave, I'm going to Twin Falls, too. My name is Myra Carter. I hope you don't snore because I'm all tuckered out, and I need some sleep."

He laughed and said, "If I do, Myra, you have my permission to kick me. You go right ahead and have a good rest."

The bus backed out of the stall and was only a block up the street when she felt the curtain of sleep descending. She thought, how good he smells.

Chapter 9

Deputy Chief Harts was about done in. It was now just after 4:15a.m, and Al Blessing was still in surgery. They had called a specialist in to work on his eye, and the chances of saving it looked slim. He had spent almost two hours with Al while they were waiting for the specialist to arrive, and Al had been insistent on talking. He claimed to not be in pain and refused any pain medication until after Donna came out of surgery. In those two hours, Al had told him in great detail about the hours with Myra. Jewels had called in a court recorder to take the statement. This would be good when he went to the district attorney since he felt the first part of this case was probably mishandled. He knew Sheriff Tate had a good reputation and had many solid convictions to his credit, but those County Mounties, as he called them, seemed, in his opinion, to be a little on the sloppy side. Jewels took great store in solid, exact police work, and attributed his rapid rise in the department to careful preparation.

Donna Blessing came out of surgery at twenty-four minutes past two and the report was that she was in stable condition. She had lost two teeth and had a dislocated jaw. There were multiple cuts on her upper torso that would heal with very little scarring. Al Blessing had cried when he heard the news and thanked God for saving Donna. Well, it was Al's turn now, and Jewels wondered if he would be so lucky. At 4:42, Doctor Otis came out of a door by the nurse station, and introduced himself.

"Chief, there was nothing we could do for Mister Blessing's eye. It was so badly damaged that we had to remove it. Mister Blessing will be under sedation for most of the day, and when he is up to it, we will inform him of his wife's condition. There is nothing more you can do here. Why don't you get some rest? You look tired."

"Thanks, Doctor, I think I will."

Chapter 10

The alarm rang at two ticks past seven, and Tate felt Darlene's warm cheek against his, as she whispered,

"Come on, Teddy, the fish are waiting. Terry has been up for an hour and has everything ready."

Tate rolled out of bed and staggered to the bathroom. He decided not to shave or shower but washed his face and hands. He was brushing his teeth when Darlene came in with a steaming cup of coffee.

"My God, Ted, you look beat. Are you sure you want to go fishing? Terry will understand. He knows what you have been through the last few days."

"Sure, sweetie, I'll be okay when I get a cup of your coffee in me and a whiff of some good morning air."

He drank his coffee as he dressed. Every move was an effort, but he knew he would be better once he got going. The drive to the lake seemed longer than usual, and Tate had a hard time keeping up on Terry's chatter. Terry and Vicki were buying a new car, and Terry was going over what a good deal he had forced out of the salesman. They arrived at the lake, and Tate was glad to see that there were several boats left. He got out of the car and just as he got to the rear bumper, he felt a pain in his chest like no other pain in his life. It knocked the wind out of him, and he went down on one knee. He thought it would go away, but it didn't, and he felt sick to his stomach. He got very dizzy. Terry came around the end of the car and saw his brother on the ground. His face was a dark blue color, and he was very still. He saw the kid that rents the boats coming towards them, and he yelled.

"Call an ambulance! My brother's sick."

The kid turned on a dime and ran for the phone in the boat shed. Terry knelt by his brother's side and held his head in his arms. Rocking back and forth he wailed.

"Oh God, Teddy, what can I do? What can I do?"

It was close to an hour before the medic people had placed Sheriff Tate in the ambulance and started for the hospital. Terry telephoned Darlene and arranged to pick her and Vicki up on his way to be with his brother. The two women were standing at the curb when he arrived and Terry wondered if they were going to be able to control Darlene. She was very upset and was demanding that Terry give her some reason why such a thing could have happened. Vicki said that Darlene had been okay until she phoned Bob and when he wanted more information than she could give him, was when she broke down. Vicki had to complete the call and she was able to calm everyone down a little. Bob was going to get there as soon as possible and this seemed to help. When they arrived at the hospital, Ted had been taken to the emergency room, and the on duty doctor had determined that he had suffered a severe attack. He had called their family physician who would soon be there and be able to answer their questions.

All the nurses said that Dr. Otis was a man of iron, but this evening he looked like he was going to cash it in.

He approached the Tates with slow, uneven steps and said, "Darlene, why don't you go home and get some rest? Ted is resting now, and we won't know any more for a few hours. He has come through the first stage of a very severe heart attack, and he seems to be doing well. If we can keep him stable for the first twenty-four hours, his chances will be better. The three of you have been here all day, and you need rest. There is no point in all of you being so exhausted that you can't be of help when the time comes."

The ride home was silent except for Darlene's sobbing in the back seat.

Chapter 11

The sun pierced through the window, and hit Myra's face. She woke with a start. Had she really been asleep all night? Her elbow pressed against the bulge in her pocket. Yes, her wallet was safe.

The still figure of Dave Miller was half turned in the next seat, and she studied his face.

Sure is handsome, Myra thought. She puckered and blew on his eyelid.

He opened one eye and smiled that killer smile. He yawned, and said, "What a beautiful way to wake up; did you sleep well?"

"Like a top, and, boy, am I hungry! When does this bus stop?"

No sooner had she asked the question than the engine slowed, and they pulled off the highway into a parking area with a big sign that said CAFE.

"Milady asks and milady receives."

Myra smiled and touched his arm. "Feed me quick!"

They found a small table in the back of the cafe and got permission from the cashier to sit in the place marked "reserved." A very slim waitress brought them coffee, and took their order. Dave ordered a full ham and egg breakfast, and Myra had French toast.

When the waitress had gone, Myra said, "Tell me about yourself."

"Nothing much to tell. What do you want to know?"

"Oh, you know, just the usual nosey stuff. Why are you going to Twin Falls? What do you do for work? You know, stuff like that."

"How about my life's story in five minutes?"

"Okay, if you can finish before breakfast."

Dave smiled and said, "Okay, here goes." He thought, *damn, she's good looking, even in the morning after an all night bus ride, she's a beauty.*

"My name is David Miller, and I'm the only son of Martha and Stewart Miller, both deceased. I had, until a month ago, one living relative, an aunt named Alma, from my father's side of the family. Aunt Alma passed away the end of June and left me her house. I'm going there to see if it's worth keeping, or if I should just sell it and spend the money on something foolish. I've heard the place is an old mansion, but I've never seen it. You know how stories can get all twisted when it comes to old houses. It's probably an old dump. However, if the place is what my Dad always said, big and beautiful, I might settle there and work. I'm a commercial artist and it really doesn't matter where I work, as long as I meet my assignment deadlines."

"An artist? Are you any good? I mean, are you famous or anything?"

Dave laughed and thought again how pretty she was. "Well, I don't know about famous, but they pay me well and I work steady. I do magazine covers mostly, but lots of other things too. I work through an agency, so I don't have to put up with all the hassle of submitting my work all the time. They do all the hard stuff for me and I have my time free to work."

Myra made a funny face and said, "Do you make lots of money?"

"Yes, little Miss Nosey, lots of money."

"Well, if you make lots of money, why are you on a bus instead of in your own car? Or even flying?"

"Oh, that's just the way it worked out. You see, when I was notified of my inheritance, I was living in a studio apartment and leasing a car from a local car dealer. When I decided to come to Idaho, I also decided to make a change in where I was living. Since I'm not sure what is involved with my aunt's house, or even what it looks like for sure, I decided to get rid of everything and this would leave me free to go wherever I wanted. If things don't go well in Twin Falls, I'm thinking of moving on to Chicago where I'll be closer to my agent. I'm not awfully keen on moving to a big city, but it's one of my choices. Anyway, I'm not due in Twin Falls for a few days and since I've never taken a bus trip before, I thought I'd try it and see what it was like. Up until yesterday it was on the boring side, but it's looking better now. What about you? What do you do?"

The waitress came with their meal, and Myra gave a little squeal of delight but didn't answer. She wondered what she would tell him when he asked her again, but that would come later.

They finished their meal in relative silence and were half way through a third cup of coffee, when the bus driver announced,

"Fifteen minutes, we leave in fifteen minutes."

The sun was now up far enough to bathe the parking lot in sunshine, and Dave suggested they sit on a bench in a grassy area in front of where the bus was parked, and soak up some "rays."

On the way to the bench they passed a phone booth, and Myra said, "Give me a few minutes will you, Dave? I should make a phone call."

"Sure thing, Myra, I'll wait on the bench."

Myra checked her pocket and found three dollars and forty cents in change. Should be enough she thought. She dug in one of the little pockets in her wallet and found a card. From the card she dialed a number and deposited two dollars and eighty cents. A voice on the other end said,

"Auburn U-Haul."

"This is Myra Carter; my number is 57-1494A, do you have any messages for me?"

"No, ma'am, we don't."

"Will you forward my locker contents to the U-Hall station in Twin Falls, Idaho?"

"Yes, ma'am we will. Stand by, and I'll give you the charges. Ma'am, the charges on forwarding your belongings to Twin Falls will be twenty-six dollars."

"That will be fine. When will you send them?"

"They will go out of here at two this afternoon and be in Twin Falls on Tuesday."

Myra joined Dave on the bench and he asked. "Everything okay? No problems, I hope."

"No, everything is just fine. I was just checking on my luggage. It's being forwarded."

Myra sat next to Dave, and he scooted as close to her as he could get and whispered, "Now it's my turn to ask questions."

Myra turned cold. What was she going to tell him?

"I suppose you want to hear my life story in five minutes."

"No, not really, not now anyway. When I hear your life story, I want it to be in front of a fireplace with a glass of good wine in my hand."

"Sounds good to me, sir, but what do you want to know now?"

"What did you do to your ear?"

"Oh, that!" She laughed,

"It was an accident. I was at a girl friend's house, and we were roughhousing by their pool. I caught my earring on a towel, and it nearly tore my ear off. I fell and scraped my head on the edge of the diving board and lost a bunch of hair too. I've always been an accident looking for a place to happen, and stuff like this is not new to me."

"Well, from now on, we'll have to see that you take better care of yourself. Can't have you destroying a girl as pretty as you."

Myra smiled.

The bus driver called, "All aboard."

They rode in silence for almost an hour. Myra looked at the watch on her wrist and thought, I wonder how that stupid Donna feels today. I've got her watch and her clothes, and I'll bet she has a headache. Serves her right, too, for trying to steal my money.

The time was 11:30, and she turned to Dave. "I hope you don't mind Mr. Miller, but it's time for my nap. I always take a little snooze at this time of the day."

"You go right ahead. I'll just lie here and watch you."

Myra smiled and felt warm and safe. She had not felt safe since she had been with Oliver, and it felt good. Poor Oliver, it was too bad he wouldn't listen.

A whish-whish sound and a feeling of unsteadiness broke the constant hum of the bus as the driver deftly pulled the large vehicle to a stop.

"Sorry, folks, I hate to tell you, but we have a flat on the front wheel, and we will be awhile. I don't know how long yet, but we'll be back on the road as soon as possible. Just sit tight. The coach will be heated, and we have limited but adequate comfort facilities on board. This coach is equipped with a radio, and there is help on the way. The closest city is Ogden, Utah, about forty miles from here. Our dispatcher says the service truck should be here in less than an hour, so just get as comfortable as you can."

Dave looked at Myra. She was curled up with that big jacket wrapped around her and smiling at him.

"Did you have a good nap? You only slept about forty five minutes."

"It was just right. I feel great. I think we have to change buses in Ogden. I wonder if this will make us miss our connections."

"I have a schedule in my jacket. Let's see."

He stood, and Myra watched him as he searched through his coat in the overhead. He was slim and well built and when he raised his arms over his head, his shirt pulled up, and she could see his stomach. He's hairy, she thought. Not at all like Oliver. He had been soft and had no body hair at all.

"Here it is. We have a ninety-minute layover. I don't see how we can make that connection now, and the next bus is at 9:50 tonight. The next one after that is at 10:30 tomorrow morning."

Myra frowned.

"What in the world is there to do in Ogden till nearly ten o'clock?"

"Oh, I'm not worried about that. We can see the sights and have a good dinner. Besides the company is beautiful, and I'm in no rush."

Myra smiled and thought this could be a great day after all.

They spent the time talking about Dave's work, and the minutes went by without notice. They were hardly aware of the service truck coming and going and were surprised when the driver announced,

"Okay, folks, we have ten good wheels under us again, and we're on our way."

It was 1:15 and the sun was warm, when the bus pulled into the nearly empty terminal. Myra watched Dave as he collected his luggage and wondered if he would question her about her not having any.

He crossed to the front door where Myra stood and said, "No luggage?"

"No. Remember the phone call I made at breakfast? My things will be in Twin Falls on Tuesday morning. Until then, I'm going to have to rough it."

"No problem then. What should we do? Any suggestions?"

"You know, Dave, I've been thinking. What I would like to do is stay over until tomorrow morning. We will be getting in to Twin Falls very late and accommodations could be hard to find. I think it makes more sense to stay here and go on in the morning. What would you like to do?"

"I think it's a good plan if you'll let me keep you company."

Myra smiled but didn't answer.

Dave said in a very low voice, "Let's find a place to stay."

Out on the street, they saw a Hilton hotel two blocks away and Dave suggested they "hoof" it. Myra enjoyed the walk wrapping her arms around Dave's free arm. As they walked, Myra thought Oliver didn't like to walk and probably would have insisted on taking a cab.

The lobby was almost empty when they checked in and Myra hoped they wouldn't ask about luggage. They registered and were given rooms 314 and 315. Dave insisted on putting the rooms on his credit card, and the clerk never batted an eye. Dave asked to have someone take his bag to his room and turned to Myra. "Let's have some lunch before we go up. I see they have a good-looking restaurant, and I could use a bite. How about you?"

"Fine with me, I'm like a baby bird. You know? Feed me, feed me."

They both had soup and salad, and much to Myra's surprise, Dave ordered tea. Myra liked tea and was always trying different ones. Oliver had said tea was a dumb, sissy drink and would never join her. Lunch didn't seem long, but suddenly they noticed the busboys were setting up for the evening meal.

Dave said, "Wow, it's four-thirty already. I guess we had better get out of here before they throw us out. Let's make dinner reservations for seven-thirty and then take in a movie or whatever, okay?"

"You have a date, handsome."

"Good. I'd like to take a shower and rest for a while, and I suppose you would like to freshen up."

"Sounds wonderful. But instead of a movie, I'd like to take a nap and be fresh for this evening, okay?"

At Myra's door, he used her key and let her in. As she passed him in the doorway, she thought for a second that he was going to kiss her, but he just smiled and said, "Here's your key; good old lucky 315. I'm across the hall. See you at seven."

Myra removed her clothes, turned back the bed, and crawled under the sheet. She went sound asleep and was startled when she heard a knock on the door.

"Who's there?"

"Room service."

"What is it?"

"I have a parcel for you."

"Just wait a minute. I'll unlock the door and when I tell you, come in and leave it on the bed. Understand?"

"Yes, ma'am."

Myra unlocked the door and stepped into the bathroom. She peeked out the door as the bellboy placed a large white box on the bed and left the room. When he had gone, she locked the door and opened the box. Inside, she found a pair of white sandals, a gray pleated skirt, a beautiful white sweater, and a dove gray jacket. Pinned to the lapel on the jacket was a note. "Hope they fit." Myra was ecstatic. How could she be this lucky? Who was this man that he should treat her this way? It was 6:05, and she had time for a long hot bath. Much had happened today, and she needed to unwind.

Promptly at seven, Dave knocked on the door. She opened it wide, and Dave gave a small whistle.

"You are sure a good looker. I see they fit. Do you like them?"

"Oh, Dave, they are just right. Where did you find them at this time of day?"

"There is a little shop just around the corner that stays open till six, and they had a shop girl that was about your size. Is the lady ready for dinner?"

The steaks and salads were perfect. They danced to a great little orchestra, and had the best wine Myra had ever tasted. Myra was relaxed and happy when she handed Dave her key to open her door. He left the door ajar, and they stood very close. He took her face in his hands and kissed her softly on the mouth. He said thank you and kissed her again. This time Myra responded and the kiss left them both a little breathless. Myra stepped into the room and pulled Dave with her. He closed the door and followed her across the darkened room to the window. They stood for several minutes with her back to him and his arms around her. They watched the traffic go by in the street below.

Myra felt warm and at ease. She turned and they kissed again. She had never felt this way before. Kissing had always been somewhat of a duty or obligation, and with Oliver it was an unmoving experience. She stood almost like a statue as Dave removed her jacket. He pulled her sweater over her head and undid her skirt, letting it fall to the floor. He undid her brassiere and pulled down her panties. She stepped out of her sandals and stood totally naked in front of him. He let out a long breath and said,

"My God, you are absolutely the most beautiful woman I have ever seen."

He removed his jacket, and she unbuttoned his shirt, pulling it over his shoulders and letting it fall. She kissed him and felt the hair on his chest. Her head was spinning. Dave slipped out of the rest of his clothes and pulled her to the bed. Lovemaking had always been a hurried affair that left her feeling cold and uninvolved, but this was not hurried. Dave was slow and easy, taking time to explore and enjoy. Oliver was always so heavy that she could hardly breath when he was on her. Dave was half again as heavy, but she felt no weight at all. She could hear her heart pounding in her ears, and for the first time in her life, she perspired. Her breath came in gasps, and somewhere in the distance, she heard a voice that she knew to be hers, making strange whimpering sounds. Her feelings were incredible, she pulled her knees up, and hugging Dave with all her strength, she felt a strange feeling in the pit of her stomach. It was like a wound up clock spring, starting small and tight in the center, and spreading out like ripples in a pond to the very ends of her toes and fingers and the roots of her hair. Dave kissed her warm and wet as the ripples receded and left her completely exhausted and relaxed. Dave lay beside her and held her close till she slipped away into a deep sleep.

When she woke, Dave was smiling at her as she lay on his arm. She kissed him and said,

"Boy, are you some kind of lover."

"Nothin' to it, little girl, especially when the object of my affection is as beautiful as you."

"Oh, you just say that 'cause it's true."

She laughed and rolled over on top of him. Coming up on her knees, she smiled and ran her fingers through the hair on his chest. She bent forward, and moving back and forth, brushed her nipples across him. It tickled.

He pulled her forward and kissed her deep and warm. She felt the clock spring winding tight deep in the pit of her stomach again.

Chapter 12

Julius Harts made a sandwich out of some egg salad left over from the day before. It was a little dry and he washed it down with a glass of milk. Jewels was not married, and he didn't think he ever wanted to be. Women, for the most part, only got in his way. They always seemed to want his time, or something, just when he had other things to do. Right now, he wanted to get out to the Blessing house and see how the evidence team was coming. The evidence team was headed by a new man, Officer Harrison. Harrison had been at the crime scene last night, and Jewels was confident that they had not unduly disturbed the evidence.

Jewels pulled up in front of 2628 Rosewood just as the county coroner's car pulled out. He saw E. W. Russell at the wheel and was happy to have him out of the way. E.W. was an old friend of Tate's, and even though he felt Russell was a good pathologist, the relationship between the two men, made him uneasy. Harrison was on his knees in front of the refrigerator, as Jewels entered.

"How are things going, Chuck?"

"Just fine, sir. We have lifted lots of good prints, and I'm sure we will be able to get a good solid match from the prints that were taken at the murder scene out at Travis Corners."

"That's good. I hope those County Mounties have their ducks in order and don't screw up a good investigation."

"Speaking of the sheriff's department, Chief. Do you know that Sheriff Tate was taken to the hospital with a heart attack?"

"My God, no. When did you hear that?"

"Just now. The coroner called his office and they told him. That's why he left. He was headed over there to see if there was anything he could do."

"If you're okay here, Chuck, I think I'll go to the hospital too."

"Sure, Chief, go ahead. I'm done here and about all that's left is to lock this place up, and I have two other officers to help me do that."

When Jewels pulled into the hospital parking lot, he noticed the coroner's car was parked in the visitor's lot. He swung into the reserved parking area by the front door marked, "Official Hospital Staff only." He thought *I'm the Deputy Chief, and I'll park anywhere I please.*
On the third floor near a sign that read Cardiac Intensive Care, Jewels saw a huddle of people. Two of them he recognized. One was the coroner, and the other was an old school buddy and son of the Tates, Bob. Bob spotted Jewels and came forward with his hand extended.
"Hi, Jewels, good to see you. Thanks for coming."
"Yes, Bob, it's been a long time. How's your dad?"
"He's doing better every hour. Dad's a tough old bird, you know. It's Mom I'm worried about. Can't seem to get her to stop crying. Why don't you speak to her? She always liked you. Maybe you can cheer her up."
Jewels eyed Mrs. Tate and remembered the time she caught him and Lois Palmer playing doctor in their basement. It was just little kid stuff, but it had embarrassed him to tears and made him feel dirty.
"No, Bob, you are all family, and I don't want to intrude. I just wanted to know how your Dad is doing, and check on some people here that were assaulted and nearly killed."
"Oh, yes, you mean the Blessings. The last we heard is that Mr. Blessing lost his eye, and Mrs. Blessing was out of danger but unable to talk. What kind of a nut worked them over?"
"We think it was a girl. If it's who we think it is, we also are looking at her as a murder suspect. The woman we are looking for could be on parole from another state and as such be in the jurisdiction of the FBI. We might need some help from you people. Can I call on you?"
"Gosh, Jewels, this is outside of my district, but I will do anything I can to help. I'm going to be here for a week or so. Why don't we get together on Monday, and I'll see what I can do to help."
"Thanks, Bob. I won't keep you from your family any longer. Give my best to every one and let them know I wish you all the luck in the world."
"Thanks, old friend, I'll be in touch."
Jewels beat a hasty retreat. He had no interest in getting deeply involved and besides he just saw that dumb deputy of Tate's, getting off the elevator. What was his name? Oh yes, Paul, a real dummy.

Chapter 13

Dave woke with the sun in his eyes and looked at his watch, 9:15. Good lord, I've over slept he thought and rolled over in bed. Instead of being next to him, Myra was dressed and sitting in a chair against the wall. She was dressed in her traveling clothes, and looked so small and vulnerable in that big jacket with the bulgy pockets.

"Good morning, Mr. Miller. It's about time you were waking up. You just have time for a shower and a cup of coffee before we have to leave for the bus station. If you'll give me your key, I'll go across the hall and get your suitcase and while you're in the shower, I'll get you some coffee."

Dave would normally have been embarrassed to be naked in front of anyone, especially in broad daylight. But he felt nothing like that when he stood, and took her hands, pulled her out of the chair and wrapped his arms around her. He just stood there for several minutes, and then he realized she was crying.

"Gosh, baby, what's the matter?"

"Nothing, you big boob. Don't you know when a girl is happy? Go on now, take your shower."

He turned the water as hot as he could stand it and tried to think. *What was he going to do? This girl stirred feelings in him he had never felt before. Oh, sure, he was no virgin but never had he so completely lost it. Last night had been like a dream. He wondered how she felt.* He heard the door open and close. He turned the handle all the way to the left, and gasped as the water turned ice cold. When he came out of the bath, he sipped his coffee, and saw she had made the bed, placed his soiled clothes in a plastic bag, and laid out fresh underwear and sox. While he dressed, she packed away the rest of his things, and setting the suitcase next to the door, went into the bathroom. When he finished dressing, she was standing by the open door and as they left the room, he noticed she had cleaned the bathroom and folded the towels in a neat pile.

They walked to the station, checked their tickets and his suitcase with the agent, and boarded the bus with hardly a word. They found two seats in almost the same place as the day before, and sat rather stiff, until the bus pulled onto the street.

"What's the matter, Myra? Are you feeling bad about last night?"

"Oh no, Dave, I've never felt so good about any thing in my whole life. I know we have only known each other a short time, and this probably sounds silly, but I feel I have known you forever, and we are on our honeymoon. I have never been so happy, never. I was sitting watching you sleep this morning, and was scared to death that you were going to dump me, or that you were married, or something awful like that. You aren't, are you?"

"No, not even close. Myra, last night was magic. I don't know where we will go from here, but I feel the same fright as you over the thought of your leaving or being married. You aren't, are you? Married, I mean."

"No, never!"

They rode for over an hour without talking. She curled her arms around his arm and put her head against his shoulder. She went to sleep like a child.

The bus rolled on for hours. It was mid-afternoon when the driver called, "Twin Falls."

Dave rented a car, and they checked into a motel on the edge of town. She stood by his shoulder as he registered and noted that he only used his name. There was no mention of her at all, except that there was a 2 marked in the spot where it asked for the number of guests.

"We have a pool-side room with a king-sized bed; I hope you like it."

"A pool, how wonderful! I need to find a place to buy a bathing suit, and I need to pick up a few essentials. You know, girl things. I noticed a small mall right next door to the motel, and I should be able to find what I need there. Why don't you go to the room, and I'll go shopping. I won't be long."

"Okay. Do you have enough money?"

"Oh yes, I have plenty. It's only a block to the mall and I think I'll just walk. Do you need anything?"

"Can't think of a thing. Have fun."

The department store had a complete women's section, but before she went there, she purchased a medium-sized overnight bag with a key. Next, she found a two piece bathing suit that wasn't too risqué and then went to the shoe department. After changing her mind several times, she selected a pair of low-heeled pumps in dark blue. Should go well with the things Dave gave her, she thought. In the cosmetic department, she found all the toiletries she wanted, and some good smelling stuff. Last, she bought a bra, several pair of panties, and two pair of panty hose. After loading all her things in her little bag, she started for the motel. Half way across the parking lot, a police car passed in front of her, and in her mind, the officer gave her the once over twice. He's probably just girl watching, she thought. Even though the car didn't stop or even slow down, it brought to mind that she was literally on the run, and that they would probably soon have every cop in the world looking for her.

Picking up an extra key at the desk, she let herself into the room, to find Dave already in the pool. She placed her case on a little stand and got out her bathing suit. She changed quickly, and grabbed a towel from the bath. As she left the room, she removed her wallet from her jacket pocket and locked it in the case.

Myra paused by the sliding door, and watched Dave in the pool. He was very trim and muscular, with large arms and shoulders. His bottom was small, and he had great looking legs, how different from Oliver. She stood by the pool waiting for Dave to notice her. When he did, he gave a low whistle and smiled that killer smile.

"Come on in, beautiful. The water's great."

She dove in and came up right in front of him. He put his arms around her and kissed her for so long, it left her breathless. They swam for nearly an hour, and even though she was a good swimmer, she could tell Dave was even better. Just think, a powerful, gentle, man. Wow!

Myra stood by the edge of the pool and looked at her prune-wrinkled fingers.

Dave came up behind her and said, "Time to eat?"

"Boy, you got that right. Feed me. Feed me!"

As they went to their room, Dave said, "What would you like for dinner?"

"You'd only laugh if I told you."

"No, go ahead. What would you like?"

"Tacos! I saw a Taco Bell across the street, and I want tacos."

Dave roared with laughter. "You too? I really like tacos. I can't get enough of them."

Inside the room they stood very close, and Myra could tell she was going to be kissed again. Her head was spinning as they stepped out of their wet suits and stood cold and naked against each other. They kissed and Myra thought it was a real spring winder. She almost giggled with pleasure and wondered where this strange and exciting fun had been hiding. She pulled back from Dave's embrace and said teasingly,

"Well, are you going to feed me or not?"

"The last one dressed has to pick up the food and bring it to the table."

While Dave was getting his sox on, Myra pulled on her jeans with no underwear and stepped into her sandals. Grabbing her coat, she pulled it on and zipped it up as she opened the door and stood in the hallway.

"I win! You have to be my servant for the night."

"No problem, I'll be your slave if you want."

Myra ordered the tacos, one at a time, and made Dave go after each one. They laughed and played and teased about Myra not having any clothes on underneath her jeans, and what the public would say if they knew. The early evening taco crowd thinned out, and they found themselves to be the only customers in the place. They sat at a corner table and talked for hours. Myra told him of her first job in a local library, and how this one special friend had gotten her interested in art and music.

It was 11:15 when they left the Taco Bell, and walked back to the motel. After closing the door, they stood in the dark and just held each other.

Finally Dave said, "Tomorrow is going to be a busy day. I have to contact the attorney that is taking care of Aunt Alma's estate and find out what I have to do. But even before I do that, I want to go see the old house. Maybe I don't even want the place."

Myra was only half listening. She was wondering how tight the spring would have to wind before it broke.

Chapter 14

David Cline had a short morning in court and he figured he had about an hour before all the law enforcement people that were working on the John Martin murder would be in his office. This new thing about a family named Blessing being involved was making the case hard to follow. He now had to go through reports from the sheriff's department and the city police and try to keep a perspective of the overall picture. Now Deputy Chief Harts had called and left a message that he also wanted the FBI to sit in on the meeting. He picked up a coffee cup on his side bar and took a sip. Whew, it was cold and stale. The door opened, and Lois, his secretary, entered with a large thermos of fresh coffee and a tray of cups.

"Since you have so many guests this morning, I guess we should have some non-two-day-old for them. Don't you agree?"

"Thanks, Lois, I never know quite how to ask for things like coffee because of all the bad press. You know, women's lib and all."

"Don't ever let those kinds of things bother you. I'm all for women's rights, but I see this as part of my job. You deal with lots of sensitive situations in this office, and I think it's my duty to see that the atmosphere is as low key as possible."

"Thanks for those kind words, Lois; you're a doll."

Her eyes twinkled and from behind his back, she said, "Watch it, Mr. District Attorney, that doll stuff will get you in trouble. Speaking of trouble, there's an FBI Agent named Tate in the front office. He says he's here to attend a meeting of the local law enforcement people with you at 11:00. I asked him if he wanted to see you now and he said he thought he should wait until the others show up."

"Will you re-invite him to come in? Hold it a minute. Do you know if this Tate is related to our sheriff?"

"Yes, sir, he is. He went to school with my brother and Jewels Harts. I'll see if he's tired of waiting yet."

On the way to the outer office, Lois stopped by her desk and checked herself in the mirror. Her thoughts went back to the time when her brother Don was an inseparable part of the threesome of Harts, Palmer, and Tate. The three boys did everything together. Jewels became a football hero, and she had had a real crush on him as a kid. In fact, she still saw Jewels once in awhile, but he would never give her the time of day. Neither Jewels nor she had ever married. She often wondered if Jewels had ever given her a chance, would she have said yes.

"Bob, Mr. Cline would like to see you unless you insist on waiting for the rest of your party."

"Oh, thank you, Lois. I didn't mean to snub him. I just thought since I was kind of an outsider that it would be better if we all went in together."

"No, No. Don't worry about that. He wants to see you."

"What kind of a guy is he, Lois? Do you know him well?"

"No, not really Bob. He's only been here a few weeks, and we are just getting acquainted. He inherited me from the previous administration, but it looks like we will be a good match when we get settled down."

"I had hoped that Jewels would be here to introduce me since my Dad can't, but I guess it will be okay."

"Where's your dad?"

"I thought you knew. He had a heart attack on Saturday and is still in the hospital."

"Oh my God, Bob, is everything going to be all right? How's your mom?"

"Mom is fine and Dad will be coming home on Wednesday if all goes well. He's up and around a little this morning, and they are still taking tests but everything looks good."

"Well, you will give your mom and dad my best when you see them, won't you? Come on in, Mr. Cline wants to meet you."

Lois escorted Bob into the inner office and introduced the two men. She told Cline about Sheriff Tate being in the hospital, poured them each a cup of coffee, and left the room.

"Sorry to hear about your dad, Bob. I've only talked with him a few times, but he seems like an up-standing citizen."

"That he is, Dave. He's kind of a do-it-yourself guy, but I guess that's all being part of the "old school."

"Old school is right. How long has he been sheriff?"

"Over twenty-six years now, I think. I was only three when he was first elected. He's seen a lot of changes since he started as sheriff and has made a lot of friends. I grew up around cops of every sort. Both my dad and my grandfather were law enforcement officers, and I guess it was their influence that attracted me to the bureau."

"Well, you give him our best wishes. By the way, Bob, what is your interest in this Martin case?"

"Well, none, really. I came to see Dad last Saturday night and ran into Deputy Chief Harts. He thought the Bureau might be interested in this case since the prime suspect is on parole from another state. I'm on a week's family leave, and I told Jewels that I would sit in on this meeting as a favor. I called my superior last night and gave him the story. He asked me to attend this meeting and pass any information on to the local agent in charge for further action."

"I see. Well, I guess the only thing to do is hope everyone can make it on time. They are due now."

Almost before the words were out of his mouth, the intercom buzzed and Lois said,

"There are several people here to see you, sir. The deputy chief, the coroner and a sheriff's deputy, Paul Bench."

"Thank you, Lois, show them in please."

Bob Tate thought they looked like a bunch of boy scouts marching in to receive a merit badge. E.W. Russell took a seat next to Bob, and Jewels sat at the end of Cline's desk as close as he could to Cline. Paul Bench sat almost at the far end of the room on a leather couch. David Cline spoke first.

"Thank you all for coming. I have learned this morning that you men all know each other and I'm somewhat of an outsider. However, since I asked for this meeting, I'll just start off by telling you why. Many times in the early stages of an investigation of this sort, police officers get so deeply involved they forget that one day they just might have to go to court and place all their hard work in the hands of an attorney. Since that attorney will probably be me, or one of my assistants, I think it might be well if we keep the lines of communications open and prevent the possibility of a mistrial or having the case thrown out because of the lack of admissible evidence. I have asked each unit involved to deliver its report at the earliest possible hour so that my staff and I will have a chance to go over them and plug any holes we might find. I see by the pile on my desk that you have complied with my request and my work has been cut out for me. Since we are all together, I would like each of you to tell me now if you have seen anything that you think could cause a problem."

Jewels spoke, "Sir, I invited Bob Tate to attend this meeting since I am quite sure that the person we are looking for is a parolee from Washington State, and if so, this case could fall into the realm of the FBI. If the FBI becomes involved, it could add greatly to our problem-solving capabilities for blood and fingerprint identification. From the looks of things, we could be dealing with a person who has killed several times and we will probably find ourselves under the bright lights of the news media. I hope we can persuade Bob to help us bring the FBI into this case and give us a hand. How about it, Bob?"

Bob Tate thought same old Jewels spouting off like he was running for dogcatcher,

"I don't know, Jewels. It's up to my boss and the local agent. I will tell you that the district chief is already looking at this and will make a determination right away."

Cline said, "Very well, I have all your reports. Now is there anything of any importance you can think of that is not covered in your reports?"

Paul spoke, "Since Sheriff Tate is in the hospital, I will have to fill in for him a little. Most of his reports are on your desk, but he didn't get a chance to finish them and I have no idea what he might want to add. I spoke to the doctor about an hour ago and the sheriff will probably be able to answer our questions in two or three days. Other than that, the only thing I can think of that might cause a problem is that I can't find the axe handle the sheriff found at the crime scene."

Jewels spun around in his chair. His face was livid. "What do you mean you can't find it? That's probably the murder weapon. That's the dumbest stunt I've ever heard. Can't Tate's Mounties get anything right?"

Jewel's face turned blank. He realized he had forgotten himself and spoken out of turn but before he could make any kind of an apology, Paul came at him with a red face and clenched fists.

"Damn you, Harts, don't you call me dumb and don't you say a word about Sheriff Tate. He was sheriff when you were wearing three-cornered pants and he knows more about police work than you or your entire department!"

Russell stood and stepped between the two men, "Okay, you two, calm down. I know you have all been working overtime on this case and your nerves are a little on edge, but it doesn't do any good to get testy. I know where the handle is and there is no problem. Now you two boys calm down and go back to work. Go on now, shake hands and get out of here."

The two men shook hands and mumbled something in the way of an apology. The three of them trouped out the door leaving Russell and Cline shaking their heads. Russell said, "Sorry about that, Dave. Young Tate is okay, but those other two are just a couple of clowns. I'll get out of here too and let you get at those reports. The whereabouts of the axe handle is in my report. Tate probably didn't have it in his records that my office was making some tests. I'll have some things to add when I finish some of the tests tonight, and I'll bring you up to date tomorrow. I sure hope Tate gets back soon and keeps these young bucks in place. Oh, by the way, I won't mention this blow up to Chief Denny, if you won't, okay? See ya."

When Russell left the courthouse, he went to his car and headed for the hospital to see his old friend.

Chapter 15

Dave stood in the bathroom door and watched Myra as she lay on the bed. She had the sheet pulled over her middle and had one leg on top of the cover. Her full, perfect breasts rose and fell in the even cadence of one in a deep sleep. Her hair framed her face and she looked like a young child. How beautiful she is, Dave thought.

He tried to sort out the last two days. There didn't seem to be any reason that he should feel this way so soon. He had had other relationships. All of them were short except one and that had lasted only two months. She had moved in with him and things were okay until she had gotten in the way of his work. He took his work very seriously and when she began to demand more of his time than he was willing to give, she left.

Now here was Myra, sweet and gentle and full of fun. She didn't seem to have the hang ups that other women seemed to have, and he attributed most of this to the chance that she really liked him, all the way.

It's time I got her up anyway he thought and crossed the room to sit on the edge of the bed. He bent over and kissed her on her throat. She stirred and pulled him down on top of her. She cradled his head on her breasts and whispered.

"Good morning, lover. Are you going to feed me before I wither away?"

"Come on, get up. We have a full day. I want to get out to see Aunt Alma's old house before we meet with the attorney at 3:00 this afternoon. Is there anything you want or have to do?"

She leaped from the bed and ran to the shower. "I'll be ready in a shake. What should I wear?"

"Let's wear jeans until after we see the house. Then if we feel we should, we can come back and change."

It seemed to Myra that they had driven much further than the map showed, but what a drive! Everything was so green for this time of the year. Very few trees had started to turn color, and they still had all their leaves. They passed a golf course and a country club with tennis courts and a large pool.

"Well, here we are. I think it's the place on the right. It looks like a picture Dad had when I was a kid."

Myra was breathless; what a beautiful place! There was a sweeping drive that seemed to Myra to be a mile long. The grounds were magnificent, and looked like they had been manicured. The house was two or maybe three stories, and there was a huge porch with columns. Behind the house was a four-car garage and an old fashioned carriage shed. On the other side and down a gentle slope, was a pond with a small stream running through it. And a Gazebo!

"Oh, Dave, can this be true?"

"I don't know. I don't see a mailbox or anything. Let's drive in and see."

They had driven a little past the driveway, and Dave had to back up to make the turn. As the car started to move, they heard a shout.

"Whoa, watch it, young man, you almost got my foot. Are you looking for someone?"

"Yes, sir. We are looking for the Alma Morgan residence."

"Well, you found it. I'm the caretaker. May I help you?"

"My name is David Miller; Alma Morgan was my aunt."

"Oh, by golly, I was expecting you but not for another week yet. My name is Jack Potts, and I watch out for the place, or at least I did, when your aunt was alive. I did the gardening and handyman work for her, and my wife did some of the housework and shopping. We got paid and were given this little house over here to live in as part of our wages."

He pointed to a small four-room house on the left side of the road.

"Did my aunt own property on that side of the road too?"

"Yes, sir, three acres on the left and twelve on the right." He went on, "I've been working on the big house this morning. Getting it ready for winter, you know. The doors are all open. Why don't you and your wife look around? When you're through, come by the house and we'll have a cup of tea. My wife will want to meet you both."

"Did you hear that, Dave? He called me your wife. Are you going to tell them different?"

"Sure, why not? No use giving them the wrong impression."

Dave parked the car by the back door and they entered through the kitchen. Myra was shocked. The place looked like a restaurant, everything in the world to cook with. It was huge. There was a large room-size pantry, and a huge walk-in freezer. Dave went to a small doorway that had stairs to the next floor, and observed that it must be the servant's way to the upstairs. Myra gasped as she looked in a buffet at the far end of the kitchen. It was shuttered on the kitchen side and was stocked with dishes and glassware that could be accessed from the dining room side. They went through a large swinging door next to the buffet and came into a great dining hall. The table would easily seat twenty, and the chandelier over the table must have weighed a ton. They went through a pair of sliding doors and crossed the great entry hall through another set of sliding doors into the most wonderful living room Myra had ever seen. There were six, no seven, arm chairs, and three davenports, several tables, and a bar. In the front corner under stained glass windows stood a real grand piano, and on the far wall was a fireplace big enough to park a car in. They went from room to room: a den with another fireplace, a small green room, and a sewing/sun room. Up the circular staircase on the second floor were six bedrooms and three baths. The master bedroom was directly over the living room, and was the same size, also with a fireplace. There was a king-size bed and three settees. One wall was lined with floor-to-ceiling bookcases, and there was a roll-top writing desk. The bath in the master bedroom had two sinks, and a tub and a walk-in shower. In a little alcove, there was a stool and a bidet. Next to the bathroom were two large dressing rooms with full length mirrors everywhere. Every room in the house was spotless and furnished with the most tasteful things. They found a door leading upstairs to a large attic room that was a complete gymnasium. There were exercise machines of every sort and a hot tub and Sauna. Their tour took them out the back door again and to the garage. Behind the car stalls was a complete workshop and behind that a greenhouse. The room over the garage was a large artist's studio with skylights, hardwood floors, and a full bedroom and bath.

"Oh, Dave, it's so beautiful I could cry. What are you going to do?"

"Right now, I want to talk to the caretaker, and see what kind of arrangements my aunt made with him."

They drove over and parked in front of the little house and were met at the door by Dora Potts. She was a raw-boned woman with gray hair and the look of hard work about her.

Jack and Dora talked for over an hour and told Dave all about themselves without asking one question about him.

Finally Dave said, "Thank you for the tea and your time. I have an appointment in an hour with Alma's attorney, and I'll be back tomorrow to let you know my plans. Just so you don't worry, I will make every effort to see that you are treated right when I figure out what I'm going to do. Good afternoon and I'll see you tomorrow about noon."

Myra sensed that Dave was preoccupied and let him drive in silence all the way back to the motel.

"Myra, if you don't mind, I would like to see the attorney alone. I don't know what I'm going to do yet or how I'm going to do it, but I have some important decisions to make."

She went directly to their room and turned on the television. She felt sick. She got the feeling from Dave's attitude that he was going to dump her. She cried real tears and felt empty.

The ten o'clock news was on when Dave came in. He had a big bag of Kentucky Fried Chicken, and two milkshakes. They ate in silence and with hardly a word went to bed. Dave held her close in those big protective arms, and she went to sleep. She woke many times during the night and each time Dave would kiss her gently and stare into the darkness.

Chapter 16

Lois rubbed her shoulder. It was always the left one that gave her trouble. She tapped the stack of eighty-one sheets of paper on her desk and slipped them into a folder. She looked in a little booklet in the center drawer of the desk and copied a case number onto the tab of the folder. She had had a long day and was looking forward to quitting time. Cline had given her three dictation tapes to transcribe, and with all the other things on her mind, the day was a blur in her memory.

Her intercom buzzed and she pushed the button.

"Yes, sir."

"Lois, I just spoke to the coroner's office, and Russell is on his way over here with Harts and Bob Tate. They have just had a meeting and want to bring me up to date. I hope you don't have plans."

"No, sir. Do you want me to stay and take notes, or will you be putting it on the recorder?"

"I'd like you to stay, if that's all right."

"Yes, sir. Will you want fresh coffee?"

"I don't think so, Lois. If we make them too comfortable, they will stay all night."

The men took the same chairs they had occupied the day before, and Lois sat next to the file cabinet at a little student's desk.

Russell spoke, "I'm sorry to barge in on you so late in the day, Dave, but my work load is getting out of hand, and I need to get this sewed up, at least for the time being. To get started, I have made tests on the blood samples we found on the axe handle, at the crime scene and in the cabin by the bed. There is no question that they are all the blood of the suspect, Myra Dillon. We got her blood type from known records of the state institution in Washington, and it matches. Next, we got a fingerprint match from all the same sources, plus the ones we got from the Blessing house, and they match the ones on file in Washington State. All this has taken place in a very short period of time, due to the efforts of Bob here and his FBI sources. There seems to be no question that the woman we know as Myra Dillon is our murderer. There is some question now, however, that this is who she really is. When she was arrested in Washington for the murder of Oliver Dillon, they were known by all to be man and wife. For some unknown reason this fact was never questioned. Since it was such an open and shut case, their union was never investigated. It seems strange that in all the questioning that was done, she was never required to give her maiden name. Bob spoke to two of the investigators on the prosecution team, and they both admit to this oversight. They say it was because she was caught so red-handed at the crime scene with the smoking gun in her hand that the background investigation was let slide. The fact that no one knew her maiden name got buried so deep in the records that even when she was released on parole, it was not questioned. She claimed that her only living relative was her husband and this also was not questioned. The FBI has, so far, been unable to find a marriage license for the Dillons. Her social security and driver's license are both under the name of Myra Dillon, and were both originally issued under that name. As I said, these findings are all preliminary, but for now, we seem to be looking for a ghost. We will do all in our power to find this woman, but unless she uses the name of Myra Dillon or gets into trouble somewhere and her prints show up at the FBI, we are stumped."

"Well, thank you all very much. As district attorney, your investigation and the apprehension of a suspect establish my position. Without a suspect in custody, I must proceed with a coroner's inquest and seek a preliminary indictment using the name of Myra Dillon and or parties unknown. Mr. Harts, do you have anything to add?"

"No, sir. I will see that we circulate photographs and a description but until something happens, I don't have any idea where to even start looking."

"How about you, Bob? Do you have anything to add?"

"No, sir. We have already given all this to the local office, and, of course, placed her prints on the hot sheet. If she's a bad girl and her prints come in from anywhere in the country, we will be alerted."

"I hate to ask this of you, Jewels, but have you rechecked her previous jobs and old friends?"

"Sir, there just aren't any. The only job we can identify is with a public library in Tacoma, Washington, and they only knew her as Myra Dillon. She was a volunteer working on a part time basis, and they had no other helpful information. This woman, whoever she is, has disappeared like a puff of smoke."

Chapter 17

Even after a shower, Dave felt groggy. The night had been long and troublesome; he had so many decisions to make.

He sat on the bed and faced Myra. "Gee, kid, I hate to leave you again today, but I just have to get this house deal settled. The attorney tells me we have a ton of papers to sign, and we have to go before some kind of a probate judge. All this is going to take most of the day. Is there something you would like to do?"

"My yes, Dave, don't you remember? I am supposed to pick up my belongings today."

"That's great, Myra. I hate to leave you alone again, but if you have something to keep you occupied, I won't worry. Why don't you take the car and drop me off at the attorney's office, go do your thing, and pick me up about three this afternoon?"

Myra parked the car in front of a sign that read, "Timothy Timmons, Attorney At Law." The place was almost in the center of town, but it looked like a suburban ranch house.

She still felt funny about the way Dave was behaving, but as he left the car he took her hand, kissed it, and said, "Have a good day, Myra, and by tonight, I'm sure things will look better. Pick me up at three, okay?"

The kid at the counter in the U-Haul office had long hair and didn't seem too smart. She had asked for her things and he didn't seem to know what to do. A woman came from the back room, looked at Myra, and said, "What's the matter, Sammy?"

"This woman wants her stuff, and I don't know about the paper work. Her name is Myra Carter, and we have her stuff out back."

"Where did you put the shipping envelope, Sammy? I need it for the signature card."

"Right there on your desk."

"Good boy. Now go get her things so you can help her load them in her car. Now, let's see. What is your mother's maiden name dear?"

"Pike!"

"Okay, If you will sign this card, we'll have you on your way in no time."

"Myra signed the card, and handed it back." The woman compared the signatures, and put the cards in a file box.

"Okay, everything is taken care of except the money. That'll be $26.00, please."

Sammy came by with a hand truck and three cardboard boxes. He loaded them in the back seat and held the car door open for her.

She drove out the same road that they had taken to the house the day before and finally found a place she had seen that was perfect for her needs. The sign said,

Kiwanis Picnic Park
(Closed for the season)

She had no trouble driving around the sign, and went clear to the back of the park. She found a spot out of sight behind some trees and pulled up by a picnic table. She unloaded the boxes and placed them on the table. There was an empty garbage can nearby and she pulled it closer. Two of the boxes were loaded with papers and old photos that she looked over, and, one at a time threw in the can. When it was full, she started a fire and burned everything she had discarded. The job was more difficult than she had anticipated. She was throwing away her past. All the letters from her friends and family were read once more, and the pictures were set to a final memory. Her last task was to empty her wallet and burn all her cards.

There, she thought, that's the last of Myra Dillon. She burned the boxes and all that was left were her birth certificate, her high school diploma, and a social security card, all under the name of Ardith Myra Carter.

Dave was standing on the curb when Myra pulled up at three o'clock on the dot. He slid into the passenger side and said, "Only one little box, is that all you have?"

"No, the rest of the things didn't fit any more, so I got rid of them. Where to?"

"Let's go have a taco. I'm starving, aren't you?"

This trip to Taco Bell was less festive than the previous visit. Myra was quiet, and Dave talked mostly about the fantastic offers that had been made for his property. He said the country club had offered five hundred thousand cash, and that was just for the twelve acres on the north side of the road. Dave ate four tacos but Myra had only one and a half. She felt so badly that one more bite would have made her ill. They finished in silence, and when they walked out to the car, Myra couldn't even look at Dave for fear of crying.

At the car, Myra handed Dave the keys and said, "Here you had better drive. I forgot that I don't have a driver's license, and I don't want to get into trouble."

While they were in the restaurant, it had started to get dark, and a cold wind had come up. Myra shivered, pulled her jacket close around her, and said, "What now?"

"Let's go see Mr. and Mrs. Potts. I want to see what we can work out with them."

Myra's heart stopped. Why would he have to work anything out with them unless he had decided to sell the house? They rode in silence until they passed the country club gate, when Dave said, "Look. The house is dark."

They pulled up in front and saw a note pinned to the door. Dave got out of the car just as it started to rain and returned with the note giving it to Myra to read.

"We have gone shopping and over to see our daughter. Will hope to see you in the morning," J. Potts. "PS: The house is unlocked."

"Nuts, I was hoping to get things settled with them tonight so that tomorrow would be free. Well, that's okay. I guess I'm not in that much of a rush. I tell you what, Let's go back to the motel, get our things, and spend the night in the house. Could be fun, right?"

"Right!"

They rode in silence back to the motel. Dave settled up in the office, and Myra loaded their things in the car. By the time they were ready to leave, it was raining very hard and they both got soaked. They got even wetter when they took things into the house. The house was dark but warm, and they shed their outer garments in the kitchen.

"Come on, Myra, I'm chilled to the bone. Let's take a shower and build a fire in the bedroom fireplace. It looks like a great night for it."

They climbed the stairs and put their things on a stand by the bed. Dave went to a small closet in the hall and came back with an armload of wood for the fire. In no time he had a good blaze going.

Myra was first in the shower. It was larger than any shower she had ever been in, and it even had a bench. The chill left her in ten seconds, and she tried to get her mind off things by scrubbing hard. She was all pink and soapy when the door opened and Dave stepped in. He took the soap from her and lathered himself all over. Then he put his arms around her and held her so tight she could hardly breath. They stood there all soapy and warm, and Myra started to cry. Not just a cry, but real body-jerking sobs.

"Oh, baby, what's the matter?"

"I'm so sad, Dave. You're going to sell this beautiful place, and I would give anything, ANYTHING, to live here."

"Oh, Myra, my love, you can live here. I want you to marry me and live happily ever after right here in this house. I want this to be our home. What do you say?"

"Yes, yes, oh yes, I do, I do."

They stood and clung to each other like they were holding onto a lifeline.

Myra started to laugh.

"What now, you silly girl?"

"Here I am, standing naked in a shower, all wet and covered with soap, and I've just been proposed to by a naked man that must be out of his mind. Don't you think that's funny?"

They stepped from the shower, and wrapped themselves in two very large Turkish towels. Myra sat on the bed, and Dave told her not to move from that spot until he returned. He disappeared for a few moments and came back with a bottle of wine and two glasses. He poured the wine, lay out on the bed and said,

"Now. Tell me your life story."

Myra felt that clock spring wind.

Chapter 18

Myra woke. It was cold outside and there was frost on the window. The long Indian summer was over, and winter seemed to be everywhere. The trees had lost their leaves, and the grass had started to turn its winter brown. A cold, heatless sun shown through the window and illuminated the room in a flat shadow-less light.

She had started her period the day before and it felt good to lie close to Dave. He always seemed to be a degree warmer than a human ought to be, but at a time like this, it was truly wonderful.

She smiled as she pictured the last two weeks in her memory. They had spent the first four days in their new home in almost total seclusion with the exception of a few hours with Jack and Dora Potts.

Myra had never been so happy, and her new home was like heaven. She explored every square foot of the house and grounds with squeals of delight at every step. Old Aunt Alma must have known she was coming to live here. There was nothing that Myra would change. The furnishings, the kitchenware, the carpets, and the wallpaper, were just what she would have selected. Even the selection of Mr. and Mrs. Potts was a stroke of genius.

The first morning, Myra had gone down to the kitchen at the first show of daylight because of the smell of fresh coffee. She found Dora in the kitchen, starting a vegetable soup for lunch. They talked for two hours, and Myra fell in love with her. Later when Jack showed up and Dave came down, the arrangements were made for them to stay on just as if there had been no change in the master of the house. Everyone seemed happy with the arrangements, and Myra was ecstatic.

Dave stirred and rolled over to face her. She felt a small irritation over not having Dave's warm back to cuddle up to but decided not to be bitchy about it.

"Good morning, lover. How's my big handsome knight this morning?"

"I'm thinking about what I should do today. I think I'll go see that friend of Jacks about building the covered walkway over to the studio. I really need to get that done right away and start working. I made arrangements with my agent to take a month off, and if I lay in bed with you all day, I'll never get the job done in time to go back to work and meet my deadlines.

"Well, by all means, let's get started. What can I do to help?"

"I don't know that there is anything you can do to help with the construction, but if you want to take Dora and select some furnishings for the studio office, that would help. I'll take care of the studio itself, but I would like some help with the office."

"Oh Dave, can I really? I'll get up right now and get started. I'll call Dora, and we'll go to town this morning. I want to see about getting a driver's license anyway. I can't ask Dora to drive me around forever. I can hardly wait till you get back to work, and I can go to work for you. I'm a fair secretary, and I think I'll be a passable bookkeeper because I'm very good with money."

Dave pulled her to him and kissed her. She felt so lucky she couldn't believe it, and the cramp in her stomach was gone.

"Come on lover, I'll scrub your back in the shower, if you'll scrub mine."

On the way to the shower, she could smell coffee. Dora must be there.

In the shower Dave suddenly turned and held her close.

"Myra, let's not delay any longer. Let's get married a week from today. It's my birthday on the fifteenth, and that way I'll never forget our anniversary. If we do it then, we'll be married before Thanksgiving, and we will be able to spend the holidays as old married folks."

"The first thing I'm going to say, Dave, is yes. Then I'm going to back up and ask you if you are sure. We have known each other such a short time, and I want you to be really, really sure. I have waited for twenty-eight years for the right man, and I want you to be positive I'm the right woman. I only want to do this once."

"I'm sure! I'm positive!"

He continued to hold her, and after several minutes he felt her shake with laughter.

"Now what?"

"Nothing at all sweetheart, It's just that every time you propose something to me, I'm all wet and soapy and standing naked with a man that's obviously lost his mind."

Timothy Timmons had been Alma Morgan's attorney for nearly ten years, and Jack Morgan's friend and attorney for many years prior to that. When Jack died back in the 70's, Tim took over as advisor and financial consultant to Alma and had been largely responsible for her substantial portfolio. She had followed his advice in most matters, and along with her uncanny knack with real estate, she had amassed a fortune of over nineteen million dollars. Her will had set aside her house and land, and two and a half million, for her nephew David Miller, and the remainder went to an orphanage in Bay City, Michigan. The bequest was in the form of a trust fund, and he had been made executor of the fund. She had made arrangements for ample payment for his services, and he figured his basic retirement needs were taken care of with this single charge. There had been some kind of friction between Alma and her brother, and he had never seen Stewart Miller or his son David. The friction seemed to increase after the death of David's mother some ten years before, and Alma would never mention their names. This was why he had been so surprised, when she had changed her will to include her nephew David. As far as he knew, the only contact between them had been an annual Christmas card from David. The cards always came the week before Christmas, and they were one-of-a-kind works of art. Alma had always shown them with pride over the holidays, but then they were put away and never mentioned again. Alma seemed to enjoy the cards but had never responded.

Now here was David accepting his inheritance and wanting to move in to the old house on the first night. He had asked for Timothy's help in making some decisions about the caretakers and wanted to see they were taken care of. After all these years, Alma had left them only one thousand dollars and nothing more. David felt that their loyalty should be more recognized and wanted to see that the little house was theirs as long as they wanted to live there. He had written a contract that would allow Jack and Dora to be in the house, rent free, as long as they lived and occupied the dwelling. There was also an employment clause, but the house agreement, was not contingent on their continued employment. He told Dave that he thought he was going a little overboard, but Dave had insisted, and since it was well within his financial means, he let it go at that.

The thing that really worried him the most, was this sudden desire to marry this Myra. He admittedly had only known her for a very short time, but this didn't seem to matter at all. He was going to marry her and that's all there was to it. When he had suggested to Dave that he consider a prenuptial agreement, Dave only said that if he had met her, he wouldn't even think of something like that. Nevertheless, he took it upon himself to contact a private detective to see if there was any thing about this woman that could cause a problem. He would do this on his own as a favor to his old friend Alma, knowing that it was exactly what she would have done.

Chapter 19

Jewels was thinking about tonight and his date with Lois. He had seen her several times in the past few weeks, and he looked forward to seeing her again. His intercom buzzed, and he picked it up.

"Chief, there is a woman out front who says she has some information on the wanted poster for Myra Dillon. Do you want to see her?"

"I sure do. Keep her there and I'll be right out."

As he came across the office, he saw a woman at the counter in her late to mid-thirties. She was a little on the seedy side, and was dressed in clothes of a decade ago or more.

"I'm Deputy Chief Harts, ma'am. How may I help you?"

"I came, 'cause you have this here poster up that says you are looking for Myra. Is there any reward?"

"No, ma'am, there isn't, but you would be doing your community a great service if you would give us whatever information you have."

"Shit, I don't care about the damn community. What's in it for me?"

"What would you like?"

"How about twenty?"

"I think that could be arranged if what you have is any good."

"Oh, it's good all right. I know Myra well."

"Okay, come on back to my office, and we'll see."

He asked her to have a seat and closed the door. He opened his top drawer and took out a pack of cigarettes, and offered her the pack. She had a waitress uniform on under her coat, and under the logo "Sandy's" was the name Sharon. He offered to take her coat, but she said she would rather keep it on. Leaning across the desk, he lit her cigarette, and at the same time, pushed the record button on his recorder.

"Now, what do you know about Myra?"

"Not till you give me the twenty."

He pulled a twenty-dollar bill from his wallet, and laid it on the desk in front of her.

"If what you have is worth it, you can pick it up."

"You damn cops are all the same."

"Let's start with your name, and if you really do have the goods on Myra, there could be another ten in it."

"My name is Sharon Mills, and I first met Myra when we were in the hospital together. We shared a room, and got to be real good friends. She was in there for shooting her husband, and I felt sorry for her, 'cause she didn't seem to fit in a place like that. She was not like the other women in that dump. She was, you know, clean cut. All the time we were roomies, she never made a mess or caused any trouble. She worked in the library, and all she ever did was read, read, read. She taught herself to type and take shorthand, and read everything she could get her hands on. She used to sit in front of the TV at night, and take shorthand notes of what everyone said on the program. Then the next day, she would type it all up. She got to where she hardly missed a word."

"Did she ever tell you about her background? Where she came from, and things like that?"

"No, never. She acted like there was nothing in her life before she met her husband. I got the feeling that she didn't hate him or anything, she just got mad and shot him. She said it was over money, and I don't wonder about that. She had a real thing about money. She had several hundred dollars on her when they arrested her, and all the time I knew her, she worried about that damn money. I got tired of hearing about it and told her to knock it off. She didn't say any more about it, but I could tell it bothered her that they wouldn't let her keep it with her."

"Are you sure she never said anything about her family?"

"No, never a word. She never had a visitor either, not one in all the five years we were together. She was just a nice, sweet girl. Or that is, she was until she pitched a fit over a lousy buck tip."

"What was that about?"

"Well, we got out of the joint on the same day, and on the bus into town, she told me she had no where to go and no job. She was going to be living at the 'Y' and was all-alone. My brother Sandy owns a small restaurant over in Pecos, and he promised me a job when I got out. Well, I felt sorry for her and told her I would ask my brother about a job for her when I got down here. My brother is not the easiest man to work for and always needs help. Anyway, I wrote her at the 'Y', and a week later, she showed up. She had never done waitress work before, but she was a quick learner, and Sandy liked her. She worked there about a month, and one day she thought one of the other girls had pinched a buck tip off one of her tables. She pitched a fit. I had never seen her like that before. She was like a mad woman. She even pulled a knife on this other gal, and Sandy had to break them up. There was nothing to it you know. The other girl had picked up the tip while she was cleaning off the table. She was only doing Myra a favor by cleaning off the table, and had put the tip in a box by the register, where we keep tip money in cases like this. It didn't calm Myra down though, and Sandy had to can her. The last I saw her, she had asked some old man for a ride into Wagon Mound, and she was climbing in his old car."

"Do you know who the old man was?"

"No, never saw him before, but he was an old guy about seventy, and he was driving an old Chevy. They took off up Highway 25, and I haven't seen her since. That's all I know. Do I get the thirty?"

"Yes, you sure do. Tell me where I can reach you, and if you can think of anything else, there could be another sawbuck in it for you. Thanks, Sharon, you take care now."

Jewels took the tape out of the recorder and put it in his safe. He was late for his date with Lois and had to hurry.

Chapter 20

Dora collapsed in the big chair in the front room, and said to Jack. "I don't know how I'm going to keep up with that girl. She's like a whirlwind. Where does she get all that energy? I thought at first it was because she is young, but I can't remember that much snap in my garter, ever."

"Hey, woman, you're getting too old to remember. It's only been a few years ago that my mother said the same thing about you."

"Well, your mom was a lot older than me, and she was sick a lot. Do you know what she's doing right this minute? She's turning all the mattresses and changing all the bedding."

"What's wrong with that?"

"She's doing it in all six bedrooms, and none of them have been slept in for months."

Myra puffed as she pulled the king-size mattress halfway off the bed. She flopped in a chair and caught her breath. Wow, this was the last of the bunch, and the house would be ready. Clean from top to bottom.

Her wedding was only five days away, and she wanted everything to be perfect. Tomorrow night they were going to meet the minister and have a little talk about the pitfalls of married life. Huh, big joke. Oh well, it would make the padre happy and it wouldn't hurt anything. Dave thought it was a bummer too, but he was Jack and Dora's pastor, and he didn't want to offend them.

After the little talk, they were going to have a party and had invited Alma's attorney and his wife over for a few drinks. This was the first time she was to meet the great Timothy Timmons and she wondered what he would be like. Myra had the feeling he didn't approve of her and Dave getting married, but whether he did or didn't, made no difference at all.

Her eye caught some writing on one of the slats on the bed frame, and she got up to have a closer look. What was written on the slat was. "Two turns right to 56 – one turn to the left past 56 and stop at 13 – two turns to the right past 13 and stop at 80 – Open Sesame." That, she thought, is a combination to a safe. But what safe? She had seen no safe and there was no way of telling where that writing came from or how long it had been there. Well, back to work!

As she made the bed, her mind went back over the week since Dave had asked to get married on his birthday. She and Dora had picked out the best looking furniture for the office, and Dave had purchased all new art tables, and accessories for his studio. The covered walkway between the kitchen and the studio was being completed today, and the men were out there now, cleaning up the construction trash.

Dora had started making a few things for the party, and she had picked out a dress she wanted to wear. She thought white would be good and had found a really spiffy looking, off-the-shoulder number that Dora said was a real showstopper. The hem had to be let out just a little, and she had to get in to town first thing in the morning and pick it up.

She would have Dora drop her of at the driver's license place for her driving test first and then pick up her dress and be home by noon to finish getting ready for the party.

There, the job was done. She stood back and looked at the room. What a beautiful bedroom it was. It was a bedroom all right, but it was more than that. It was a library, a sitting room, and a Roman bath, all behind one door, and she loved it. She and Dave had come there the night before and closed the door. Dave had taken her in his arms, and said he wanted to always feel they could come here and close out the rest of the world. Did she want to get married and live in this gorgeous house with this gorgeous man? You bet I do, she thought.

Going downstairs through the little stairway off the stair landing and into the back of the kitchen always gave her a little thrill. She didn't know why, it just did. Dave said it was made that way so the servants could get around without being seen in the main part of the house. Stepping into the kitchen she found Dora Just going out the back door.

"Hi, Myra, the men have finished out back, and I'm going to drag Jack home before the storm that's coming gets here. Have you seen the weather change in the last few minutes? I'll bet it snows before morning. Boy, look how the wind has come up."

As she went out the door, Dave came in. "Burr! It's getting cold out there. I'm going to jump in the shower and then I want to eat. Would you like to go in town for a taco?"

"Sure, if you'd like, but Dora made some pot pies for us and I can make a salad in a flash."

"Okay, I'll clean up and be right down."

"Why don't you make a fire before you shower? I'll put everything on a tray, so we can have dinner in our room."

"Wonderful! How good can life be?"

"Just so! just so."

There was just a skiff of snow in the morning. The wind was still blowing when Dora drove her to the license bureau and parked the car in a spot that said, "Drivers taking the driving test, park here." They went inside, and she watched Myra and the examiner drive away. Myra had seemed a bit more flustered than she usually was about things, but Dora guessed that would be normal since she was getting a license so late in life.

When the test was over, Myra parked the car in the parking spot and the examiner said, "You did very well on the test. Are you sure you've never had a license before? You drive like an old hand."

"Oh, I didn't say I had never driven before. I said I had never had a license. I was raised on a farm, and I have been driving since I was just a little kid. I never drove on the road much though, and we never had just a car. All we had to drive were trucks, and my brother always took me where I needed to go in town. Besides, my dad always said that driving was, or should be, left to men, and he never encouraged me, or my mother, to drive off the farm."

Myra got her license, drove to the dress shop, picked up her dress, and drove home. On the way home, the conversation lagged, and Myra thought the license was the last of the documents she needed to bring back Ms. Carter. *Next week when I'm Mrs. Miller, the transition will be complete.*

Dropping Dora off at her door, she put the car in the garage and ran into the house. It was freezing. Dave was not home and she guessed he was with Jack someplace. She made a cup of spiced tea and sat looking out the window as Dave drove in the drive with a car she had not seen before. He parked it in the garage next to the rental car and came in the house.

"What do you think of our new car? Do you like it?"

"New car? Oh, Dave! Let me see."

She grabbed her coat and ran outside.

"It is a beauty. What kind is it?"

"It's a Mercedes Benz."

"My god, Dave, isn't that awfully expensive? Can we afford it?"

"Sure, Myra. No problem!"

"I was getting worried because we were spending so much money on the house and everything. Now you come home with a new car."

"Well, we have had the rental for several weeks now, and we sure can't afford that, now can we?"

"Dave, you're making fun of me."

"No, no, Myra. I'm telling you there is no problem."

"Okay, Dave, but if you start running short, let me know. I have a few dollars, and we won't have to starve."

"Starve? okay, Myra, I was going to tell you at my birthday party, but I guess I'd better tell you now."

"Tell me what?"

"That Aunt Alma didn't leave me just the house. She also left me two and a half million in cash."

"You mean DOLLARS?"

"Yes, dollars."

Myra didn't understand it, but she suddenly felt that clock spring wind tight in the pit of her stomach. She ran to Dave, threw her arms around him, kissed him like she was going to eat him alive, and said, "Dave, take me up to our room and make love to me. Now, Dave! NOW!"

Betty Timmons watched her husband comb his hair. She was always a little jealous over his hair. His hair had turned pure white just after he was forty and hers just looked like it was dead. His was full and wavy while hers was thin and straight. Somehow it didn't seem fair.

"If you didn't want to go to this shindig, why did you say we would?"

"You know why, Bett. It's because I feel I owe it to Alma. Besides, this young man might need me someday. I think he is a little on the impetuous side. He must be nuts, marrying this girl after knowing her such a short time."

"Oh, I don't know Tim. You said you knew you were going to marry me after our first date."

"That was different, Bett, and you know it. We grew up in the same town, and our families knew each other for years, and we didn't meet in a damn bus station!"

Timothy continued to comb his hair and look at the man in the mirror. *Was Betty correct? Was he making too much of a big thing about Myra. After all, the detective found nothing, nothing at all. But why nothing? Betty was right, he was a suspicious old man.*

"Come on, Tim. We're going to be late; it's almost 7:30!"

Tim parked the car in front and thought how good the old place looked with all the lights on. This was the way it was so often when Jack was alive.

Dave met them at the door, and as he took their coats, a strikingly pretty woman came up behind him and held out her hands.

"Welcome, Mr. and Mrs. Timmons. I'm Myra. It's so good of you to come. I've been looking forward to meeting you. I've heard so much about you from Dave."

The evening couldn't have gone better, Myra thought. The little talk from the minister was very short and not at all as offensive as she had figured it would be. The Potts fit in well, and the Timmons were delightful company. Mr. Timmons was very good looking for an older man, and Betty was a premier guest. She was an excellent musician and spent most of the evening at the piano, playing old favorites.

It was just 11:00 when the guests departed, and as they climbed the stairs to their room, Myra said, "Just think, Dave, only two more days. Are you scared?"

"No, not a bit, I've never wanted anything more in my whole life."

Before the car was out of the driveway Tim said, "What did you think of Myra?"

"I thought she was a delight. Very obviously comes from a good background and has a good knowledge of music and literature. I think Dave has made a good choice. I don't need to ask what you thought of her. You couldn't get your eyes off her body for a second."

"Boy, ain't that the truth. Did you ever see a shape like that? She could be a model. Other than that, I have to admit she is just a sweetheart. No wonder Dave is so nuts about her. If I were younger and single, Dave would have a problem. I'd run after her till her legs gave out, and he wouldn't stand a chance."

Betty jabbed him in the ribs, and they both laughed.

"You know I'm the only woman in the world that ever turned you on. Admit it now, admit it!"

"Yes, dear."

It was all in fun, but she was right. One hundred percent.

Chapter 21

Myra was alone in the house when the phone rang. It was the Telephone Company wanting to install the phone in the studio. Myra told them to come as soon as they could, and they said they would be there in twenty minutes.

She went out to the studio through the covered walkway, and for the first time understood why Dave had gone to so much trouble. The weather outside was just plain nasty, and it was almost warm in the passageway.

Dave was working on a magazine cover with racecars and grandstands on it. She had to admit he was good and was surprised at the realism.

"Do you get a lot of money for this kind of work?"

"I think so. I have done work for these people before and my standard fee is $3,000.00. The agency gets 15% and my share is about $2,500.00. I average close to ten jobs a month and I make more on some and less on others. Last year I had a taxable income of $131,000.00 and now that I'll be working out of my home and you will be the bookkeeper, we will probably make even more."

Myra stood dumbfounded. "Wow, and I thought sixteen thousand was a lot of money. We're rich."

"Sixteen thousand? Why sixteen thousand?"

"Oh, no reason. I had that much at one time and felt rich, but a hundred and thirty thousand, WOW!"

"Now my little darling, get out of here and let me work. I have to finish this and get it in the mail before I can take time out to get married."

"You said the magic word. I'm gone. By the way, the telephone men will be here to install the phone in the office in about ten minutes."

"Good – Now git."

Back in the house, Myra sat in the kitchen and looked at all the gleaming fixtures. This kitchen was a cook's dream. It had everything, and she thought about her mother's kitchen with its wood stove and chipped sink. Myra felt alone in the quiet house, and the thoughts about her mother gave her a lump in her throat. She went to the den and closed the door, picked up the phone, and dialed.

"Hello, Mamma? This is Ardith."

"Oh Ardy, I'm so glad you called. It's been so long. All these years I've been so worried about you. Are you all right? Where are you?"

"I'm just fine, Mamma. I'm in another state. I'll write you soon and give you my address. I just wanted to call and let you know I'm getting married."

"Married? Oh, Ardy, I'm so happy for you. Is he a nice man? Will he be good to you?"

"Yes, Mamma, he's wonderful. He's handsome and kind and rich and I'm so much in love with him that it hurts. Are you okay, Mamma? Do you need anything?"

"No, honey, I'm just fine. I still have some money left from the farm and I get Dad's social security. Aunt Madge and I live in the little house in Irondale, and we get by just fine. Tell me more about your young man. What's his name?"

"His name is Dave, Mamma. And he's smart and talented and I'm so very happy. We will be married on Friday and we have the most beautiful home. I'll write you when we get more settled and tell you all about everything, okay? Got to go now, Mamma. You take care of yourself and I'll write soon. Bye, Mamma, I love you."

"Bye Ardy; I love you too."

The first call on the new phone in the studio was from Timothy Timmons. Dave spun around in his chair and picked it up.

"Hey, Dave, this is your last night of bachelor hood. I'd like to invite you out for a drink. You live right next door to the country club, and we could go there. We have a swell bunch of fellows in the club, and I'd like to introduce you around. You will probably want to join as soon as you get settled a little more and this would be a good time to look us over. Besides, Betty wants to bring some of the gals from the club over while you're away, and give Myra a little shower or bachelorette party just to let her meet some people and get acquainted."

"Sounds like fun, Tim. I'm sure Myra will have fun with the women, and I would like to meet some of the locals. What time?"

"Let's make it early. How about seven; I'll pick you up."

"Fine, see you then."

Dave went into the house and found Myra sitting in the den with the lights off and the door closed.

"Is there anything the matter, babe?"

"No. It was quiet in the house, and it felt good to just sit. I haven't had my usual nap for several days now, and I think I went to sleep for a while."

Dave told her of the call from Tim and that Betty wanted to give her a little party/shower so she could meet some of the women from the club. Myra beamed.

"Isn't that wonderful, Dave? We are going to have neighbors. Does this mean we will join the club?"

"I think so; Tim wants us to."

"Will you teach me to play golf and tennis?"

"I think you would be better off taking lessons from their Pro. I'm just a duffer and about all you would learn from me is bad habits."

"Oh posh! Anyone that's as good in bed as you are just has to be good at everything."

She saw him blush as she curled her arms around him and held him close.

"Gosh, I love you, Myra."

"Me too, Dave. I want to be a perfect wife for you."

Dave laughed and said, "Do you know what a perfect wife is, according to my dad?"

"No, what?"

"She has to be a helper in the field, a lady in the parlor, and a harlot in the bedroom. Can you be all those things?"

"Sure! come on upstairs and I'll prove it to you."

Dave was surprised at the size of the clubhouse. It didn't look this big from the outside. There was a large dining room with a dance floor that would easily accommodate two hundred people and a large bandstand with its own sound system. The bar was almost magnificent, and the huge Olympic size pool could be covered in winter. There were eight tennis courts and an eighteen-hole championship level golf course. The pro-shop looked well stocked and the Pro had enough trophies on the wall to impress anyone.

Tim was obviously known by all and introduced Dave to so many people there was no way he could keep track. Dave had three drinks in the evening and Tim lost count. Tim appeared to be smashed and invited at least twenty people to "good ol' Dave's house", for his birthday party, at 4:30 the next afternoon.

At 11:00 on the nose, Tim announced that he and his old buddy Dave were going home. He took Dave's arm and headed out the door. Once they were outside, Tim's demeanor changed. He was stone sober!

"Why the act, Tim?"

"Oh, that's just good for business. There were about a half-dozen attorneys in that room, and if they think I'm a bit of a lush, it gives me an advantage over them, when we meet on the legal playing field. That's the reason I'm better than they are. I'm devious."

Dave thought, *I guess so. I'll have to watch myself with this guy; he's tricky.*

Ten minutes later, they opened the front door and ran into a covey of ladies. Tim went into his drunk act and tried to get them all to come back in the house for a drink. The women all laughed at him, and one woman said he'd better go home and sober up so he could be ready for Dave's party the next day. They were all invited!

When the chatter died away with the exit of some twenty women, Tim and Betty and Myra and Dave all stood in the entryway in a small circle. Tim put his arms around Dave and Myra from one side and Betty from the other. He was again stone sober and in a pleasant but serious tone, said, "Well, it looks like we have you launched into the local social set. You will find them to be a fine bunch as a whole, and they will very likely be your friends. Your aunt and uncle were friends to most of them, and they want you to follow in their footsteps and be a real part of the community. Betty and I loved your Aunt Alma and Uncle Jack, and we are looking forward to a wonderful relationship with you.

As for tomorrow, there will be many more birthdays, but only one wedding, and we wish you, Myra, and you, Dave, all the happiness in the world. May the two of you find the love and consideration for each other that Betty and I have been blessed with, and care for one another all the days of your lives."

The door closed behind the Timmons, and Dave took Myra in his arms. She was crying openly, and Dave had a lump in his throat.

"My god, I love you, Dave"!

"I love you too, Myra, more than anything, or anybody in the world. I want the same things for us, as Tim just said, only more."

As they climbed the stairs, Myra thought, *I will never have to be afraid or alone again. I'm safe.*

Chapter 22

At 11:00 sharp, on the fifteenth of November, Myra and Dave were married.

Myra was surprised, when the minister asked for a ring, and Dave produced a solid gold band. He handed it to the minister, and the inscription inside was incorporated in the ceremony. When the part about the ring being a symbol of God's never ending love for them, and their never ending love for each other came, the minister paused and gave the ring to Dave, saying,

"Read the inscription, and repeat after me."

Dave read, "All my love forever", and repeated, "with this ring, I thee wed." It was large and heavy but fit her finger perfectly.

Myra wore her new white dress, and Dave wore a dark gray suit. Jack and Dora Potts stood up with them and witnessed the marriage certificate. Jack, who professed to be a sterling photographer, took several pictures of the bride and groom. They had a small lunch that Dora had prepared, and by noon, the newly-weds were alone.

"Do you know what I want to do, Dave?"

"I'm almost afraid to ask. What?"

"It's past my naptime, and I'm beat. Let's take a nap and be ready for all those guests this evening."

They closed the door of their room on the world and undressed. They were naked and held each other close.

"Myra whispered. Happy birthday, David Miller."

"Thank you, Myra Miller. I love you."

They both fell into a deep, exhausted sleep.

It was the wonderful smell coming from downstairs that woke them both. Dave's watch said 3:35, and he knew Dora was in the kitchen. Dave bent over and kissed her softly on the throat, and lifting her small naked body from the bed, carried her to the shower. They playfully washed each other under water that was so hot it stung and then dried with those big towels that Aunt Alma had left. Myra dressed in the skirt and sweater that Dave bought her, and he wore slacks and a sport coat.

Their noisy entry into the kitchen made Dora laugh, and Myra was shocked at the food her friend had prepared. There was a large ham, with three salads and fruit dishes. Several kinds of sandwiches and six different hot and cold hors d'oeuvres. Myra was about to question Dora about the maid's uniform she was wearing, when Jack entered the room wearing a butler's garb.

"Why are you two dressed like that?"

"What do you mean, Mrs. Miller? This is our job. We served Mrs. Morgan for years, and Mr. Miller was good enough to keep us on."

"No, not now, not ever. Yes, we will pay you for the work you do, and if you want to help me with the house as a friend, or even as a relative, that will be fine. But at social functions, you will NEVER be treated as servants, EVER. My god, you two. You just stood up for us at our wedding. You are not servants; you are like family. I would accept help from my mother, and if you are willing, I will accept help from you, but never as a servant. Now get out of here and change your clothes. We have guests coming soon, and we want you to help us celebrate David Miller's, thirty-first birthday."

Dora Potts smiled and put her arms around Myra,

"Thank you, dear. Let me help get the food out, and we'll go change. It's almost four-thirty and people will be arriving any minute."

Ten minutes later Dave came in the back door and Myra met him in the kitchen.

"Brrr, it's getting cold again."

"What in the world are you doing outside?"

"One of the yard lights was out, and I put a new one in so it would light the driveway better. By the way, I saw Dora almost running down the drive, and it looked like she was crying. Did something go wrong?"

"No, not really. Dave, do you think of Dora and Jack as servants?"

"So that's it. Myra, I want that relationship to be guided by you. This is your home and you are the mistress here. Whatever you say goes."

"Oh, Dave, I love you. They went home to change their clothes, and when they come back, they will be helpful friends and not servants."

Dave thought the party couldn't have gone smoother. The buffet was perfect, and everyone had a good time. Betty Timmons spent the entire evening at the piano, and much to everyone's surprise, she was joined by Jack Potts, who proved to have a smashing Irish tenor voice.

During one of the "Happy birthday" toasts, one of the club members asked Myra if she played golf, and she said no, but Dave did. Dave was quizzed about his handicap. He admitted he was just a duffer and didn't even have a handicap. Tim said, "Well, as soon as you folks get settled a little, we'll have to change that. Both of you will be old pros by summer."

Dave remarked that they would like to join the country club as soon as they were invited.

"What do you mean invited? You have been a member since the day you were born. Don't you know that when your aunt and uncle gave the club the land for the golf course? They provided for all the blood members of their families to be automatic lifetime members. Not only are you and Myra members, but you don't have to pay dues. For as long as the club is in existence, you and all your progeny are automatic members."

The party slowed down at eleven-thirty and soon after twelve, all the guests were gone. Myra and Dave were alone again.

"So help me, Dave, I've never felt so welcome. The party was a success, and there didn't seem to be a phony in the crowd. Then there's that thing about being life members of the country club. Your aunt and uncle must have had a crystal ball to have known how happy this would make us. Just think. All our children will be members too. How many members shall we contribute?"

They climbed the stairs together and closed the door of their room on the world.

Chapter 23

At Thanksgiving they ate for the first time in the dining room. At Myra's coaxing Jack and Dora had invited their daughter Ruth and two children for dinner. Ruth was a single mother and had no family other than her folks. Her husband was an orphan and had been killed in a construction accident when the youngest child was four months old. Ruth had money from a fairly large life insurance policy and a settlement from the contractor's insurance. She was no financial burden to her parents, but she was lonesome and depended on them for a lot of moral support. Myra thought Ruth was somewhat of a clinging vine, but Dora didn't seem to mind, and she loved the two grandchildren with a passion. Myra had to admit the children were well behaved and a delight to have around.

The house had been warm and filled with laughter and good smells. Before sitting down to eat and at Dave's insistence, they had stood in a circle and held hands. Dave thanked each person by name for being there, and then said, "God bless this house and all who come here."

Myra cried.

The following day was gray and cloudy, with little flurries of snow now and again. Myra was seated on a stool looking out the kitchen window and drinking a cup of tea. She was trying to picture what Sam Fields would look like.

Sam was Dave's agent and was arriving that day to meet with him. The mental picture she drew from Dave's description was that he was a very dignified person, meticulously correct in everything he did. Dave left at 8:30 to pick him up at the airport and she didn't expect him back for another hour.

She saw Dora coming up the drive and waved to her through the window. Dora came in stamping her feet and shivering from the cold.

"It must be ten below out there. Jack is watching a ball game on TV and I wanted to get away from the noise; what are you up to?"

"Nothing, Dora, I'm just having a cup of tea and thinking about meeting Dave's publisher. Want a cup?"

"Sure, but you sit still. I'll fix it. Why is this man coming all the way from Chicago at this time of the year?"

"Dave says he's a bachelor and doesn't have anything better to do than work on holidays. Besides, I think he wants to meet me. I'll be doing a lot of Dave's correspondence and I'll bet he just wants to give Dave's entire operation the once over."

"How long is he going to stay?"

"I think three days."

"Will you need any help?"

"No, I don't think so, I've got the house all cleaned up and fresh linens on the beds. Since he is a bachelor, he probably doesn't get leftovers much, so I'll have plenty to feed him. He'll probably spend most of his time in the studio anyway.

Dora had been gone about a half-hour when Dave's car came up the drive. The man with him was smaller than she was. This Sam Fields was barely five feet tall. She met them at the front door and took Sam's hat and coat. He introduced himself and held out his hand. His grip was strong and she felt almost like he could x-ray her with steel blue eyes.

Dave passed her with two suitcases and announced he would put them in the front bedroom. Myra guided him into the living room and asked if he had had a good trip.

"Yes, indeed I did. It's always nice to get out of the big city. I think your home is beautiful. I would like to see the rest of it as soon as you can find the time."

"How about now? We can start by showing you your room, and letting you get settled. Would you like to rest awhile or freshen up first?"

"No, I'm not tired, but I would like to get out of this monkey suit and put on something comfortable."

"Fine, I'll show you the way."

When Myra came down, Dave was just coming in from the studio.

"What were you doing out there?"

"I was just taking care of the art portfolios he brought with him. I have no idea what he has in them, but there are six of them, and they took up the whole car. He's got enough gear with him to stay a month."

"Dora and I made some sandwiches for lunch do you think he would like a sandwich? I'll go set them out in the kitchen and when he comes down, ask him."

Myra set up three places on the kitchen table and laid out a lunch of veggies, pickles, chips and dips and sandwiches. She started water for tea and sat on her stool to wait. What was this guy all about? He was small in stature but seemed to be almost a giant in other ways. For instance his voice was like a tuba, low and penetrating. The two men entered the room and seated themselves at the table. Myra poured the tea and sat with them as they ate. Sam talked to Dave about work, the load of work he had lined up, and what a busy year they could look forward to. After lunch they all went out to the studio and Sam was very impressed.

"What a super place to work. No wonder you are so creative. I am so pleased to see you working together. I thought perhaps when you got married your production level would change, but I can see this is not so. I have some things I was going to get to later, but I think I'll cut to the chase, and let you know why I came all this way to see you."

He went to his stack of portfolios and selected one. He removed the artwork and placed it on one of the worktables. Myra recognized it as work Dave had done and then noticed it had a large seal on one corner that read "1st Place."

"This is the work I entered in the commercial artist's show in New York while you two were getting married. As you see, it took first place. I have two others here that took second place and fifth place. No other artist in my memory has ever taken three places in one show, and you are the talk of the industry. Already my office has been swamped with work for you, and I think we should decide what kind of work you would like to settle on. There will be far too much work for you to handle, so you will have to pick and choose. From now on your work will command a much higher price. All the hard work of the past years is really going to pay off. Your artistry is also going to make me very rich because I will be getting work in that I will be able to steer to other clients. My commissions will go out of sight. I have so much summer work coming in already that I need an answer right away. I set aside three days for us to work out a program so I can go home with all the input you can give me, and hopefully, make the best of this great opportunity."

Dave and Myra stood speechless. They stood and looked at this little man as if he were a mountain. Sam spoke again.

"Why don't we relax tonight and get to know each other better. Tomorrow, we can get to the meat of the decision. For now, Mrs. Miller, why don't you show me the rest of you lovely home?"

Myra and Dave walked him through the house and ended with a quick cold trip to the gazebo. They returned to the kitchen just as the yard lights came on and Sam suggested a drink. Dave built a fire in the living room fireplace, and they settled down to some soft classical music on the stereo. The conversation drifted from one subject to another and finally settled on Sam. After several drinks he almost told them his life story.

He had started in the art business representing his sister, who at that time was famous in the fashion world. She was his only client for several years until she became very ill with cancer and just faded away and died. He had to make a living and started working with young commercial artists like Dave. He was a hard working, clever man and in a few years had built one of the leading agencies in the country. Now with Dave's success, he planned to expand his agency by taking on several new clients. This would allow him to bring on new talent and have them take over the bread and butter part of the business while Dave would handle the cream of the crop. At first Myra didn't care for the feeling that he was using Dave, but it soon became apparent that this was not the case at all. Yes, he got a commission on all Dave's work, but he found and contracted the work, and was responsible for keeping Dave in the public eye. Sam admitted he had come here to try and talk Dave into coming east with him, but after seeing their home and studio he had changed his mind. He now felt the atmosphere here was most conducive to bringing about the best of Dave's talents. They talked into the wee small hours of the morning about how to set up the books that Myra would keep, and ways to keep the overhead down. Sam even made projections about their forthcoming income. With the new clients, he felt their money would more than double in the next few months and that it could possibly triple in the next two years.

They climbed the stairs as the sun was coming up and went to bed. Dave was out like a light but Myra couldn't sleep. She could only think about all that money and that she would help to earn it.

Myra slept until eleven and when she awoke she found the men had been up for hours and were in the studio going over the work Sam had brought with him in those huge folders. When she came down stairs, she found Dora making lunch for them and was ready to call the men to lunch. Myra headed for the studio just as Dave and Sam were coming in the house. Dave said, "Do I have an agent or what? This guy is a dynamo, Myra. Do you know he was up at eight and out in the studio?"

"It's easy to do when you have someone as talented as your husband to work with, Mrs. Miller. We have covered in a few hours what I had planned to spend several days doing. There is nothing more I can do here and I would like to start for Chicago as soon as possible. I have checked the schedule, and if I can leave here by 2:00, I can make the late flight out of Boise for Chicago and be home in the morning."

They ate a hurried lunch and Sam packed his things. Sam said his goodbyes and with Dave at the wheel they headed for the airport.

When they had gone, Dora whistled and said, "Now there goes a little atomic bomb if I ever saw one."

"I think you are right, Dora. I just hope we don't get burned by the radiation fallout."

Chapter 24

The days went swiftly by and Dave found Myra to be the best secretary he had ever had. They spent much of their time alone except for Jack and Dora.

Jack occupied most of his days working on the house and grounds, and when Myra didn't beat her to it, Dora kept the house spotless.

The work that Sam Fields had dumped on them during his short visit was completed a piece at a time and sent with great care to Chicago. Myra did all the correspondence and started an efficient bookkeeping system. Not only did she keep track of the money and expenses, but also set up the accounting to keep track of materials and the time it took to complete each job. Two of the jobs were returned for revisions, and Dave was working on them now.

By the end of the week, they would be caught up on all the work, and Dave wanted to take a little break over the Christmas, New Year holiday.

On the 19th of December they packed a bag, and leaving the Potts in charge, they went to Boise on a shopping trip. Dave had made reservations at a fine hotel, and they were looking forward to the first night away from the house since the day they had arrived in town. The hotel room was a suite overlooking a park, and it was, in Myra's eyes, the ultimate in luxury. During the day they shopped, and at night they had dinner in the best restaurants. They went dancing and made love. The best night was the night they ate dinner at Taco Bell. On that night they promised each other they would never part, and that no thing or person would ever come between them.

Myra felt she was buying out the town. She purchased seven dresses and pairs and pairs of shoes. She bought sweaters and slacks and golf and tennis outfits. She splurged on underwear and nightgowns, blouses, and scarves. Never had she felt more pampered or loved.

Dave picked out presents for Jack and Dora and had a woman in a department store help him select two dozen stocking stuffers to give to unexpected guests, if there were any. He also bought a complete camera and darkroom set to complete a little darkroom he started in a storage room in the back of the studio. They arrived home the evening of the twenty-third and found that Jack had set up a tree in the living room. There was a note pinned to the tree telling them where to find the trimmings. The Potts would be spending the next four days with Ruth and the kids.

They were both out of breath by the time they got the car unloaded and collapsed in chairs in the front room. Dave felt they must be on some kind of a high because neither of them could stop laughing.

"What is it, Myra? Why so happy?"

"Because I *am* happy. I'm the luckiest girl in the whole wide world. Let's start a fire and decorate the tree."

In front of a blazing fire, they decorated the tree and drank some wine. They laughed and sang, and just after midnight, made love on the rug in front of the fireplace.

Hunger finally drove them to the kitchen the next day about noon, and they found a stack of mail left there that morning by Dora.

"Look here, Dave, Dora must have come in while we were sleeping."

In the mail were cards from the Timmons, and all the people who attended Dave's birthday party. There was a large card from "The Fields' Art Agency", and a card from the country club, announcing their annual New Year's Dance RSVP.

Christmas day was partly cloudy and windy, and the temperature never got over 26 . The house and studio were warm, and Dave spent the day installing the new darkroom. He found enough plastic pipe to hook up the sink and enough copper tubing to bring water through the wall from the bath on the other side. All he needed was a sink, and some counter top, to complete the project. The next day they went to town, found the items for the dark room, and had tacos for lunch. By mid-afternoon they were home, and Dave had the darkroom ready to try out.

He took several pictures of Myra seated in the front room window and at the piano.

Myra had never seen what went on in a darkroom, and was fascinated with the procedure. By dark, Dave had dry negatives, and called her in to watch the enlargement function. She couldn't make sense out of the negatives, but when the picture came up in the developer, she was like a kid with a new toy.

The picture Dave had selected to print was one he had taken by the window. Myra had never seen a picture of herself that was anything like this. It was like a painting, and she could see the talent and artistry of Dave in the finished picture.

"Oh Dave, it's beautiful. I can hardly believe it's me."

"It's you all right. Let's see what the rest of them look like."

There were sixteen pictures all together and Myra thought they were all great.

"Gee, Dave, they're all so good. You could make a living as a photographer."

"No, sweetheart, that's not my thing. I want to paint. I have stayed with the commercial art since I needed to pay the rent, but now I would like to paint, and I want to start with you. Would you be willing?"

"Sure, honey, whatever you want."

"It's not going to be that easy, Myra, you will have to spend some long hours holding a pose. It's been a long time since art school. I will probably be very slow and have to do everything over and over."

"No problem, Davy, just tell me what you want, and I'll turn into a statue if I must. When do you want to start?"

"How about tomorrow morning? We can get an early start, and use the early daylight that comes through the east windows."

They picked up and cleaned up the darkroom, and had a snack in the kitchen before going upstairs.

They showered together, and Myra thought the clock spring in her stomach was going to break before she could hold him close.

The next morning Dave was up before the sun, and was sitting on the edge of the bed, when Myra pried her eyes open. He held a small jewelry box in his hands, and when she sat up, he opened it and removed a jade necklace.

"Where did you get that?"

"It was my mother's. It's yours now, and I want you to wear it for your portrait. Come on, get up. I want to catch the early light in the studio."

"My god, Dave, it's gorgeous. It must be worth a fortune."

"I don't know what it's worth now, but my Dad had it appraised in 1939 and it had a value then of $6,000.00. It's probably worth much more now. I really don't care what it's worth, Myra. This was my mother's pride and joy, and is the last of a collection that had been in the family for a long time. This is the only thing left to me by my mother, and it was her wish that it be given to my bride. Come on, hurry! Will you wear the white dress you got married in?"

As they crossed to the studio, it was just breaking day, and Dave seemed to be impatient to get started. He asked her to fix her hair the way she wore it at his birthday party, all piled on top of her head.

While she fixed her hair, Dave went to the house, and returned with the master's chair from the dining room. It was ornately carved, and had a floral pattern in the upholstery. He placed the chair facing the north windows, and smiled as Myra sat.

"Beautiful! You look like a princess."

After four hours of sitting still, Myra knew what Dave meant when he warned her about the long hours. Her shoulders ached, she was hungry, and she had to pee, but she never moved. At 12:05 Dave laid his brush down, and said, "Let's take a break for an hour or so, and have something to eat."

"Can I see what you've done?"

"Sure, I guess so, but don't criticize. It's not done by a long shot."

Myra felt almost like that time she touched the electric wire in her dad's shop. Her stomach got a strange tickling feeling and for just a second she thought her heart stopped.

There was much to do on the body part of the picture, but the face was like it was alive. It was her all right, but she had never seen herself this way before. The eyes had a haunting gaze that said so many things, and the mouth was warm and sensual, with just a touch of a smile.

"Dave! Oh, Dave! I love it. Do you like it?"

"I'm having a real time getting it the way I want it. Do you see the problem?"

"No, what is it?"

"It's in the mouth; I can't get a certain hardness out of it. I've done it over several times, and I just don't seem to be able to get it right. Don't you see it?"

"No, don't change a thing, sweetheart; it's me!"

"I'll only need you a little longer, and I'll be able to finish it without you having to sit so still. If we can have another two hours this evening, I'll be able to finish the dress part. I want to get the shadows just right."

Myra finally gave up at eleven-thirty and went to bed. Dave promised to follow, as soon as he got this one fold in the dress just right. This was the first time since they had been together that she had gone to bed without him, and she was not sure she liked what was going on. She knew he was dedicated to his work but this seemed to be overdoing it.

She felt him come to bed at three-thirty, and she waited for him to reach out for her. When he didn't, she turned to face him and found he was already sleeping. She smiled and thought, *The honeymoon must be over.*

Dora watched as Myra finished dressing for the dance. She was wearing a new dress that looked so good on her that she didn't seem real. It was just a shade off from the color of that gorgeous necklace Dave had given her, and Dora thought how most people don't wear green well, but Myra did.

"You're going to make all those women at the club jealous."

"They have nothing to fear from me, I wouldn't touch any of their poopy old men for all the tea in China."

"I didn't necessarily mean the men. You and Dave are such a beautiful couple and have so much going for you that some of them will just naturally be jealous."

"Thank you, Dora!"

"You're welcome. You'd better hurry now. Dave is waiting."

They sat at a table with five other couples, but Dave hardly knew they were there. The orchestra was great, the dance floor was not crowded, and he was dancing with the most beautiful woman in the world. During dinner, Betty Timmons introduced Myra to June McKay, and Jean Sackman. June and Jean were about Myra's age, and they hit it off from the first hello. June's husband was the owner of the largest appliance store in town, and Jean and her husband owned the Sackman Ford agency. The four women talked a lot of small talk, but they all agreed that they should get together and take advantage of the covered pool during the winter. They made a date for January tenth to meet at the club and spend the day in the water. The men all talked about their work or businesses but when it came up that Dave was an artist, they had nothing to say. Dave felt like a fifth wheel.

The clock struck twelve and Dave took Myra to the dance floor and held her close.

"Happy New Year, love of my life. May you find nothing but happiness in the year of 1986 and all the years thereafter.

"They sang Auld Lang Syne, and Myra cried.

Chapter 25

Paul Bench sat in Sheriff Tate's chair, and wondered what was going to happen now that the sheriff was not coming back to work. He was the acting sheriff, and he was not sure he liked it all that much. He had always been able to turn to Tate when the going got rough, and he didn't like the politics at all. There was talk of some guy on the city force by the name of Harrison who was being considered for the job, but nothing for sure. Paul thought he would like the money and the name, but not what went with it. Besides he would have too close contact with Jewel Harts and he didn't like that a bit. That guy was the biggest bag of wind in the world.

Margaret came in with the 911 report and Paul looked at the pages like he had never seen them before. That's another thing, Paul thought, *all this new paper work. What was wrong with just calling in or going through the operator?*

Tate sat in the living room and tried to read. He could see Darlene's back as she stood at the sink and felt as lucky as he could get. The doctors all gave him a clean bill of health as long as he didn't go back to the stress of the job. This meant he and Darlene could take early retirement and do some traveling. Darlene seemed almost elated over his heart attack since it got him out of the job of sheriff. She had tried to hide it all these years, but Tate knew she was never happy with his choice of careers. He grinned and thought what she would think if she knew where he spent yesterday afternoon. Terry and Vicki were there for Thanksgiving and on Sunday before they went home he had taken Terry's new car for a spin. On the drive Terry wanted to gas up for the trip home so they stopped at a station at 35th and Fernwood. Terry wanted to check the oil and everything else on the car. Tate thought he was behaving like a new father with his first child, and got out to have a Coke, while Terry went through his routine. The station was rather busy and Tate didn't see him until he spoke.

"Hi, sheriff, how are you?"

It was Al Blessing. Tate hadn't seen him since they were in the hospital together and hardly recognized him. It was almost impossible to tell he had a false eye and he seemed to have put on a pound or two.

"My god, is it really Mr. Blessing? You look great. How's your wife?"

"Oh, Donna's okay; she still has a bad time if she hears the name Myra, but it's not that common a name that she has to worry much. What have you people found out about that dame? Have you found her yet?"

"No, not yet. I don't have much contact with anyone on that case anymore. You see, I'm on medical leave since I got sick, and I probably will never go back to work. You are more apt to know what is going on than I am. Have you heard any thing?"

"Not since that young cop named Harts told us they had found where she worked, and who some of her friends were. I figured he had her in his back pocket the way he talked. Well, I can't worry about her today. I have had a promotion, and we are moving to Phoenix, Arizona. You take care, Sheriff, and good luck."

"The same to you, Mr. Blessing. Give my best to Mrs. Blessing."

Tate knew Darlene would have a fit, but he just might drop by the station and see what was going on with the investigation. After all, this had been his case to start with.

It had been two weeks since he ran into Al Blessing, and he had not been able to get his mind off Myra Dillon for more than a few hours at a time. He just knew they were missing something that would give them a lead on her. He had called Bob to say hello on his birthday, and in passing asked him if he had any new thoughts about her. The only thing Bob had to say was that Jewels had been a pest about calling him for information, until he got rid of him by giving him the name of an agent in the fingerprint ID section in Washington. This agent, Bob said, was an old maid like Jewels, and they would probably get along well together. Bob was like Darlene and scolded him for not taking it easy. Bob felt he should let go and leave things up to Jewels.

He said, "You know, pop, you shouldn't stay involved in stuff like this. It's too frustrating and you don't have enough to go on. The best thing for all of you is to hope she stubs her toe, and has her fingerprints taken for some reason. Her file is kept on top of the pile by the constant inquiries of Jewels Harts, and if she pops up he'll know in a matter of hours."

Bob was right of course, but he still felt there was something they had overlooked. Well, for now he would set it aside and check again after the first of the year.

Chapter 26

Myra had been in town all morning looking for a new bathing suit and finally bought two because she couldn't make up her mind. When she drove in the drive she could see Dave waving to her from the studio window. When she entered the studio, Dave was standing by his easel and holding up a glass of wine.

"Join me, my sweet?"

"What are you up to, you devil?"

"I have completed my masterpiece."

"How wonderful. May I see it?"

He stood aside and pulled a cloth from the front of the painting. Myra took a deep breath and whistled.

"Whew, it's beautiful. I'm beautiful! I think I'm too beautiful. How will I ever be able to stand next to it, or let anyone see it, if they have to look at me afterwards?"

Dave poured her a glass of wine and they sat for a long time just looking at it. Finally Dave said,

"You know I'm not altogether satisfied with it, don't you?"

"No! Why?"

"Well, there's something about the mouth I think that I just didn't get the way I wanted it. I can't put my finger on it, but there is something hard about it, that I just can't seem to get out."

"Oh, Dave, you're wrong; it's wonderful."

"You know what I'm going to do? I'm going to send it in with the shipment to Sam tomorrow, and see what he thinks. He's got a good eye, and he'll be honest."

"How could he help but like it? It's the best work I've ever seen outside of one or two of the masters, and then I'm not so sure it's not better."

"Say, babe, I'm hungry is there something in the house to eat?"

"You bet there is, I made a big pot of stew and it should be just right now. Come on in, and after you eat I'll model my new swimsuits for you."

"Speaking of swim. Jean Sackman called while you were out, and wants to know if we will join her and her husband for a drink and a swim at 4:30 this afternoon. I told her you'd call."

"Gosh, that sounds like fun, Dave; would you like to?"

"You bet I would. I'd like to talk to her old man anyway. I think it's time we got you your own car."

"Wow! Can we really? You know what kind I want?"

"I'll bet you want a convertible."

"No, I want one of those little pickups."

"O.K., you got it. Give them a call, and we'll talk about it at the club."

Mike Sackman, was shorter than Jean by over two inches, and was starting to go bald in the back. He was not the best looking guy, but what he lacked in looks, he more than made up for in humor and wit. Dave thought he was the best-humored fellow he had ever met, and he seemed nuts about Jean. After they had a drink, they changed into their suits and met by the pool. Dave was surprised when he saw Mike without his street clothes on. He was built like a rock, and Jean was about the same. Their bodies looked like those body building pictures you see in magazines. They swam for over two hours, and Myra invited them over for a steak and salad dinner. The dinner was great and they spent the evening in the living room getting acquainted. Dave spoke to Mike about the pickup that Myra wanted, and they arranged to go see about one the next day. The Sackmans were leaving at 11:00 and Myra asked Dave if he would mind if she showed her picture to Jean. Dave said he would be proud to show it, and they went to the Studio. Mike said "WOW" and Jean said, "My god, Myra, it's beautiful. I knew Dave was talented, but I didn't know he was this good. Mike, get Dave to do one of me. Will you, Dave?"

"I don't know Jean. This is my first serious work, and I'm not sure where I'm going with it. Give me a few weeks and we'll see, okay?"

The next day Myra and Dave were at the showroom door as the agency opened. They were looking at a half-ton pickup, when Jean drove up with Mike. They all said hello and agreed to meet for lunch after the car dealing was complete. Jean had a hair appointment and would be back about 11:30. After looking at several pickups, Mike said, "You know, I have a small pickup, that I think might be just what you are looking for. It's used, but only has a few miles on it, and you can't tell it from new. It's a trade-in on a larger truck.

The fellow who traded it in found it wouldn't do the job for him and hardly used it at all. It's loaded with everything in the world as far as accessories go, and I can let you have it for what we allowed him for it."

The little Toyota truck was parked in the wash rack, and was as clean as a pin. The color was a soft blue, and Dave said, "Myra, it's you."

Myra agreed it was just the thing, and they closed the deal with a shake of the hand. Dave was shocked by the strength of Mike's handshake and could feel the vice-like grip for several minutes after the contact. The two men started for the office to complete the deal. Myra said,

"Dave, would you mind if I let you two take care of the paper work, and I took the car for a drive? I'm sure it's what I want, but I haven't even driven it yet."

"Oh sure, baby, I'm sorry. We seem to have been buying a car for you, and then we left you out of it. You go right ahead and take it for a drive. Stay as long as you want."

"Thanks, Hon, I'll be back in plenty of time to meet you guys and Jean for lunch."

Mike got the keys and checked the gas. Holding the door for her, he smiled and wished her well with her new truck.

Myra drove out of town, and found herself on the road by the Kiwanis Picnic Park where she had spent the day burning her past. She drove around the closed sign and parked down by a little pond the kids had been using to ice skate on. She examined the interior of the little truck, and saw there were only 2,300 miles on it, The factory paper floor mats were still in place, and not even soiled yet. She wasn't familiar with the name of Toyota, but Dave said it was a nice little pickup and that was good enough. It had air conditioning and cruise control and a stereo sound system. The previous owner had installed a canopy that gave the look of being low and sleek. The deluxe bucket seats fit her perfectly, and she felt giddy with pride over owning her very own truck. She was thinking of her father, and what he would have thought about her having such a vehicle. Her thoughts were far away when she became aware of someone standing next to her. She looked up to see a man in a sheriff's uniform.

"Is everything all right ma'am? Are you okay?"

"Yes, everything is fine officer. My husband just bought this truck for me, and I'm just looking it over and getting acquainted. Am I doing something wrong?"

"Not really ma'am, but this is private property, and it is closed for the season. We try to watch over the place, 'cause the kids come in here and skate on the pond. It's more than a little dangerous, and we worry. Do you live in the area?"

"Yes, sir, I'm Mrs. David Miller, and I live in the house next to the country club."

"Oh, yes, you're the new people in the old Morgan mansion. Jack Potts is a friend of mine, and he says you are great people to work for. I'm Sheriff Virgil Johnson, and I'm very happy to meet you."

"Thank you, Sheriff, is it okay if I go now?"

"Yes, ma'am, it sure is."

As the little truck pulled away, Sheriff Johnson thought what a good-looking gal. Wonder why she acted like I caught her with her hand in the cookie jar?

At lunch Myra bubbled over about her new truck, and after three glasses of wine, was feeling no pain. She remarked about Mike's build and how strong he was. Jean told them that she and Mike had met at a bodybuilding club, and that Mike was runner-up in the Mr. Iron Man competitions of five years ago. Myra told them about the complete gym in their attic, and that they had never yet used it.

After lunch, Dave said, "Come on, darlin,' give me a ride in you new pride and joy. We can go out to the house, pick up the shipment to Chicago, and put your truck to some use. Those big shipping flats don't fit in the car well, and this little truck will be just the thing."

They all thanked each other, and in parting promised to come and check out the attic gym as soon as they could. Dave braced himself when he shook hands with Mike and thought perhaps that Mike was putting a little more into this strong man thing than was needed.

It was the next Monday when Mike called and asked if they could come over and check out the gym. They arrived at 7:30 and were very impressed with the setup. After a good thirty-minute work out, Mike was showing Dave how to work the muscle group he called the "Abs". He was kneeling beside him with one hand under his neck and the other on his stomach. Myra and Jean were standing next to Mike when Jean exploded,

"Damn you, Mike, don't start that shit again."

She turned, scooped up her outer clothes, and ran down the stairs. The three of them stood in shock, and finally turned to Mike.

"What was that all about, Mike?"

"Hell, I don't know Dave, she's been on the peck lately, and it's hard to tell what's wrong. I'll go settle her down, and we'll see you later."

It was the end of January when they saw the Sackmans again and you would have thought it was yesterday. Jean gave her a big hug and Mike patted Dave on the shoulder and gave Myra a peck on the cheek. They were at the club having dinner and to meet the new tennis pro. He was a young man in his early thirties and had the most unlikely name of Jeremiah Paul Jones. He preferred to be called Jerry and except for a few gentle ribs from his students this is what everyone called him. Except for Tim Timmons. Tim said Jeremiah was his grandfather's name and it was too proud a name to be hidden by Jerry. As usual, Tim appeared to be drunk, and Dave wondered how much he was faking this time, and for what purpose. Myra liked Jerry at once, and before the evening was over, had, along with four other women, signed up for lessons that were to start the next week.

Dave and Myra played their first game of tennis on Valentine's Day and Dave was pleased at the progress she showed after only one week of lessons. After the game they walked the quarter-mile to their back door. As they entered the house, the phone was ringing. Myra answered the phone and said, "Oh hi, Sam, how are you? Sure, Sam, he's right here. Here, Dave, it's Sam Fields, he wants to talk to you and he sounds so serious."

"Hi, Sam, what's up?"

They spoke for almost an hour with very little being said by Dave. Myra was beside herself with curiosity and was having a fit when Dave finally hung up. For several minutes after the call ended, Dave just stood there and smiled.

"Darn you, Dave, you tell me what's going on or I'll die."

"Great news! Sam submitted your portrait to a local gallery in Chicago, and they liked it so much they sent it on to New York for a showing in the most prestigious gallery in the United States. It won second place in the winter artist's convention and was chosen as the most promising work of a new artist by an international convention of artists. There will be an awards banquet that I am to attend on March 17th in New York City. I am to be introduced at the ceremony and honored by some three hundred of my peers. Sam says this is about like getting an Oscar in the movies and will turn everything I do from now on into gold."

Chapter 27

Saint Patrick's day was still a full week away, and in Julius Harts' thoughts, Lois was all hepped up about the costume party at the Elks. Jewels was not looking forward to getting all dressed up in some stupid costume and going where there were so many people he couldn't breath. It must be the preparations that got to him because he always seemed to have a good time after he got there. This year would be a change from the other years, when he had gone with a different date each time. This year, he would be going with his wife. Strange, he thought, how those words were still unfamiliar. He and Lois had been married two months and two days ago, and he still wasn't thinking like a married man. He guessed his thoughts would change when the honeymoon was over; whenever that would be. Lois occupied much of his time, and many of his thoughts since he discovered what she said she knew all the time; that he was in love. They had been to a New Year's Eve party, and they were sitting in the car saying goodnight when Lois suddenly turned to him and said,

"Well, are we going to go on like this till we're old and feeble, or are you going to admit you love me and let me set the date for our wedding?"

He was a little stunned by the abrupt approach, but he smiled and said, "Okay, I love you, now what?"

"Damn you, Jewels, why have you wasted so much of our lives to tell me?"

Her kisses were warm and he remembered feeling his heart beating in his ears.

The intercom rang and the desk officer told him that Sheriff Tate would like to see him. Not again, he thought. This was the third time in a month that old Tate had been to see him about the John Martin murder. He wondered why the old war-horse wouldn't let go of it. He was retired now, and the new sheriff was in office. Why did he keep looking for this Myra Dillon? There was no new evidence, and the dead end was still a dead end. Chuck Harrison was now the sheriff, and why didn't Tate give him the grief. He punched the intercom and said,

"Tell Mr. Tate I'm busy, and I will be tied up for several days. Thank him for coming in and tell him we can probably get together next week sometime."

It was kind of a dirty trick, but what was he to do? He had to get rid of the old boy somehow, and he was sure this would give him the picture.

Tate entered through the side door of the sheriff's office, the door he had used so many times in the past. It didn't seem the same somehow, must be the new paint. From the hallway he could see Paul Bench seated at the front desk reading some sort of file. He found it hard to come here today or any day for that matter. He had avoided the office since he retired. It brought back too many memories. Margaret came out of the file room, and almost bumped into him.

"My goodness, Sheriff, what a surprise, how are you? Paul, look who's here, our old boss."

Paul almost ran to greet him, and instead of the usual handshake, he put his arms around Tate, and patted him on the back. "Good lord, sheriff, it's good to see you. We thought you were mad at us for some reason. Come on in, and say hello to everyone. Sheriff Harrison is out for the moment, but he will be back soon, and I know he will want to talk to you."

Margaret had to take a phone call, and he was left alone with Paul.

"How are things with you, Paul?"

"Couldn't be better, Sheriff. I am staying busy, and I really have gotten to like the new sheriff."

"I was worried about that, Paul. I kind of thought you would go after the sheriff job."

"I thought about it at first, sheriff, till I got to know Harrison a little better. He's a real good man and is so much more suited to the job than I will ever be. I couldn't take the politics of the job, and he seems to really like it. We both signed up to run for the office, and one night we were working on that train car accident that killed three people, and got to talking. Before the night was over, I could see he was the man for the job, so I told him right on the spot that I was backing out and would back him in the election."

"Good for you, Paul, it takes a good man to know what is the best thing to do, and then have the intestinal fortitude to follow through and do the right thing."

"A little thing I learned from you, Sheriff. Gosh, it's good to see you.

How's Mrs. Tate?"

"Just fine, Paul, and, by the way, don't ever tell her I was here. She gets upset with me because I still think about the job."

Paul let a little smile show through and said, "Don't worry about me, I'll never tell."

"Speaking about the job, Paul, what's new on the John Martin case? Have we learned anything new about Myra Dillon?"

"Not a thing, Sheriff, she seems to have evaporated. We have her fingerprints and picture with the FBI, and I check with them every once in a while, but no luck. Jewels Harts jumped into this like he was going to set the world on fire, and then he just quit. We have the jurisdiction over the murder case, and all he is really responsible for is a felony assault robbery charge. I'm not sure there is much to the robbery thing either, since the only ones that ever saw the money are the Blessings, and they have moved out of state. As usual, Jewels is being a big bag of wind, and if there is nothing in it for his career, he won't even talk about it."

"Yes, I found that out three weeks ago, when I tried to see him."

"Did he give you the brush off?"

"Yeah, I guess you could say that. Say, Paul, I wonder if you would check and see if there would be any objections to my coming in and looking over the notes on Myra Dillon. I still can't help feeling I missed something, and the answer is right under our noses."

"I'm sure there won't be, Sheriff. When would you like to see them? It will take an hour or so for Margaret and me to dig them all out, but you can see them any time."

"How about May first? Darlene and I are going to take a little trip to see my brother, and we should be home by then." "You bet, Sheriff. We'll have them all in one place and ready to go over whenever you want."

Paul watched Tate as he left by the front door and walked down the steps. He was reminded of the words to an old song, "Our steps are less sprightly than then." He could remember when Sheriff Tate took those steps two at a time, and now he was holding onto the handrail.

Chapter 28

Myra felt she was the happiest soul in the entire world. Her days were filled with work in the studio, and playing tennis with Dave and her friends. Her nights were filled with love and passion in the arms of the most wonderful man in the world. She reflected every day about how much she loved Dave, and what her life would be without him.

Her tennis game improved day by day and her friendship with June McKay and Jean Sackman deepened into an almost sisterhood relationship. The three women swam every morning and took a tennis lesson from Jerry every day the weather permitted.

On the afternoon of March 12th, Myra met June coming in from her lesson with Jerry, and asked June to meet her in the lounge when she finished her shower. When she came into the lounge, June and Jerry were discussing her backhand and it seemed to Myra that it took forever to get rid of Jerry. She finally asked Jerry if he would pardon them while she had a few words with June. Jerry seemed put-out but left them alone.

"What is it, Myra? Do you have a problem?"

"I don't know, June, I'm not sure. I'm asking you in confidence, because you have children and have a family doctor. I think I'm pregnant, and I don't have a doctor. I would like to know the name of your doctor. Would you call him and make an appointment for me."

"You bet I will, Myra. Does Dave know yet?"

"No, not yet. I thought I would wait until I knew for sure."

"When would you like to see him?"

"Well, our plan is to leave for New York on the 15th, and I would like to know before we go if possible. I wouldn't bother you now, except that I had a little problem yesterday, and I think it's time I checked to make sure."

"How far along are you?"

"About two and a half months, I think."

"You sit right here, hon, and I'll call my doctor. His name is Lester Long, and he is a jewel. You'll love him."

Myra was a million miles away in thought when Jerry came back to the table.

"Pardon me, Mrs. Miller, I don't want to intrude or make a big deal out of anything, but I hope you aren't mad at me for being thick headed and not knowing when to get lost."

"No, Jerry, everything is just fine. Don't give it another thought."

"I'm sure glad, Mrs. Miller. I really like you, and I don't want to upset you in any way."

"I like you very much too, Jerry, and every thing is fine."

"You know, Mrs. Miller, I sure like your house. It's the most beautiful place in town and I would give anything to live in a place like it. I wonder, if some day when you're not too busy, if you would show it to me?"

"Why sure, Jerry, you come by any time."

"Thanks, Mrs. Miller, I will. See you later, Okay?"

June returned, and Jerry waved as he headed for the pro shop.

"What did the eager beaver want?"

"Oh, he just wants to see our house some day. He thinks it's nice. What did you find out?"

"Doctor Long can see you now. If you go in right away, he'll see you. I explained that you were planning to go out of town, and that you were concerned because you had a little problem."

"Thanks, June, you're a dear. Keep this under your hat for a while, will you?"

June hugged her and said, "Your secret is safe with me. Good luck, Myra."

The office was small, and the waiting room was empty. She was met at the door by a nurse in her 50's, wearing a name tag that said Betty.

"Mrs. Miller?"

Myra nodded and was ushered into the inner office. Doctor Long was tall and looked very fit for a man in his mid 60's. Myra had seen him at the club but had never been introduced.

"I understand you think you are pregnant, and you might be having a problem?"

"Yes, Doctor."

"Is this your first pregnancy?"

"Yes."

"Okay, let's have Betty get all your paper work done, and get you ready. Then we'll see, okay?"

Betty came in, and while Myra got into a gown, took down all the usual information.

"You'll like Doctor Long, Mrs. Miller. He's a great doctor, and a fine man. He's a little off his stride today though. He has been at the hospital all day with an old friend and patient. He cancelled all his appointments and planned to spend the day with his friend. At 10:30 this morning his friend died, and it left him with some sad thoughts. He was not going to see patients today, but changed his mind when he thought you might have a problem."

After the examination, Myra dressed and sat looking out the window for what seemed to be an eternity. Betty came in and said, "Doctor would like to see you in his office, Mrs. Miller. Would you come this way?"

The office was larger than the rest of the rooms would indicate, and Dr. Long was seated behind a large desk that was covered with papers, and family pictures. Betty held a chair for her then left the room.

"Well, Myra, you are pregnant, but you also have some problems, and we have to discuss them up front. You will have to cut out all heavy lifting and strenuous activity. It could be, that to carry this child to full term, you will have to spend a good deal of your time in bed."

Myra went numb. She sat there, and listened to all the medical reasons why this problem had come about, but all she could think about was how much she wanted, or didn't want a baby, and how this extra care was going to affect Dave.

"Will I be able to make the trip to New York with my husband next week?"

"No, Myra, I don't think you should. I don't have all the tests back yet, but from what I can tell now, if you want to carry this baby to term, you'll have to stay close to home for the next six months. I'll want to see you nearly every day for a while, till we see how things go. I'll make arrangements to come to your house if necessary. Do you have someone to stay with you while your husband is away?"

"Yes, I do."

"Good. Then I would like to see you tomorrow about 4:00. By that time your blood work will be back from the lab, and we'll see what needs to be done next."

It was dark when Myra parked in front of Dora's door, and waved to her through her kitchen window. She motioned for Dora to come out and turned the radio off so they would not be interrupted. Dora sat quietly while Myra told her about what the doctor said, and cried when Myra asked if she would help.

"Myra, my child, you don't have to ask. I'll be there any time you need me. I'll not say anything to Dave as you asked, but I have to tell Jack. He won't say anything though and when you get ready, we'll all take good care of you. Are you going to tell Dave before he leaves on this trip to New York?"

"No, not unless I have to. I'd like to see him have a great time and get this award. He has worked so hard and I want to make sure as few things as possible disturb his getting this justly deserved reward. I'm going to tell him I have a problem, and I don't feel good. I'm going to say that I have to have some tests to find out what treatment I have to have. I don't want him to feel it's anything but a minor female problem that will probably be cleared up by the time he gets home. You stand by me, Dora, and I think we can send him on his way with only a mild case of disappointment."

"You got it, honey. Whatever you need, you got."

It took two days to calm Dave down and get him to agree to go to New York without Myra. Dora was the one that seemed to turn him around. She told him what was wrong was women's business, and he had no part in it. Although Myra made her daily visits to see Doctor Long, she always returned home cheerful and in good spirits. Finally, on the morning of the 15th, Myra took Dave to the airport. She intentionally made them get a late start, so there would be no time for hard to handle planeside goodbyes. Dave said, "I'll call you every day." Myra wished him well with his acceptance speech that he had been practicing for a week.

Promptly at seven each night, Dave called, and Myra assured him all was well. They talked for over an hour and Myra was reminded of a couple of school kids and a first love affair. Nevertheless, she went to bed with a warm feeling and slept well.

Chapter 29

On the morning of the 17th, Myra returned from seeing Doctor Long, and after parking the car, stopped to look at the tulips that were in bloom. Jack Potts was surely the best gardener in the world. The entire yard looked like a show place. As she started towards the back door, she heard a horn honk, and looked up to see Jerry Jones coming up the drive.

"Hi, Mrs. Miller, I haven't seen you for a few days, and wondered how you were doing?"

"Oh, we are just fine Jerry. How are you?"

"Just great, Mrs. Miller. Gee, your place sure is beautiful. Have you got time to show me the house today?"

"I guess so, Jerry, why don't you come in and have a cup of tea with me, and I'll give you the grand tour."

Jerry leaped from his car and followed Myra into the house. He sat at the kitchen table and watched as Myra made the tea. He admired the kitchen and asked if he could help. Myra told him no, and said,

"While we are at the club, Jerry, it's all right to call me Mrs. Miller, but when we are in my home, please call me Myra. I would like us to be friends."

"Myra. What a beautiful name, to go with a beautiful woman."

Myra thought how youthful and clumsy he was and turned to get some cups from the cupboard.

The first thing she felt was the strength of his hand as he spun her around and holding her very close kissed her full on the mouth. She didn't struggle or respond, she just stood there in a state of shock, her hands at her sides and out of breath from the surprise of it all. She just stood there and said nothing. Jerry kissed her again and this time she tried to push him away.

"Stop it, Jerry. What has come over you? Stop it"!

She tried to free herself, and they spun around, so that she was bent backwards over the butcher block. He was very strong and he was hurting her back.

"Stop it, damn you. What's wrong with you?"

"What's the matter, Myra, don't you like what you have been asking for? Twitching that tight little ass around like you were trolling for a salmon, and now you want off the hook?"

Kissing her again, he forced his knee between her legs. With one arm he held her fast, and with the other, he almost tore her blouse off. He shoved his hand up under her brassier, and onto her breast. The rage that Myra felt held no bounds. She reached in back of her to find something she could use to drive him off. Her right hand grasped the handle of a large butcher's steel. Pulling it from the pocket in the butcher's block, she swung it as hard as she could, and struck Jerry on the left side of his neck. He screamed with pain and staggered back. She hit him twice more on the side of the head, and he fell to the floor. Just for a moment he lay still and gave Myra a chance to get her feet under her. She came after him again and struck blow after blow. Jerry tried to get to his feet, and made a dash for the door. The steel had broken the skin and cut deeply into his flesh; there was blood everywhere. As he crawled to the door, Myra struck him again and again. She continued to hit him all the way out to his car. As she followed him out the door and down the steps she screamed, "Damn you, you son of a bitch, you can't rob me. No one will ever rob me of my pride again. You will not rob me or take my money ever again. Do you hear me, Christopher?"

He finally got to the car and started it. He almost ran over Myra as he tore off down the driveway. Myra stood panting for several moments as she watched him drive away.

She was sitting on the porch steps, when Dora and Jack arrived. The steel was in her hand, and there was blood on the steps, and the walkway, and from the amount of blood on Myra, it was hard to believe it was not from her.

"Good lord, child, what happened?"

"Christopher tried to hurt me again, and I had to stop him again."

"Who is Christopher?"

"Oh, I mean Jerry Jones."

"You mean the tennis pro from the country club?"

"Yes."

The pain was almost unbearable, and Jerry was not sure how he made it to the hospital emergency room before he lost consciousness.

He fell to the floor as he came through the door and was taken immediately to the emergency room operating table. Several large cuts on his neck and shoulders were bleeding profusely, and the emergency room doctor had a time getting them closed up. The attendants took him to x-ray and took several pictures looking for skull damage. The ER nurse said,

"What do you think happened, Doctor? Did he have an accident?"

"I don't think so. It looks more like he was beaten. I think we had better call the police. The x-rays show he has several small skull fractures, and a broken collarbone. His face is badly cut, and he will probably need a lot of surgery if we are ever to see his real face again."

Jerry first became aware of the pain, and then of a police officer, a doctor, and two nurses standing over him. The officer asked, "Can you speak, Mr. Jones? What happened to you?"

"Myra Miller. Mrs. Miller hit me."

"Why? Do you know why, Mr. Jones?"

"Just tried to kiss her."

"Is that all?"

"Yeah!"

"Where does this Mrs. Miller live?"

"Next to the country club."

"That's outside the city, Mr. Jones. Is that where it happened?"

"Yeah."

The police officer said, "I have to make a report on this, Doctor, but it's outside the city, and I will have to call in the sheriff's department. While I write up the report, will you have one of your people call the sheriff's department to send someone over here? Is it possible this man might not live?"

"I can't say for sure until we make some more tests, but he is in a very serious condition."

Sheriff Virgil Johnson stood at the nurse's station reading the hospital and police report on the victim, Jeremiah Jones. The head nurse hung up the phone, and said, "You can add to the report, Sheriff, that I have informed his next of kin about his injuries, and they are on their way here. I notified his parents, and they are flying here from San Francisco. I hope they have insurance, 'cause that young man is going to need it."

Deputy sheriff Johnson scanned the police report, read the medical report carefully and then went back to the police report. Myra Miller? This was the woman he met at the Kiwanis Park about a month ago. He thought how small she had seemed. He had seen her around town several times since, and she was always ready with a smile and a friendly hello. He spoke to the nurse,

"I see by the report here, that your staff took pictures of the victim when he first came in. Is that correct?"

"Yes, sir, we usually do when the reason for the injuries is not known, or when there could be an insurance problem that could involve the hospital. They are instant pictures, but they are pretty good. They are right here. Would you like to see them?"

"Good lord! I had no idea it was this bad. Are you sure he's going to live. Look at this. His face is a total mess. Are you sure he wasn't in a car accident?"

"Yes, we are quite sure. The same instrument, something like a poker inflicted all the wounds. The wounds were made from being struck from all sides, and the front and back. This type of injury is not consistent with an automobile accident. I worked for six years in a pathology lab, and this type of wound is consistent with one person beating another. The victim said it was a woman who did this, but I wonder. These blows were struck with great strength and because of the number of blows, whoever struck them, must be psychopathic."

"May I see the victim?"

"Yes, but he won't be able to talk to you. The doctor doesn't have him fully sedated due to the skull injuries, but he will be out for hours and the doctor wants him kept quiet."

Johnson walked to his car and felt the first drops of rain.

He drove out Country Club Road, and when he got to the mansion, it was dark. There was only one light on over the garage and that had a photocell on it, so it was probably automatic. He looked over at Jack Potts' house, and it was also dark. The rain was coming down in torrents, and he decided to let it go until tomorrow. No use getting soaked to the skin and ruining a fresh uniform. As he turned in the driveway, he could hear a phone ringing. It rang fifteen times, paused, and started ringing again. It was still ringing when he pulled away; the time was 7:40 PM.

Chapter 30

Betty Timmons was making coffee when the phone rang. It was only 8:15 and Tim was not up yet. She went to the foot of the stairs and called to him.

"Are you home? Tim, are you home?"

"Yes, if it's someone we know."

"It's Dora Potts and she sounds like she's crying. She says there is something wrong with Myra. She's in the hospital."

"Hello, Dora. How may I help?"

"It's Myra. Mr. Timmons, she had a miscarriage early this morning, and I'm worried about her. Not just because of the baby, but the police are here, asking her all kinds of questions about that tennis pro guy, Jerry. He did something to Myra that caused her to hit him with a butcher's steel and they think he might be going to die. I don't know what to do. Mr. Miller isn't due home until about 4:00 this afternoon, and I'm afraid she might say something in her condition that will be a problem."

"I'll be there in twenty minutes, Dora. You keep everyone away from her as best you can and tell Myra I'm on my way. Is her doctor there? Do you know who he is?"

"Her doctor is Doctor Long, and he's been with her since early this morning."

"Good, I'll want to speak with him first thing. Make sure he knows I'm on my way, and that I want to speak with him."

Tim had known Les Long for twenty years, and was glad to hear Myra was in his hands.

There was a small traffic tie-up at the overpass, and for the first time in his life, he honked his horn for someone to get out of his way. He had to park in the outer lot and was out of breath when he got to the front door.

Myra was in room 315. Just across the hall, he spotted Dr. Long at the nurse's station, dressed in his scrub blues and looking at a chart.

"What's the story, Doc? I'm here as Myra Miller's Attorney."

"Hi, Tim. Well, I guess I'd better start from the beginning. Mrs. Miller came to me a few days ago, believing she was pregnant but feeling there was something wrong. The tests showed she was about three months along and that there were complications. I was seeing her every day, and I was convinced she was going to have a very difficult pregnancy. She didn't want her husband to know yet since he was scheduled to be in New York yesterday to receive some kind of an award. I saw her yesterday morning, and when she left my office about 1:30, she was in good spirits and was going to do everything she could to take care of herself and the baby. Last night at 5:30, I got a call from Dora Potts, telling me that Myra was experiencing some abdominal pain, and was bleeding a little. They were on their way to the hospital, and could I meet them there. I called ahead, had a room readied for her and got to the hospital at 6:20. There was not much I could do. There was no heartbeat from the fetus and she miscarried at 7:40. When I left the hospital at 10:00, she was resting, and I felt there were no serious complications. The fetus was about three and a half months, and was normal in every other way."

"Are you aware of the problem Myra had with a young man named Jones?"

"Yes, I am."

"Would you say, Doctor, that what took place between your patient and Jeremiah Jones was the major cause of the miscarriage?"

"No, Tim, not really. It was touch and go as to whether she would go full term right from the start. I'm sure whatever happened could have hurried it along, but to say it was the major cause, no."

"Is it all right if I see her now?"

"Oh, yes, she's awake, and even had breakfast. She might be a little woozy still from the medication, but she's young and seems to be doing well."

Tim spent the rest of the morning with Myra, and Dora Potts came in for a while. The two women told him the story in great detail, and he made a book full of notes. The police came in about one-thirty wanting to take a statement from Myra, and Timmons almost threw them out. He told Sheriff Johnson, he didn't give a hang about his paper work. He was to leave his client alone for a full thirty-six hours unless the so-called victim died.

"I'm not sure who the victim is in this case anyway, Sheriff. Has your 'victim' made a statement yet?"

"Yes, he has, Mr. Timmons, but this is a felony assault case, and I need statements from both parties."

"Then I guess your 'victim' is going to live, and the charges will be, at the very most, assault."

"Yes, sir, that's the way it looks now."

"Very well, come back tomorrow, and we will cooperate fully under the law."

Dave was due in at 4:00 on the shuttle flight from Boise, and Tim decided he should be the one to meet him. Dave was the first off the plane and was surprised to see Timmons.

"What's the matter, Tim, is Myra okay? I tried calling her until after midnight last night, and there was no answer."

"Yes, Myra is all right. She is in the hospital but all right. Come on, let's get your bags and I'll explain on the way."

Timmons gave Dave a complete rundown on what happened, and when they came into the parking lot of the hospital, Dave got out near the front door.

"You park the car. What room is she in?"

"Three Fifteen."

When Tim got off the elevator, the first person he saw was Donald Frost, a young local attorney. Don was a member of the country club and was one of the attorneys that Tim always put on his drunk act for. As he got off the elevator, Tim pulled his tie loose and put on a show of trying to tuck in his shirt. This was done in one smooth movement, but left Tim looking a little disheveled and confused. Don was standing with two people, and Tim noted the woman had been crying.

"Hi, Don, what's up?"

"Hello, Tim, you're just the man I want to see."

"Oh, really? What's on your mind?"

"Mr. Timmons, I would like you to meet, Mr. and Mrs. Jones. They are the parents of Jeremiah Jones. You know him, he's the tennis pro at the club, and the boy Myra Miller beat so badly. I know you are the Miller family attorney, and I would like to speak with you, and them, about taking care of the medical needs of Jerry. They flew in from San Francisco today because of the serious condition of their son. After seeing their son and talking with the doctors, it has become glaringly apparent that their son's injuries are extensive. He will require a great deal of medical attention, both now and in the future."

"I see, and what do you expect to gain by holding court in a hospital waiting room? I think we should be in front of a judge and jury, if we are going to convict Mrs. Miller of any thing."

"Mr. Timmons, I have spoken at great length with Jerry, and so have the police. There seems to be no doubt that Myra Miller was the person who inflicted this horrible beating, and since Mr. Miller is a man of more than modest means, we thought a public display in court could be avoided."

"And what if we say no? Do you intend to pursue this matter in court?"

"Yes, sir, we do."

"Mr. Frost, have you spoken to Mrs. Miller?"

"No, we have called her home, but got no answer, and the sheriff's department will not say where she is at this time even though they admit they know."

"I see. Would you folks mind stepping in the family room here? I think we can settle this right here on the spot."

Tim was sure he saw a glint of greed on the face of Attorney Donald Frost.

They were alone in the family room, and in one smooth motion Timmons tucked in his shirt and straightened his tie. He turned and faced the three. He lost all the bumbling, hesitant mannerisms and his voice became piercing and cold.

"Well, since you don't know where Mrs. Miller is, it is clear that you don't have all the facts. So, let me tell you a few. First, let me say to you, Mr. and Mrs. Jones, I'm very sorry your son is injured and I think that all cases of violence are shameful. But what is even more shameful is your attitude about Mr. Miller being a man of means. Just because Mr. Miller has a few dollars you have seen fit to find yourselves a fool of an attorney and come here with all the greed of a pirate ship with its flag up. And now that we are through with the introductions, let's cut to the chase. Your son, Mr. And Mrs. Jones, was beaten by my client, as a result of his attempt to forcibly rape her. At the time of his attack on my client, she was three months pregnant. As a result of the stress placed on her by your son's criminal act, she miscarried at 7:40 last evening, and the baby died. Now I'm going to suggest, Mr. and Mrs. Jones, that you spend the rest of the day having your fool of an attorney explain a few things that sound like manslaughter. Then tomorrow you spend the greater part of the day getting your son ready to get the hell out of town. I will be with my client during this period, trying to convince him that bringing suit against you would not only be a waste of time, but that it would probably not be good for his childless wife. Are there any questions? No? Good."

Timmons departed, and left behind a very angry but whipped attorney, a very downhearted father, and a sobbing, heartbroken mother.

When Dave entered room 315, Myra was sitting up in bed combing her hair. Myra dropped the comb and held out her arms. They clung to each other and broke into tears. They cried openly for close to twenty minutes when, suddenly, Myra sat up straight and dried her tears.

"Sweetheart, it's over now. The doctor says I'm young and healthy, and there is no reason we can't have a baby any time we want. He says I have to stay here until tomorrow, and then we can go home. Here comes Tim now. Why don't you two go get drunk or something and let me get some rest."

The two men walked slowly out to their car, and Tim said, "Drink, Dave?"

"No thanks, Tim. I think I'd just like to go home."

Chapter 31

It was breakfast time the next morning when Sheriff Johnson stepped off the elevator on the second floor and dodged around several food carts to get to Jerry Jones' room. Jerry was sitting up and it looked like he had just had his bandages changed. Some of the swelling had gone down, and his right eye was now completely uncovered.

"Good morning, Jerry, do you remember me?"

"Sure, Sheriff, how could I ever forget you?"

"I came by this morning to see how you are and to check with you on the progress of this case. I spoke to your parents last night, and they are of the opinion that you want to drop all charges against Mrs. Miller. Is this correct?"

"I never wanted to charge her in the first place, Sheriff. All this lawsuit stuff was my folk's idea. That crazy dame almost did me in, but I guess you could say I asked for it. She's such a foxy little thing. You know the way she walks and all. Looking back on it, I really misread her and ended up way off base. I can't tell you how sorry I am that she lost her baby, but who would have guessed that little thing was pregnant? This morning looking back on the whole mess, I think she could have accomplished getting rid of me with one whack, and I think she must be off her rocker."

"That's the thing that bothers me, Jerry. Why would she follow you clear out to your car and keep hitting you even after you got the car door open? Did she say anything to you at all while she was after you?"

"You know, Sheriff, now that you mention it, she did say something that was strange. Oh, sure, she called me a few names I've been called before, but she also called me Christopher."

"Christopher? That's strange. Did she say who Christopher was?"

"No. What she said was that I was never going to rob her of her pride or money again and then called me Christopher."

"That's all she said?"

"All I can remember, but then I was a little busy trying to duck and run."

"Okay, Jerry, I'll go now, but I'll see you later."

"No, I don't think you will, Sheriff. My folks have talked to the doctor. They are going to charter a plane and fly me home tomorrow morning. There's a doctor in San Francisco that's a real whiz at the kind of treatment I'll need, and they figure the sooner he gets to work on me the better."

"Well, good luck then, Jerry. But before I go, there is just one thing I have to say. Take it easy on the ladies. Doing what you did is against the law."

Dave picked up Jack and Dora and got to the hospital at 10:00. Myra was ready to go, and they went home. She seemed in very good spirits, and wanted to know all about Dave's trip to New York. When they got home, they dropped Jack and Dora off at their door, with a promise to call if they needed anything at all. They parked the car in the garage, and entered the kitchen. Once inside, Myra turned, put her arms around Dave, and broke into uncontrollable sobs.

"Oh, Dave, I'm so sad. We almost had a baby."

"Yes, Myra, I know, I know."

He picked her up like a child, carried her to their room and closed the door on the world.

Chapter 32

Dora saw Dr. Long coming to the front door and hurried to let him in before he rang the bell.

"Good morning, Doctor. Mr. Miller is in the studio and Mrs. Miller is still sleeping. I know it's ten o'clock but I thought I would let her sleep until you got here since it's her first day out of the hospital."

"That's just fine, Mrs. Potts, she should have her rest. I think it's time we woke her up though, and later today we should make sure she gets on her feet, even if we have to force her a little."

"Oh, that won't be a problem, Doctor. If we have a problem at all, it will be to hold her down once she gets going. Come along, I'll show you to her room."

Myra was sleeping soundly until the doctor touched her hand. She came awake with a sigh and smiled at him.

"Good morning, doctor. Hi, Dora. My, don't you two look serious?"

"Good morning, Mrs. Miller. What a great way to start my rounds with a smiling face and a cheerful attitude from one of my patients. Now, how are you really feeling?"

"I'm still a little tired Doctor, but other than that, I feel good. I got up to go to the bathroom when Dave left this morning, and I was pretty weak in the knees, but everything else was just the way you said it would be."

"No abdominal pain, headache or upset stomach?"

"No, none of those things. The only thing I found a little funny is that my wedding ring seems about two sizes too large. I waved goodbye to my husband this morning and it fell off. Could I have lost that much weight in such a short time?"

"I wouldn't worry about that, Myra. The medication I gave you usually causes a short term water loss, and that will some times look like a loss of weight, but when the drug wears off, all will return to normal in a short time."

"That's good. I was afraid I was going to have to have it resized so I wouldn't lose it. It's so beautiful. I couldn't stand it if something happened to it. It's solid gold, you know."

"Well, Myra, I think you are going to come out of this just fine. I would like you to take it easy for the next few days and come in and see me on Monday. Eat normally and drink plenty of water. You have Mrs. Potts here to look after you, and you do what she tells you. I'm going to leave some pain pills with her for you, just in case you have a little discomfort. If you feel more than just mild pain, or show any signs of abdominal discomfort, call me right away, understand?"

"Yes, Doctor, I sure do. Thank you."

Dora and the doctor went down stairs, and as he went out the door, he said,

"It is normal and part of the getting-well process for women to have some signs of depression after a miscarriage, and she is not showing any. This only means she is holding it in. Get her to talk about her feelings if you can. If she spends the next day crying, it would be good medicine."

"I know, Doctor, but she and Mr. Miller are very close, and he told me this morning that they both cried themselves to sleep last night."

"Good, I know you'll take care of them both."

"Yes, I will, Doctor. Let me walk you to the door."

"By the way, Mrs. Potts, where is Mr. Miller?"

"He's out in the studio. He works very hard and you are apt to find him there at any hour. He went out early this morning so that Mrs. Miller could get some rest. He will be coming in for lunch soon, and I should fix something for him."

She let Doctor Long out the door just in time to keep Sheriff Johnson from ringing the bell. The two men said hello and goodbye, and the doctor left.

"Good morning, Dora, how are you? Is Mrs. Miller up to seeing me for a few minutes?"

"I guess so, Virgil, if you don't stay too long. Let me go ahead and make sure she's decent."

Dora went upstairs and in a moment or two came to the head of the stairs and motioned for him to come up.

"I think you two know each other, Sheriff, so if you will pardon me, I'll go fix Mr. Miller's lunch."

Sheriff Johnson stood in the doorway and looked at Myra for several moments until Dora's footsteps could no longer be heard, and then said "Good morning, Mrs. Miller. How are you feeling?"

"Just fine, Sheriff, what did you have in mind?"

"I just wanted to get the loose ends of the past few days cleared up. I have just come from the hospital and saying goodbye to Jerry Jones and his folks. For a while, they were thinking about charging you with assault but have decided to not do that and just go home. Since there seems to be two sides to the events of the past two days, I wondered what your thoughts were about bringing charges against Mr. Jones."

"What do you think I should do, Sheriff?"

"It's entirely up to you, Mrs. Miller. If you file a complaint against Jerry, I will have no alternative but to hold him here until the matter is placed in front of a judge. Is it your wish to file a complaint?"

"No, Sheriff, it is not."

"Good, then I'll tell the Jones family they are free to go, and that will be the end of it, okay?"

"Yes, Sheriff, that will be fine."

"Thank you, Mrs. Miller, I'll be on my way. Oh, before I go, I would like to say a few words so as to clear the air. What went on between you and Jerry Jones, we will probably never know for sure. However, it seems pretty clear that you were, at first, trying to fend off an unwanted advance, and that's okay. But after you got him away from you, and he was trying to get away with his life, why did you follow him clear out to his car and continue such a savage beating?"

"Don't you think he had it coming?"

"No, I don't. The beating you gave him was uncalled for. He had no right to make improper advances to you, and you had every right to make him stop, but the beating you gave him was way beyond that. That man will be disfigured for the rest of his life, and it was touch and go for a time about his living at all. I think you went way beyond what was called for or what a sane person would do. I think, Mrs. Miller, that when you get to feeling a little better, you should have Doctor Long recommend a good psychiatrist. I think, Mrs. Miller, that you need some help."

"Is that all you wanted to talk about, Sheriff?"

"Yes."

"Very well, good day, sir."

As the Sheriff's car pulled out of the drive, Dave came in the kitchen. "What's up, Dora. Why were the police here?"

"Oh, that was Virgil Johnson, Dave. He wanted a few words with Myra before the Jones's left town. I'm sure it wasn't much. Virgil is such a nice boy. Jack and I have known him all his life, and there never was a nicer young man. Here, give me a hand with this tray. I fixed you both a bite to eat, and if you'll help me with it, you can ask Myra what he wanted while you're having lunch."

When they came into the room. Myra was sitting up in bed and gave them a big smile. "Hello, you two, are you finally going to feed me? I'm starved."

Dave said, "What did the sheriff have to say?"

"Oh, he just wanted to tell me that Jerry was all right, and that he and his folks were all going back to San Francisco. He knew I was worried about Jerry, and he wanted to let me know everything was going to be fine. Now what's for lunch?"

Chapter 33

All Myra could hear was, "Oooh – aaaah, It's so beautiful." She was in bed reading a Flower and Shrub catalog that Jack had given her. "What's so beautiful, Dora?"

She jumped out of bed and ran to the hall. Dave was standing on a small ladder, and had just turned on a light over her portrait.

"Sweetheart! It is beautiful."

Dave had hung the portrait at the top of the stairs, and installed a light over it.

"It looks alive, sweetheart, almost like it was going to talk."

"I wish it would talk, Myra. I would have it tell me what is wrong with the mouth; I just can't seem to figure it out."

"Oh, no, Dave, it's me!"

Dave climbed down from the ladder and they all stood at the end of the hall and looked at the painting for several minutes. Dave finally said, "Say, young lady, you are supposed to be in bed. The doctor says you should stay down for another day."

"Oh, Dave, you know I'm feeling fine, and that doctor is just an old fuddy-duddy. I don't want to stay in bed another minute. I promise I'll take it easy, but I just can't stay in bed any more."

Dora shook her head and watched as Dave put his arm around her; Myra had won again, Dora thought.

The next two days were quiet in the Miller house. Dave had his work caught up and Jack and Dora were busy with cleaning out the little greenhouse getting ready for spring. On the morning of the third day, Dave got a call from Sam Fields about a rush job he had sent the day before, and Dave borrowed Myra's pickup to go get the shipment. Before he left, he told Myra he was going to stop and see Tim Timmons and would probably not be home much before dark.

As soon as he left, Myra went upstairs and started sorting through the winter clothes she wanted to put away, and figure out what she was going to wear when Dave took her out for dinner as he promised. The spring dance would be held on Friday, and she wanted to look her best for all the snoopy people at the club. She knew there had been a lot of talk even among her friends, but she didn't care, it wasn't her fault that all this mess happened. She smiled as she took stock of her things and wondered why she had them all in one little corner of the closet. The closet / dressing room was huge, and she had crowded all her things into one corner. She moved all the heavy winter things to the other corner and put her sport clothes in the center. She put all her shoes in the shoe holder on the back wall. As she moved all her dress-up clothes to the front on the other side, she became aware there was a large full-length mirror behind where all her cloths had been. The mirror was in three parts and if you pulled the side parts around it made a three sided mirror, that gave an almost 270 degree view of anyone standing in front. There was a light bar over the area, and she turned it on to get a full view of herself. She made a face at her reflection and thought, not bad. She noticed the mirror was smudged and got a cloth and some glass cleaner from the bathroom. As she wiped the edge of the center glass, the cloth snagged on something, and she had to put her finger behind the mirror to free it. She unhooked the cloth from a thing that felt like a catch. It moved when she touched it and she tried moving it back and forth. She heard a click sound and the entire center section of the mirror swung out from the wall.

Set into the wall was a very impressive safe. It was at least two feet wide and three feet tall. Her memory pictured the safe combination she had seen on the bed slats, and her heart started to race over some wild feelings she could not hold back. She felt Dave didn't know about this, and wondered if anyone in the world did, now that Alma was gone. She found a piece of paper and a pencil, and slid on her back under the bed. She copied the combination, and came back to the safe. She turned the dial several times to the right, and stopped at 56; one turn to the left and past 56 to stop at 13; two turns to the right past 13, and stopped at 80. She held her breath and tried the handle. It moved with smooth precision and the door swung open. Myra felt her heart beat and her hands shook as she opened the smaller inner door. Inside was a strong box about 12 inches long and 9 inches deep and high. There were several large manila envelopes, and a leather pouch. On the bottom shelf was a shiny silver colored revolver, and a box of bullets in a 357 caliber. She removed the things from the safe and placed them on the bed.

First she looked at the gun and saw that it was loaded. It was a Ruger Security Six and looked as though it had never been fired. There were six shells missing from the box of bullets, and they were in the gun. She opened the strong box with the key that was in the lock, and spread the paper contents on the bed. She looked at several of the documents, and they were all the same. She counted them out and found there were one hundred Bearer Bonds with a value of $5,000 each. Her hands were shaking to the point she could hardly gather the bonds together, and place them back in the box.

My lord, she thought, *there is a half a million dollars here!* From what she knew about this type of security, they were negotiable, and just like cash in the right hands. She felt a little drunk. Her mind was not functioning, and she tingled all over. What did all this mean? Did Dave know? What should she do, she had never seen so much money. If she kept it, how would she cash it in? She thought about Dave. This would really make them rich. How much tax would there be if they tried to spend it? Would they be able to hide it and never tell?

For many minutes she sat frozen in thought and then her eye caught the name Timmons on one of the large envelopes. She removed the contents and started to read. It was well after noon when she laid the file of papers down and gave a long whistle. The file went back almost forty years and covered dozens of deals that Tim and Jack Morgan had been involved in, and in later years, Alma. She found that the $500,000 came from a deal during World War II, where the government purchased some land in New Mexico from a Company called Jamor, Inc.. Dave's uncle Jack and Timmons had controlling interest in Jamor, with Jack holding most of the stock, and Timmons having just enough to be an officer in the corporation. There were government officials involved and almost two million dollars was paid under the table. Timmons got $75,000 and Jack cleared $610,000. Timmons had advised Jack to hide the money in Bearer Bonds, and had helped purchase them, so there would be almost no way to trace them. The remainder of the under the table deal, about $1,250,000, was paid to the campaign funds of five elected officials, and there was a detailed file on each name listed. All five envelopes were sealed and written across each seal was the word DECEASED and a date starting with 1958 and ending with 1973.

My God, Myra thought, *these people were all a bunch of crooks!* There was enough evidence in these files to convict a preacher, but Myra guessed it was way past any statute of limitations, and besides the only one still alive was Tim Timmons. So, even old honorable Tim had feet of clay, and Myra wondered if he knew these files were still in existence. She could tell from the dates on the envelopes that the records had been well kept long after Jack Morgan had died, and this meant Alma had to have known all about everything. It was also clear that Tim was well aware of the bonds but had not mentioned them in the probate of the estate. Did Dave know? Had Timmons told Dave?

There was a white folder in the stack, and Myra opened it. It was full of letters, and several birth certificates. One by one, the letters told a story of Dave's father and Alma. Dave thought they were brother and sister, but the documents showed they were only half-brother and sister. They had the same father but different mothers. Alma had been a little on the wild side when she was young and her sister-in-law (Dave's mother) had been a little rough with her. Alma had gotten pregnant and wouldn't tell who the father was. The baby was still born, and a year later she married Jack Morgan. There was a letter in the file from Dave's Dad (Stewart) to Alma, asking for financial help when Dave's mother was sick and dying. Stewart had pleaded with Alma for temporary help, so that he would not have to sell most of the family jewelry and keepsakes to pay the medical expenses. Alma had turned him down and referred to Dave's Mom as "that woman". The last thing in the file was a sympathy card from Alma to Dave's Dad when Martha died. In large bold letters on the front of the envelope was written, "Return To Sender". Myra got a lump in her throat and thought about her own family. It seemed so sad that there were bad feelings in Dave's family too. If people would stop trying to take from each other and give from the heart, all this sadness could be avoided.

The leather pouch caught her eye, inside she found a small cardboard box about three inches square. In the box was a round clear plastic container with a gold coin in it. Myra could see that it was a twenty-dollar coin with a date of 1915 on it. She twisted off the top, and held the coin in her hand. It was heavy like her wedding ring and except for the date, seemed to be new. She had heard about gold coins before, but had never seen one. It was beautiful! Rolling over she held it under the bedside lamp and examined it closely. There was not a mark on it, and the detail was amazing. It had the same warm gold color as her ring, and it was easy to see why some people collected them. If this is what real gold was like, Myra wanted a bucket full, like the bucket of gold at the end of the rainbow. As she returned the coin to its little box, she saw a folded piece of paper under the cardboard insert. She slid the paper out and unfolded it. Written on the inside were the words 1915 St. Gaudens Proof (60).

Myra placed all the things back in the safe and taped the combination to the back of the mirror. She closed the mirror door over the safe, and after making sure it was latched, went to the kitchen. It was almost dark and Myra was hungry. She decided she would have a cup of tea and not eat until Dave got home. This would be a good night to go in town and have tacos. Her mind was racing around in circles when Dave pulled into the driveway. How should she handle this? Should she just tell him what she found, or hold off, and see if she could tell if he already knew. She grabbed her jacket and ran out of the house. She met Dave as he got out of the pickup and hugged him hard as she kissed him.

"Take me to town and buy me a taco?"

"You bet, sweetie; Let's go."

On the way to town, Myra sat as close as the bucket seats would allow and held her cheek to his shoulder. When they parked in the Taco Bell parking lot, she pulled Dave to her and kissed him long and hard.

"Wow, what brought that on?"

"It's just that I'm so happy, and I love you so very much. Were your parents happy, Dave?"

"Yes, they were, Myra. They were devoted to each other and they loved me very much. When my mom died, I thought it would kill my dad. He never seemed to get over her death, and I think he finally died of a broken heart."

"Can we be as happy as that, Dave?"

"I already am, Myra. You are my life, and I never want to be without you."

Myra felt like crying but instead she changed the mood and kissing him quickly on the cheek, she jumped from the pickup and said, "Well, if you love me that much, you had better feed me before I dry up and wither away."

As they ate their tacos, they sat close, and watched a group of young people at the other end of the room. Dave told her he had received a large shipment from Sam, and that they would be pushed for time in the next week or so.

"I want you to run interference for me and see that I'm not disturbed by phone calls or anything until I get on top of this pile of work."

"How about the spring dance?"

"Oh, there will be time for that, but no disruptions during the day."

They turned on the radio during the ride home and found a country western station. They sang along with the radio, to the tune of Cold, Cold Heart, and Dave had to admit to himself that he had never been so happy.

Dave parked the pickup in the garage, and arm in arm they went into the house, up the stairs, and into their room. They showered together and went to bed. Myra lay close to Dave until she heard his steady, deep breathing and knew he was asleep. She rolled over and stared into the dark. She thought about all the events of the day and was sure Dave knew nothing of the safe, or it's contents.

Chapter 34

Myra spent the morning working on the books and cleaning up the dark room. When she finished, she peeked in at Dave, saw him busy at work, and slipped quietly out of the studio. Dora and Jack were working out behind the greenhouse, and she walked over to see how they were doing. Jack was trying to start a gas-powered sickle-bar mower and Dora was sorting plants. Myra smiled as she approached and heard Jack use some bad words to show his frustration with the machine.

"What's the matter, Jack? That thing got the best of you?"

"Sorry, Myra, I didn't see you coming. Every year this thing gives me problems until I run it a little. I want to get it going and clean up the edge of the pond, before it starts to grow and get thick."

"Sounds good to me, Jack. I wonder, Jack, if it would be possible to trim along the edge of the creek too? That's such a pretty area and it's all overgrown."

"Sure, Myra, I can trim it back as far as the woods if you'd like." How far back from the water would you like to have me trim it?"

"Oh I think a nice wide path would be good. How about ten or twelve feet?"

"No problem ma'am, I'll even use some of some old grass seed we have, and turn it into a nice little parkway."

Jack gave another yank on the starter cord, and the engine sputtered and roared to life. Jack idled the engine back to an irregular purr and with the smile of a conquering hero, steered the beast in the direction of the pond. Both women stood laughing while Jack and his noisy contraption faded in the distance.

Dora said, "Boys and their toys," and Myra smiled.

Myra turned to Dora and with her best pleading tone asked,

"Dora would you mind fixing something for Dave's lunch? I would like to rest for a while and go to town this afternoon."

"Sure thing, honey. Is there anything wrong?"

"No, nothing at all, I just want to be alone for a while. Maybe write a few letters, you know, stuff like that?"

"No problem, Myra, I'll take good care of things. You get a good rest and if I'm not in the house when you leave, find me and let me know, so I can answer the phones and keep Dave from being disturbed."

Myra stopped in the kitchen long enough to make a pot of tea, and placing the tea, some lemon, sugar, and some cookies Dora had made on a tray, headed for the bedroom. Once in the room, she rolled a standing mirror over to where she could see anyone coming up the stairs from the bed and opened the safe. She removed all the items from the safe and spread them on the bed. This was the third time she had gone over the items in the safe, and except for knowing the present value of the bearer bonds and the gold coin, she knew the documents by heart. She liked the feel of the pistol. Its weight gave her a feeling of power and control. Even more than the feel of the pistol, she liked the sensation of warmth the gold coin gave her. The coin was room temperature, but when she held it in her hand, it felt warm. She had not handled the coin since the first day with her bare hands, since she felt there could be things on her hands that would discolor it.

This time when she replaced the plastic holder, a wave of urgency came over her, and she felt as though she should hurry to, or from, some unknown source of excitement. She jumped from the bed, and from the back of the closet dug out her suitcase, got the key from her wallet on the dresser, and removed her old wallet from the case. She sat on the bed, and counted the money inside. There was a little over twelve thousand dollars, and just touching it, made her feel flushed. With hands that were almost trembling, she placed the old wallet and the money in the safe and then placed the paper with the coin description on it, in her new wallet. She scooped up all the items on the bed except the pistol and placed them in the safe, spun the dial and closed the mirror. She went to the back of the closet, found the denim jacket old John had given her, and slipped it on. It was big and bulky, but it felt good and protective. She slid the pistol into the inside pocket, and looked at herself in the mirror. She turned this way and that, to see if it showed. Not a sign! There was no way anyone could tell she was carrying a gun. A quick inspection of her wallet confirmed there were three one hundred-dollar bills in the inside compartment, and after checking the mirror, she went bouncing down the stairs. As usual she took the small back stairway to the kitchen and just as she reached the foot of the stairs she could hear Dave and Dora talking. She paused for a moment and listened as Dora said, "Do you think I should wake her, Mr. Miller? She said she wanted to go to town this afternoon."

"No Dora, let her sleep if she wants. There's nothing in town that won't last until tomorrow."

Myra burst into the room like a teen-ager and almost jumping into Dave's arms, exclaimed, "Caught you talking about me, huh?"

Her laugh was infectious and Dora paused in her lunch making to enjoy the two in an open display of affection. Teasingly, Myra pushed Dave away and said,

"Well, I'm off to town. I want to do some shopping and pick up some 16x20-photo paper. We're almost out of fixer and I want to see if they have some of that new fine grain developer we were reading about."

Dave and Dora watched as Myra skipped across the drive and bounced into her little pickup.

"Can you beat that, Dora? A few weeks ago she had never seen the inside of a dark room and now she runs it like an old pro. Where does she get all that energy?"

"I think she's just happy, Mr. Miller."

"I hope so, Dora. I hope so."

Chapter 35

Tate slowly turned the coffee cup in its saucer as he watched Paul Bench leave the coffee shop and cross the street to the courthouse. He was tired and feeling a little down in the mouth about the two days he had spent going over the Myra Dillon file. Jewels Hart must be right. There just wasn't anything to look into. His thoughts were miles away and he was surprised by a tapping on the window next to his booth. Standing outside was Sandy Longtree from the credit union. She had a big smile and motioned that she wanted to talk to him. Tate waved her in and stood as she slid into the booth.

"Finally, sheriff, I've had you on my mind for almost a month, but I didn't know how to approach you. I called your house several weeks ago and Darlene almost took my head off when I told her I had had an inquiry on that Dillon dame you asked me about. I was going to speak to Jewels Harts about it, but he's such a puke that I decided to wait till I could find you alone out of reach of Darlene."

Tate smiled and said, "Now don't you go cutting up the girl I'm nuts about."

"I didn't mean anything bad about ducking Darlene, Sheriff. It's just that I know her so well and I know when to run for cover. When she was on the board of directors at the credit union, I learned to respect her every wish."

Sandy dug deep in her purse and came up with an envelope with some writing on it.

"Here now. As I said, several weeks ago, I got a call from a young man who was working for the collection agent for Shell Oil. He was new on the job, and as is usual with new people the company had him working old dead recovery accounts. It's a thing that collection agency people do with new trainees and he was just getting his feet wet. It gives the new people good training in skip-tracing and every so often they turn up an old account that can be talked into paying. Anyway, he found where we had made an inquiry of the credit bureau last year and was checking to see what we knew. As is also usual with new people, he talked too much and I got him to tell me all about the account he was collecting. It only amounted to sixty some dollars and was made up of five credit card purchases. The only thing that stuck in my head was, that all five of the charges were made in a station in a small town called Chimacum, Washington. These five charges were all that was ever charged on the account and they were spread over almost a year. There was never a payment made on the account and a pick-the-card-up order went out. The card was never used again and the account was turned over for collection."

"Okay, Sandy, what importance do you see in an old credit card charge that could help find Myra Dillon?"

"Well, Sheriff, it's been my experience that everything we do follows a pattern, and I think that somehow this town of Chimacum is part of the pattern."

"How so, Sandy?"

"You see, Sheriff, this little town is no more than a wide spot in the road, and to have that many charges, spread over nearly a year, means one thing to me. I think there is, or was, a tie to someone in that community, and my money is on family. I'll bet there is a family tie to someone in that town and if you could find what it is, I'll bet they are still there. This gal was not much more than a teen-ager when these charges were made and I'll bet if it is a family connection, that someone in that little community knows who Myra really is. My goodness, look at the time! I've got to run. I know it's a long shot, Sheriff, but since you don't have anything else, what can you lose?"

"Not much Sandy. Thanks a lot."

"Sure, Sheriff, anything for my favorite cop. See ya!"

Tate watched as Sandy disappeared in the crowd and thought what a slim bit of information. There was no way you could call this a lead, but Sandy was right, what else did they have?

Chapter 36

Myra rolled the window down and let the brisk spring breeze blow on her face. It was a beautiful day and she felt like singing. Her little pick-up purred down the road and she had a feeling of anticipation. The photo shop was located in a small shopping center and as she turned into the parking lot, she passed a sheriff's car and looked straight into the eyes of Virgil Johnson. Her gaze was like ice and she tried to look past him as though he wasn't there. Johnson smiled and raised his hand in a kind of a one-fingered salute. Myra felt a small tinge of anger about seeing him again. It seemed as though she saw him every time she went to town, and she somehow felt he was watching her. Even though she knew this was probably not true, she still felt this way and was beginning to resent the feeling. The lot was a little crowded and she parked at the edge of the back lot and walked around the end of the building to the camera store.

On the corner next to the camera store was a small shop she had seen before but had paid little attention to. The little store had a barred window and was a bit on the dirty side. Except for a sign over the door that read open / closed, and a painted sign on the single window that was so faded you could hardly read it, there was no other marking. The faded sign read "Gold Coins" – "Gold Bought and Sold". A plastic sign in the door read Closed Until, and a little picture of a clock that indicated 3:00. Myra made her purchases at the photo store and while she waited for her things to be wrapped watched idly out the window. As she watched, a short stocky man in his fifties came around the corner, unlocked the door of the coin shop, and went inside. Must be the owner, Myra thought. He even looked like the store. His pants were baggy and he wore an old tweed sport coat that was worn almost thread bare. Myra picked up her packages and left the store through the door that went into the main part of the center. She stopped at the Orange Julius stand and ordered a drink. She sat at a little table with her drink and enjoyed a bit of her favorite pastime—people watching.

She watched a young woman with a small child trying to fit several packages into a stroller so she wouldn't have to carry them. The woman seemed frustrated and ended up almost in a fit of rage when the child moved and pushed several parcels on the floor. The woman finally got things placed properly and strode off down the mall. Myra's eyes wandered again and came to rest on Sheriff Virgil Johnson. He was talking to a security guard and didn't seem to have seen her. She dumped her drink in a trashcan and stepped out the door at the end of the mall into the back parking lot. Placing her package in the back of her pickup she stepped forward to enter the cab when she saw a light come on in the rear of what would have been the coin shop. On an impulse she put the keys back in her coat pocket and stepped around to the front door of the shop. Looking through the door window she could see the little man at the counter and started to enter – the door was locked. The little man looked up and pressed a button on the counter and an electric lock buzzed. The door came open, and Myra entered.

"Yes, ma'am, could I help you?"

Myra smiled and asked why he had the door locked. He explained that he had been robbed in the past and this allowed him the select the people that came in the store. He went on to say that he had many things of value and would only allow three of four people at a time in the store due to the danger of shoplifting. He smiled a yellow-toothed smile and asked again if he could help her. Myra gave him one of her most calming smiles and made up a little story. She related how she had this friend who had told her about a gold coin that was worth thousands of dollars and she was just curious as to whether there was such a coin.

"Do you know what the coin was?"

"Yes, it was called a Saint Gaudens Proof, minted in 1915."

The proprietor smiled and said, "Well, you sure picked a good one. Depending on its present condition, it could be worth as much as twelve thousand dollars."

Myra felt a flush come over her as she asked, "My goodness, are there very many coins like that?"

"No, not many. Would you like to see one?"

"Yes, I would. Do you have one?"

Turning to his safe, he removed a wooden box and took out a single coin in a round plastic disk. The plastic disk contained a coin exactly like the one in Alma's things.

"Oh my," Myra whispered. "It's beautiful. Where would you go to find a coin like that?"

"Most are in the hands of collectors and this level of coin is very seldom seen. When one does show up, it's usually at an auction and is sold to a collector or a dealer and is never seen by the public. In the past few years most coins are sold for their gold value and are purchased by people wanting to buy the gold as an investment and a hedge against inflation. Right now, gold is at a very low price when compared to a few years ago. Six or seven years ago at this time, gold was selling at over eight hundred dollars an ounce and now it's down to just under four hundred."

Myra was shocked. "Wouldn't this mean it would be a bad or risky investment?"

"Well, this all depends on when you bought and sold."

He had a crafty grin and Myra figured out he was kidding her.

"I had quite a bit on hand when the rush came and sold when it hit seven fifty so I did all right. I'm now back buying at about four hundred and there seems to be plenty for sale. I just came from buying a small collection of coins and I'll be able to sell the coins individually at about twenty dollars over the actual price of gold on any given day. Would you like to see them?"

"Oh, yes, could I?"

"By the way, I'm Saul Feinstein. And you are?"

"I'm Myra Miller."

"Good to know you, Myra. Now let's have a look."

Saul laid an album on the counter and opened it flat on the counter. Myra let out a slow whistle and felt a warm flush come over her. The album held coins in little plastic cases that were seated in velvet recesses and seemed to be giving off a warmth all their own.

"How much is something like this worth?"

"Oh, this collection of twelve coins is not all that valuable since all the coins are very common. But they are in fine condition and they will bring about six thousand as a collection, or a little more if I sell them one at a time. Would you be interested?"

"I don't know, Mr. Feinstein. Why don't I think it over and get back to you?"

"Sure thing, Mrs. Miller, but don't delay too long. It probably won't last more than a few days."

Myra drove home in silence – her mind on the warmth and raw beauty of GOLD.

Chapter 37

Dora looked out her kitchen window and watched Tim Timmons drive up to the front of the mansion. Timmons got out of his car and seemed to be nervous about something. He went to the front door and without ringing the bell, or knocking, took a key from his pocket and went in. How very strange, she thought. She had seen him do this many times before, but this was after Alma died and before Dave and Myra came. Always before, he had said he was checking the estate inventory, and since he was the attorney for Mrs. Morgan, she thought nothing of it. Now that the Millers were in the house, and because Timmons was acting as though he was hiding something, she felt strange about his actions. Drying her hands, she went slowly out her back door, and headed for the back of the big house.

As she reached the porch, she could hear Jack running the lawn mower out by the pond, and for a moment considered calling him up to the house. After a slight hesitation, she thought better of the idea, and went into the kitchen. She had watched Myra as she left for town a few minutes before, and she knew Dave was in the studio. The house was quiet, and she got a strange feeling in the pit of her stomach. She crossed the kitchen, and went past the sewing room, to stand in the main hallway. There were small thumping sounds coming from the den, and she stepped to the doorway and looked in. Timmons had his back to her, and was in front of the bookcase on the right side of the fireplace. He was pulling hands full of books from the shelf, and, after peering behind them, replaced them back on the shelf and took another hand full. He was obviously looking for something and seemed to be very upset at not finding it. Dora could hear him muttering some very foul language and almost had to smile at his frustration. She stood watching him for several minutes, and he finally finished looking behind all the books in the case. He turned, and was visibly shaken at seeing Dora standing there.

"My God, Dora, you gave me a fright. I didn't hear you come in."

"Is there something I can help you with, Mr. Timmons?"

"No, I don't think so, Dora. I'm looking for an old law book that I loaned Jack Morgan several years ago, and I didn't think it was worth bothering Dave over it. I knew Myra wasn't home since I passed her on the way over here. I didn't think anyone would care if I just looked for it on my own."

"Oh, I think that's no problem Mr. Timmons. Could I help you?"

"No, thanks, Dora. I'm sure it's not here, anyway. I guess I'll try to find it in the public library."

"Very well, Mr. Timmons. If I can be of no help, I'll just go start Mr. Miller's lunch."

"Thank you Dora, I'll let myself out."

Dora went back to the kitchen and before she reached the sink, she heard the front door close, and a few seconds later she saw Timmons car almost speeding down the drive. How very strange she thought. I'll have to speak to Mr. Miller when he comes in for lunch. No, she thought, I won't bother him with this. I'll wait and speak to Myra when she comes home.

Chapter 38

Myra slowed to a stop a block from several blinking lights on the top of some highway department trucks and a police car. There seemed to be some kind of ditch-digging going on that blocked the road and traffic was tied up. The bulge in her jacket pocket made her feel good as she contemplated her trip to town. She had spent the night making up her mind to buy the coin collection she had looked at the day before, and had removed six thousand dollars from her cache in the safe to make the deal. All morning she tried to make up her mind as to whether she should tell Dave or not. She finally decided not to share it with him just yet, and was surprised at her decision. She was not sure why, but deep down there was a feeling of fear. She just couldn't convince herself to bring her desire into the open even though she felt she could trust Dave. It made her feel a little uneasy to be spending half of her money on a coin collection, but once she had seen the gold pieces, her mind had been made up and now she was going ahead, no matter what. Her mind came back to her driving, as traffic going the other way started to move. About the third car in line was driven by Tim Timmons, and she tried to catch his eye as he went by. He had a look of preoccupation, and Myra felt it was just as well he didn't see her, considering her plans. As she passed the flagmen and the police car, she once again looked directly into the face of Virgil Johnson, and felt a small flush of anger as he raised his hand in that one finger salute. Was this guy everywhere? Was she over reacting? *To heck with him,* she thought, and turned her thoughts to bargaining with Saul Feinstein.

Saul stood at the counter reading the gold prices of the day, when he saw Myra come around the corner and up to the door. He pushed the buzzer and the door clicked open.

"Good morning, Mrs. Miller. Did you make up your mind about the coin collection?"

"That all depends on the price, Saul. What will it take to make you happy you sold it to me, and me happy I bought it?"

Saul laughed and laid the collection album on the counter.

"I can see we are going to be good friends, and I can look forward to selling you lots of coins. After you left yesterday, I did some research, and now that today's gold prices are out, I can let you have the set for $5,045.00. That's my rock bottom price, and I won't come down a nickel."

Myra stopped short of the counter by several feet, and partly turned, as though she intended to leave.

"I guess we don't have a deal then, because I also did some research, and I'll not go a dime over $4,500.00."

Her hand was on the door handle and Saul said, "$4,750.00?"

Myra hesitated a moment, and turning back to the counter, held out her hand and said, "Sold. Far be it from me, to try and rob an honest hard working merchant of the money he needs to put food on the table."

Saul smiled his yellow-toothed smile and took Myra's hand. She almost jerked away as she touched him. His hand was cold and sweaty, and made her skin crawl. A thought flashed through her mind, and she tried to picture what kind of a woman would be married to a dirty old man like him. She wiped her hand on the side of her slacks and reached for her wallet.

"That price will have to be cash. No credit cards. I'll have to have money or a check and if it's a check, you'll have to wait till the check clears before I can let you have the coins."

"No problem, Saul. I have the cash."

As she counted out the money, Saul hand-wrote a receipt for the coins. Saul's writing was small and exact, almost like it was printed. He listed each coin in detail and showed the sale price of each coin. Without the use of an adding machine, he adjusted the price of each coin, so that the total came out to exactly $4,750.00. Myra had the correct change, and as Saul recounted the bills, she went over the bill of sale, and was surprised at how much it looked like it had been done on a machine. Saul removed a large wad of money from his pocket and placing the new bills on the outside, folded the wad in half and slipped it back in the pocket of his baggy pants. Myra wondered if he ever used the cash register. Saul produced a dark brown cardboard box from under the counter and placed the coin album in it.

"There you go, Mrs. Miller, it has been a joy to do business with you. I hope we will be good friends, and do much business in the future. Do you expect to enlarge your collection from time to time?"

"Yes, I do, Saul, but just now, I'm not sure how much. A lot will depend on the price of gold."

"Sure I understand, but if it's okay with you, I would like to feel free to call you if I run across a particularly good deal."

"I don't mind at all, Saul, just don't discuss our business with anyone who answers the phone. Just leave your phone number and I'll get back to you. Let me give you my number."

The box that held her coins was lightly clutched to her chest, as she left the coin shop and went around the corner to the end entrance to the mall. Going directly to the ladies' room, she washed and dried her hands three times. She ran a comb through her hair, and checked her lipstick. Pulling out her wallet, she counted the money she had left, and placed the large bills in the hidden compartment. The dirty feeling she had when leaving Saul's shop was gone, and she felt a little giddy. Leaving the rest room, she walked slowly through the mall looking in all the windows, just idly passing the time and shopping. In the window of "Darlene's Designs" was a cocktail dress the color of fresh daffodils, and Myra was wondering how it would look for the club spring dance, when she heard someone call her name. Turning, she saw June McKay coming towards her, and was immediately caught up in June's infectious smile.

"Good lord, Myra, where have you been? I haven't seen you in a dog's age. Are you feeling all right? I don't know why I asked that question. You look gorgeous."

June gave her a big hug and though Myra never considered herself a hugger, found she was hugging back. The two women took seats on one of the benches in the center of the mall and spent thirty minutes getting caught up on the events of the past weeks. Myra suggested lunch and June responded by recommending tacos. Myra smiled and thought, no wonder I like this girl, we even think alike. As they started for the restaurant June said, "I see you were eyeing that yellow number at Darlene's. I tried it on, but I'm too big in the bottom, and too small at the top. I'll bet it would be dyn-a-might on you. Why don't you try it on?"

"Okay, June, maybe after lunch."

Lunch took over an hour, and both of them enjoyed the time. After lunch they went back to the dress shop, and Myra tried on the dress. When she came out of the dressing room, she drew low whistles from June and half the sales people in the store. Myra felt special and bought the dress.

Chapter 39

Myra's first thoughts were of her new gold coins. She felt rested and alive. The bed was warm, and Dave was next to her, still in a deep calm sleep. The sun was just coming up, and the room was getting light enough to see well without a lamp on. Today was the spring dance, and she felt good about her new dress. She thought the cream-colored shoes and bag would set the dress off well. Slipping out of bed, she went into the bathroom, brushed her teeth, and washed her hands and face. Stepping into her dressing room, she put on a large dressing robe and slippers. Checking the top shelf to see that her album of coins were where she put them the night before, she looked at Dave to see he was still sleeping and went down the back stairs to the kitchen. Before the last step, she could smell fresh bread and was a little amazed to find Dora already there. Dora squeaked with surprise and said,

"Lord, Myra, you gave me such a scare! I hope I didn't wake you."

"No, Dora, I just got up because I felt so good and didn't want to stay in bed another minute. In the past few weeks, I've spent more time in bed than I can stand, and besides that I'm hungry. Dave worked so late last night that we didn't have dinner. We just had a snack and went to bed. What are you making that smells so good?"

"I just took a batch of cinnamon rolls out of the oven, and I was just starting to ice them. They'll be ready in a few minutes. Would you like one with a cup of coffee?"

"Sounds great to me, Dora, but why are you up so early?"

"Oh, it's this darned hip of mine. I have a touch of the gout or something, and if I stay in bed too long, it bothers me. Besides, I wanted to give the living room a going over just in case you wanted to invite some of your friends in after the dance tonight. We are going over to our daughter's place today One of the kids is having a birthday and they are having a little party, so we won't be here all day."

Dora finished the rolls and Myra poured two big steaming mugs of coffee. They sat at the counter and were silent as they ate. Myra unwound her roll and broke off little pieces to dunk in her coffee while Dora watched her with a smile. Finally Dora spoke.

"You know, Myra, something very strange happened here yesterday after you left. Mr. Miller was in his studio and I saw you leave for town about nine-thirty. I was doing some dishes and looking out my kitchen window when I saw Mr. Timmons drive up and go in the front door. He had his own key and went right in, but he seemed to be sneaky about it. I went over to see what was going on and found him looking behind all the books in the den. He seemed to be searching for something and about jumped out of his skin when I spoke to him."

"Did he say what he was looking for?"

"Yes, he said he was looking for a law book he had loaned Jack Morgan years ago, but he acted so funny."

"Don't worry about it, Dora. He's a good friend and I trust him completely."

"Oh, I didn't say he was doing anything wrong. It's just that he acted so strange."

Dora went into the living room and Myra picked up the dishes and put them in the sink. She rinsed the plates and cups, and put them in the dishwasher. There were dishes in the washer from the night before, and Myra started the washer before she went upstairs. Stopping on the landing, she looked down and watched Dora as she dusted. *Good old Dora,* Myra thought, *she caught straight arrow Tim in the act. Now I'm sure he knows about the records in the safe. He just doesn't know where the safe is.* Continuing up the stairs, she went to the bedroom and climbed on top of sleeping Dave as she whispered in his ear.

"Come on, lazy-bones, get up. Dora has some of the best rolls for breakfast and I'll scrub your back in the shower, if you'll scrub mine."

Chapter 40

The club was crowded and everyone seemed to be letting off steam. Myra thought it must be they were coming out of hibernation and feeling the first blush of spring.

The Sackmans, McKays, Timmons, and Millers were all at the same table. Myra was having the time of her life and she was sure Dave was too. They danced, drank champagne, and talked a lot about Dave's work and his success in the art world. Jean Sackman asked again if Dave would paint her picture and June McKay soon joined in, wanting her portrait done too. The two women were having a great time kidding Dave, when Myra turned to Tim and asked if he would dance with her. Tim had not started his drunk act yet and without the slightest hesitation followed her to the dance floor. Myra was surprised by the solidness of the man and was pleased to find he was a great dancer.

"I wanted to get you alone, Tim, and thank you for the way you handled things with the Jones family. I think that situation would have been a lot worse if not for your expert hand."

"No problem, Myra. Betty and I are very pleased to know you and Dave, and class you as good friends. Anything we can ever do to help you, we will do."

They danced in silence for several minutes until Tim said,

"Did Dora tell you I was by the other day when you were not home?"

"Why, yes, she did mention you were there, Tim. Was there something special you wanted?"

Tim held her back at arm's length, looked hard into her eyes, and said, "Dave is wrong. It's not the mouth that's wrong with the painting. It's your eyes."

"Whatever do you mean, Mr. Timmons?"

"You know damn well what I mean, Myra. I'm not sure, but it's just possible that you are the smartest, most clever woman I have ever met, and you know a lot of things you have not told me yet."

"You mean things like the Jamor Corporation?"

Tim missed a step on the dance floor for the first time in twenty years.

"Does Dave know?"

"He hasn't the slightest."

"Are you going to tell him?"

"Oh, yes, but maybe not right away. I think Dave is a little more sensitive than we are, and it's possible that his confidence in you could be shaken if we don't make plans and handle this correctly. What do you think Mr. Timmons, attorney at law?"

"I think you are one crafty lady, and if you had a law degree, I'd ask you to be my partner. Come to think of it, you might be my partner now, and I just don't know it, yet."

Myra looked calmly at him and said in a soft, clear voice.

"Don't worry, Tim, you stood by us when we needed you and I will never let our little secret hurt you, or Betty, in any way."

"Young lady, you are something else. I do think we should get together soon and talk, don't you?"

"How about next Tuesday, your office, 10:00 a.m.?"

"Fine, Dave too?"

"I think not just yet, Tim. Let's first settle how we want to expose this long untold tale to the light of day."

The music ended, Myra stood back from him, and said,

"You dance divinely, Mr. Timmons. Thank you."

She curled both her arms around his and walked back to the table with a smile that would have melted a marble statue.

Everyone agreed it was the best spring dance ever, and not everyone went home sober. Dave invited all the couples at their table over the next afternoon for a barbecue, and Tim invited five or six more. The next morning, as usual, Myra was up at six and was in the kitchen at seven-thirty taking steaks out of the freezer when Dora came in. Myra explained about the barbecue and Dora started planning a menu. She would pre-bake some potatoes, make a salad, and fix some baked beans.

"How many will there be, honey?"

"Well, including you and Jack, I'm countin' on sixteen for sure and another two possible. I got out ten of those big steaks and that should be plenty if we cut them in half. With all the other stuff you have planned, I'm sure no one will go away hungry."

Jack Potts came through the door and gave Dora a slap on the backside before he realized Myra was there. Dora made a wild swing at him and good-naturedly said, "Jack, you old fool, stop that. Can't you see you're embarrassing Mrs. Miller?"

"Don't you worry about Mrs. Miller. Just worry about getting me something to eat. The weather is going to be beautiful today and I want to finish cleaning up around the Gazebo."

"Okay, but you hurry up with what you are planning, 'cause there's going to be a barbecue here at 2:00 and we're expecting close to twenty people."

"Don't you gals give it another thought. I'll have that place looking like a park in an hour. And I'll get out the big grill and get it cleaned up and started in plenty of time. That big grill hasn't been used for years, not since Jack Morgan died. It will do up to thirty big steaks all at once."

Dora placed a bowl of cereal and some toast and jelly in front of Jack, and Myra poured him a cup of coffee. He seemed to inhale his food and almost ran out the door to get started on his appointed tasks. As he went out the door, Myra said, "Gosh, Jack, you don't have to hurry so much you can't take time to eat."

Jack was beaming with enthusiasm and was grinning like a kid.

"Don't fret about me, Mrs. Miller. This is just like old times. You know, with parties and all. Mrs. Potts and I are sure glad you young folks are here, and the old place has come back to life. It's been a long dry spell. Yup, too long."

Myra left Dora in the kitchen and went upstairs to wake Dave. As she came onto the main stair landing she could hear him singing in the shower. She tiptoed into the bathroom and slipped out of her clothes. Waiting until his back was to the shower door, she quickly stepped in behind him and hugged him close. In moments they were all warm and soapy, and Myra had never felt her spring wind so quickly or so tight.

Tim and Betty were the first to arrive. They came, as Tim said, bearing gifts. He and Betty had been to Canada just before Christmas and had brought home some twenty year old Rye Whisky, that Tim said was so smooth, it could be used as a lubricant and he intended to get well oiled.

The steaks were perfect and the rest of the food was served up like a well-planned banquet. There was music from a boom box that Jack found someplace and they danced in the Gazebo. The twenty-year-old whiskey, went almost untouched in favor of beer and every one went home tired, sober, well fed and in good spirits. By the time the last guest had departed, Dora had everything cleaned up and put away. Of course, the last one to leave was Timmons and he made another of his little love and togetherness speeches. After he was gone, Dora said, "Boy, that guy is something else."

Myra agreed, Tim Timmons was something else.

Just before eleven o'clock, Dave and Myra, with arms around each other, went slowly upstairs into their room and again closed the door on the rest of the world.

Chapter 41

Monday morning was overcast and it looked like rain. Dave finished a project he had been working on for several weeks and got it in shipping flats to send to Sam fields. Myra helped with the packing and asked what he would be working on next.

"I don't have anything. I've caught up on all that mid-summer advertising stuff, and right now I don't have a single job on hand. It's all right with me though. Did you see what the contract price was on this last job?"

"Yes, I sure did. That Sam is a real salesman. He got more money for this last job than you made all last year, and I think it's great. I think it's great that I'm married to the greatest commercial artist in the world."

Dave wrapped his big arms around her and held her warm and close for several minutes. Myra was happy!

They loaded the shipping flats in Myra's little truck and headed for the airport. Myra laughed at Dave's little joke about their being off to "Ship the shipment to Chi", and they laughed and sang to and from the airport. Just as they arrived home, the sky cleared and the sun came out.

Dave said, "I have an idea, let's have lunch at the club and see what's going on over there. I could stand a round of golf, if I can find a partner, and maybe you can find someone to play tennis with."

Lunch on the veranda was a special delight: the food was excellent and the weather was unbeatable. Just as they finished, June McKay and the Sackmans entered the bar. Mike Sackman came over with his usual wide grin, and said, "What a surprise to see you guys here. I didn't think you ever took a day off. I sure hope when you do take time off you find you are free on Mondays. I take a lot of Mondays off because I work on Saturdays, but nobody else seems to, and I find it hard to find a partner."

Dave allowed as how he would like to take Monday and a few other days off and would be happy to shoot a round any time Mike was willing to be defeated.

The two men headed for the locker room, totally ignored by the women who were already deep in girl talk about the spring dance.

June went home about four o'clock and Jean and Myra played tennis until they saw the men coming in about six. They decided to have dinner together and found it was well past ten-thirty when they decided to call it a day. The last hour was spent discussing how, and when, Dave would start on Jean's portrait. They agreed to meet the next day, take some pictures and perhaps even start on a sketch.

Dave seemed very pleased about his new task and getting back to working on a specific project. He admitted to spending a lot of his free time painting still life and scenery. Myra was a little shocked when Dave announced that he had completed over fifteen canvases and made a mental note to spend more time in the studio. As they walked arm in arm upstairs to their room and closed the door, Myra was sure that no one in the entire history of mankind had ever been this happy.

Soon after Jean came the next morning, Myra gathered the file folders from the safe and arrived in front of the Timmons law office promptly at ten o'clock. She had left Dave and Jean totally engrossed in what they were doing and she doubted if they even knew she was gone. She opened the door and was waved into the inner office by Betty. She was surprised when Betty remained in the room and took a seat next to Tim. There was a moment of silence and then Tim spoke.

"Since our talk at the dance the other night, I have filled Betty in on all the details of Jamor Corporation. She knew some of what took place, but not everything, and I wanted to make sure there were no more secrets. Have you told Dave?"

"No, not yet. I thought I would go over things with you first and see what you advised."

She handed Tim the white envelope with all the birth certificates and correspondence and said, "Would you look these things over and tell me what you think?"

Tim spent close to a half hour going through the documents The room was so silent they could have heard a pin drop. Finally he closed the file and with some deliberation replaced it in the envelope.

"I don't see where any of the things in that file will ever be anything but interesting history to any one but Dave and yourself. There are things in there that will explain the stress between Alma and Dave's father, but they will have no bearing on what took place with the Jamor Corporation. Now, I see by the file you brought with you that you have all the originals of the Jamor transactions, and just so you know we are talking about the same information, I will tell you that I have copies of all those documents. As far as The Morgans and I were concerned, there were never any secrets about Jamor. Up until the other day, I didn't know where the documents were and perhaps if I could have found them before you did, I would have made them disappear."

"I see. What about the half million in Bearer Bonds, would they have disappeared too?"

For the second time in four days, Myra had caused Tim to miss a step. He acted as if she had shocked him with a stun gun.

"Wha… What do you mean a half million in bonds? I thought those were gone long ago."

"No sir, they are right here in this packet."

Tim laughed and slapped the side of his leg as though he had just heard the best joke ever told.

"Yes, sir, Myra, you are someone to reckon with."

He was out of his chair and pulling Betty to her feet went laughing and dancing like a man possessed. Betty finally pulled back from him and said, "My God, Tim, what's the matter with you? What's so funny?"

"Don't you see, Bet? What I was worried about is not a problem at all. It's only the money. What I was concerned about was my image, and how that would, or could, affect my handling of Alma's trust fund. But that's no problem at all. All Myra wants is advice on what is the best way to dispose of these old bonds and turn them into cash. Right, Myra?"

"Right. I didn't think about the image problem with the trust fund, and I was pretty sure the statute of limitations outlawed everything else. The only thing I'm thinking about now is what cut you will want out of the bonds."

"CUT? Oh, Myra, I love you. I don't want a cut. The money is all yours and you are welcome to it. All I want is to know that something I did over forty years ago is not EVER going to come back and haunt me. Now as far as the bonds are concerned, I will have to do some research on their present day value, but I'm sure it's substantially more than their face value. These bonds were originally designed to have the interest collected periodically on what they called coupons, but the laws are changing, or have changed, and I will have to do some checking to find out the best way to convert them. I know a good taxman and we will come up with a rollover, or something that will save the most money. It's my guess, Myra, that you and Dave will come out of this with well over a million in hard cash, and everyone will be happy, including the IRS. Before you go, let me get some numbers off the bonds and I'll get started on a solution."

"Okay, Tim, this all sounds very good. However, let's not tell Dave just yet. I want to break this news about his family to him very gently and I want to pick the best way and time to do it."

"Sounds good to me, Myra. You pick the time and place, and I'll help you if I can."

Tim and Betty stood in the doorway and watched Myra climb in her little pick-up and drive away. Betty said, "You seem very pleased about the outcome of what was a major concern. Are you happy?"

"You bet I am. This couldn't have worked out any better if I had planned it myself. That Myra is a wonder, one of the smartest people I have ever met. And to think Dave met her in a damn bus station."

Chapter 42

Jean Sackman's painting was coming along and Dave seemed to be pleased with the outcome. Myra expected it would take a week or so to complete, but after working on it three weeks, Dave said they were not half done. Sometimes the sittings went on for hours and in most of that time, she was stuck with Mike. He wasn't really a lot of bother though since he usually spent most of his time in the attic gym. He was very proud of his body and showed it off whenever possible. Myra wasn't sure she liked all that muscle bulged out everywhere. In those quiet times, when everyone was doing their thing, Myra would read or do some laundry. On a couple of occasions she slipped away and went to the club for a swim or a tennis session, no one seemed to ever know she was gone. Today was the 26th of May, and the house was as quiet as a tomb. Myra went to the den and curling up on the big leather couch, she dialed the phone.

"Hello, Mamma? It's me, Ardith. How are you, Mamma?"

"I'm doing okay, Ardy. Thank you for the $200.00. It will sure come in handy. Are you sure you can afford so much?"

"No problem, Mamma. I'm married to a rich man and he gives me anything I want. I can even send you more if you want."

"This man of yours seems to be a fine husband and provider Ardy. I'm so happy for you. Are you happy other ways?"

"Oh yes, Mamma. Dave is so kind and gentle and some times I can't believe I'm not having a dream. I want you to meet him soon, Mamma. How about making plans to come for a visit in September? We have a big house and there is plenty of room. You could stay as long as you want and I could take care of you. I'm worried about the way you seem tired all the time and the pain you have in your side. Have you been to see the doctor?"

"Yes, I have, Ardy, and they can't find anything wrong. The doctor gave me some pills and my side feels much better. Aunt Madge is supposed to take me to town next week for some more tests but after taking these pills for two weeks, I feel so much better, I don't know if I'll bother."

"Mamma, I have to go now. Please go see the doctor and have the tests, okay? I'll call you again next week to see how you are. And, Mamma, think about coming here in September, will you? Bye bye, Mamma. I'll call you next week; take care of yourself. Say hi to Aunt Madge for me. I love you."

"I love you too, Ardy, goodbye."

Just as she hung up the phone, it rang. She picked it up halfway through the first ring. It was Saul Feinstein.

"How are you Mrs. Miller? I wanted to call and let you know I had some very fine coins come in during the last few days and I can make you a good deal on them."

"How many do you have, Saul?"

"Just two right now, but they are quality pieces and I bought them right, so I can let you have them at a good price."

"I'm free this morning, Saul. Why don't I come in now? What price are you asking?"

"I can let you have them for $20.00 over today's gold prices and that's a good value when you see the condition."

"Okay, Saul. I'll see you in about an hour."

Myra opened the safe and removed $1,000.00 from her wallet. She felt a strange flush go through her when she saw how little money was left. To ease her tension, she removed the coin album and looked at her treasure. There they were, warm and solid in their beautiful red velvet pockets. A smile came on her lips and she dismissed all concern about the money. After all, she was trading it for gold.

She replaced the album and closed the safe. Taking her denim jacket from its hook she headed for her pickup, pulling on her jacket as she went. As the first sleeve came on, she could feel the comforting weight of her 357. Since placing the gun in the inside pocket and finding out that it could not be seen, she had never removed it. She always wore this jacket whenever she went out alone and the hardness of the gun pressing against her, gave her a feeling of assuredness. As she went out the back door, she could see Dora out in the yard with Jack, and Dave was busy in the studio with Jean. She was sure no one even saw her go and in a moment, she was headed for town, the window rolled down and the wind blowing through her hair.

Saul saw her coming and punched the buzzer before her hand was on the door.

"Come in, Mrs. Miller. I'm so happy to see you. Isn't it a fine day?"

"Why, yes, Mr. Feinstein, it's a lovely day. Do you have the coins?"

"Yes, ma'am, I do, and they will make a beautiful addition to your collection."

They were beautiful. Myra could tell they were "extra fine" and well worth $20.00 over the gold price.

"How much do you want for them?"

"I can let you have them for $407.00 each."

Myra reached for her wallet and Saul held up his hand.

"You know, Mrs. Miller, when you first came in, I didn't know who you were and wanted cash, but since then, I have found you are the Millers that live out by the Country Club and I would be happy to take your check anytime."

Myra smiled and thought about not spending her last money on the coins. There was plenty of money in the bank and Dave, to her knowledge, had never even looked at the checkbook. She paid all the bills and this small amount would get lost in the maze of checks written every month just to take care of the mansion. Why not? She wrote the check.

As she left the store, Saul offered to call her any time he had a coin or two that would be worth adding to her collection. She thanked him and headed for home.

Coming into the drive, she could see Dora in the kitchen window and was met at the door with a cheery hello.

"When did you leave, Myra? I didn't see you go."

"Oh, I just took a little drive. It's such a beautiful day."

"I was just fixing a little lunch for Mr. Miller and Mrs. Sackman. Do you want some?"

"Yes, I do, Dora. Let me slip upstairs and get rid of this coat and I'll be right down."

"Lands sake, child, why do you wear that big heavy thing in this warm weather? I should think you would put it away until winter."

Myra was half way up the back stairs when Dora spoke about the coat and almost laughed out loud. If she only knew.

In the bedroom she hung up her coat and put the coins in the safe, then went in the bathroom to wash her face and hands. She always felt dirty after being in Saul's shop.

Dave and Jean Sackman came in the back door just as Myra stepped into the kitchen. They proudly announced that the picture would be done soon and Jean seemed to be in a tizzy about how good it was. Myra had to admit that it was a true work of art. Dave had a way of capturing just the right look and the skin tones were the best she had ever seen. The colors of the flesh were so real looking, they almost took your breath away.

Jack came in and they all had lunch together. Myra felt warm with her friends and Dave was the light of her life. How could living be any better than this?

After lunch, Jack wanted Myra to inspect the work he was doing down by the creek. Myra was impressed. It was just the way she had envisioned it. It looked like a park and she praised Jack until he became embarrassed.

On the way back to the house, Myra looked up and saw Virgil Johnson pull into the drive. A cold flash went through her like someone had stepped on her grave.

"What the hell is he doing here?" she said out loud.

Jack looked a little shocked and said, "Don't you like him, Mrs. Miller? He's here to pick me up. We have a fishing date and are going to take some crippled and disadvantaged kids fishing out to Alder Lake. It's all right, isn't it?"

"Why, it most certainly is, Jack. I think it's wonderful of you men to do things like that for the children."

To go in the back door, Myra had to pass within a few feet of the Sheriff's car and again Sheriff Johnson nodded and gave her that one-fingered salute. She smiled a stiff sort of smile and brushed past him with just a nod of her head.

Jack and Virgil went fishing, Dora and Jean went home, and Myra went to their room. It was only 2:00 p.m., but she undressed, put on a pajama top and found a good book. She was about half way through the first page when Dave came in. He put on some pajama bottoms and lay beside her on the bed with a book he had been reading. They read until dark and the house cooled off. Myra went to the kitchen and made a tray of snacks and Dave built a fire. The room was cozy and warm and they read until after midnight. Finally they put their books aside and turned out the light. A warm soft glow came from the fireplace and Dave took her in his arms. Myra lay still until Dave was asleep and thought about the day and her new coins. Her last thoughts were *It must be sinful to be this happy.*

Chapter 43

E.W. Russell didn't much care for Chinese food, but Ted Tate did and he was buying. They finished lunch and had spent over an hour talking about finding Myra Dillon. For the third time in the last month, Tate had gone over the entire case in great detail and seemed to always end up in the same place; no evidence. Even after adding what he had learned from that gal from the credit union, there was still nothing substantial to go on. E. W. was growing a little weary of his friend's do-nothing attitude and finally said, "Hell, Ted, why don't you just tell them all to take a flyin' leap and go to this little town, where there might be something on this Dillon dame? I know Darlene is against it, but what the hell? You've done things she didn't like for years and you're still alive. As you say, there isn't a lot to go on, but it's better than sitting around and making yourself sick fussin' about it."

"Yeah, I know, but it's different now than when I was working. Darlene really gets on me about my health and when I resist, she really comes apart. You think I'm nuts, don't you?"

"Of course, I don't think you're nuts. You have this obsession about a case that everyone else has forgotten, but that's what always made you a super cop. You never gave up. All those years as a police officer can't be dismissed just because you are retired. It's not the way I would be if I were in your shoes, but I'm not you and I think it's bad for you to feel this way and not do anything about it. If you want, I'll take some time off and go with you."

The waiter came with their check and asked if they would settle up since the restaurant was closing until the dinner hour. Tate paid the check and they stood on the sidewalk and said goodbye.

As Tate watched E.W. walk away, he realized what a good friend was all about and felt a lump in his throat as he saw the age that was showing in E.W.'s steps.

Chapter 44

The decision to hang Jean's picture in Mike's office at the car agency had seemed strange to Myra, but standing there looking at it made her change her mind. Mike and Dave had put up a drapery that covered the entire wall behind Mike's desk and hung the picture in the center. A very large ornate frame was selected that gave the portrait a nineteenth-century look. Some recessed lighting had been installed that highlighted the picture even in bright daylight. Myra was impressed and the Sackmans were very vocal in their praise of Dave's artistry. Dave had been very quiet about all the goings on, and Myra stood back and watched his face as the finishing touches were made on the drapery. She moved to stand beside him and taking his arm, looked closely into his eyes.

"You're proud of this work, aren't you?"

"Yes, Myra, I am. It's probably the best I've done so far from a technical standpoint, and I'm really pleased with the skin tones. I was just wondering what Sam Fields would say about it."

"Why don't we ask him? He hasn't seen you for several months. Why don't we call him and invite him for a visit? He can see the painting and we can throw a party while he's here."

Dave looked at her and smiled. "Great idea, I'll phone him tonight."

Dave had come in his car and Myra was driving her pickup, so when she said, "See you later," and left, no one even seemed to notice. She drove by the mall and was surprised by all the kids running around. She parked behind the Saul's store and went in.

"Where are all the kids from, Saul? The mall seems loaded with them."

"Today is the last day of school and they got out early. There seems to be some sort of a tradition to spend their first day off from school at the mall. Not many come in here though, so I don't pay much attention to them. The only thing it means to me is that it's the second week of June and summer is on the way. Say, Mrs. Miller, I'm glad you came by, I have some coins you might be interested in. I bought them as part of a larger collection and they are nice pieces."

Saul laid a coin album on the counter and opened it. There were six coins in the album and Myra was almost short of breath at their beauty. The inside of the album was a warm brown color and it made the coins look like they were on fire.

"Oh my, Saul, they are nice, aren't they? What would they be worth?"

"I can let you have these for $2,400.00. They are probably worth a little more, but I got a good deal on them and if you take them all, I'll let them go for that."

Myra's hand was shaking as she wrote the check. She felt funny about writing a check this big without consulting Dave, but she just had to have these coins.

"You know, Mrs. Miller, the people I got these from have a large collection that I'm trying to work out a price on. They have a very nice twenty-dollar collection, with 136 coins in it. It's one of the best I've ever seen. Would you like to see it when it comes in?"

"You bet I would, Saul. When do you think you'll work out your deal?"

"I'm not sure, Mrs. Miller. Probably not for a few weeks anyway. Would you like me to call you?"

"Yes, I would Saul. I would like to see them even if I don't take them. In the meantime if you run across more like these, let me know, okay?"

The drive home was like a dream and Myra felt disembodied, almost like she was another person looking at what was going on.

She parked the car and went directly to the bedroom and opened the safe. Spreading the albums on the bed, she stood back and thought for a moment that she could feel her stomach spring winding. They were so beautiful she felt like crying.

The house was quiet and she barely heard Dave's car come up the drive. Quickly she cleared off the bed and locked her treasures in the safe.

Should she tell Dave about her collection? The guilt she felt was growing every day, and it was beginning to bother her.

Starting down the stairs, she paused at the landing and could hear Dave in the den speaking to someone on the phone.

Sliding down the last few feet of the banister, she almost ran into the den. She interrupted Dave's conversation by slipping in next to him and working in under the phone cord, started kissing him on the neck.

Laughingly, Dave pushed her away and said, "Cut it out, you little devil, I'm on the line to Sam trying to convince him to come for a visit."

"Oh goodie, is he coming? Is he? Is he?"

"Yes, dear heart, he is. He wants to clear up a thing or two and will leave as soon as he can."

Chapter 45

Sam Fields arrived on the first day of summer and by the time he got to the mansion, the temperature outside was 90 F. Dora had fixed a luncheon buffet and after getting settled in his room, Sam slouched in the corner of a large leather davenport that felt cool to the touch in the 73 F living room. He had a drink in his hand and the look of complete satisfaction on his face. Dave and Myra sat next to him.

Myra said, "I can't tell you, Sam, how nice it is that you were able to come for a visit. How long will you be able to stay?"

"Well, since I haven't taken a day off in several years, how does a month sound?"

"Oh, Sam," Myra trilled, "do you really mean it?"

"No, not really, Myra. I can only spend a week away from the office, but if you'll let me, I'll spend that entire week right here in this leather nest. With, of course, a little time off for sleeping and eating some of Dora's fine cooking."

It took several hours for Sam to show his liquor and in all this time he kept up a steady stream of conversation. He spoke about his life and the early days in his business, the hard times he went through to get the business going and about his sister and her illness. When he went to bed, he was hardly able to navigate the stairs. Myra was sure he would have a hangover in the morning.

The next day was cool and the air smelled like rain. Myra and Dave were up and dressed by 7:30. When they stepped into the kitchen they were surprised to find Sam sitting at the kitchen table with a drink in his hand and talking with Dora about baseball.

Dave smiled and whispered to Myra, "He must have a cast iron stomach."

Dora greeted them with a big smile, the offer of breakfast, and the news that Sam was in the kitchen at 6:00 when she had come in.

Sam said, "Dora tells me, Dave, that you have been doing some more painting and that you have done another portrait of a friend of yours. When can I see it?"

Dave beamed and said, "Whenever you'd like. The office where it's hung doesn't open until 9:30, but we can go right after breakfast."

Myra chirped, "Before you go to town, Sam, you should take a look in the studio. Dave has been doing a lot more than pretty girl pictures. He has some still-life work that will blow your mind. He has also done some landscapes that are breathtaking."

It was well past eleven-thirty when Sam finally agreed to come out of the studio and go to view the portrait in town. His excitement was enough to make Myra and Dave feel self-conscious, and Myra could see the pride in Dave's face. Sam went on and on about the depth and color and perspective of each piece, but always ending his comments with, "Worth a fortune, readily marketable, better than gold."

Myra smiled inwardly when she thought about the better than gold remark. As proud as she was about Dave's work, how could it be better than gold?

Sam seemed to have forgotten about going to see Jean's portrait All he could speak of was how to get all Dave's work to a gallery in New York and setting up a show. Sam's excitement seemed boundless. Myra got a feeling that there was a glimmer of greed showing through.

Myra looked at her watch. It was just two o'clock when Dave and Sam pulled out of the drive and headed for town. Myra had begged out of going along, saying she was a little tired and wanted to take a nap. Dora cleaned up the few dishes from lunch and went home, leaving Myra alone for her nap.

The house became very quiet after Dora left and Myra went directly to the bedroom and opened the safe. She spread her coin collection out over the bed and was amazed at how large it had gotten. Sitting cross-legged on the bed in the midst of her fortune, she felt a warm feeling come over her that reminded her of the times when she was a girl and went to the barn where she could be alone and satisfy the tightness in her stomach. The warm feeling was soon replaced by a tightness that amazed her.

Myra was jerked back to reality when one of her coin books fell off the bed and she became aware it was starting to get dark. *Good Lord*, she thought, *I've been here all day.* In the distance she could hear Dora in the kitchen and Dave's voice saying,

"I'm going to get her up pretty soon so she will be able to sleep tonight."

In a panic she put her collection in the safe and got the door locked. Feeling a little sweaty, she took a quick shower and dressed in a skirt and sweater that made her feel youthful and female.

CALL ME MYRA

She stepped quietly into the kitchen from the back stairs. Dave spotted her as she came through the door and said "I'll be blessed, Myra, if you don't get better looking every day. That nap must have been a good one. You look like an angel."

He came to her and kissed her warmly. Myra felt like crying and laughing at the same time. Yes, she thought, it was the best nap she had had in a long time.

Suddenly she was aware that there were others in the room, all seated at the large table and having coffee. The only one she didn't expect to see was Sheriff Virgil Johnson. Her gaze fell on him like a block of ice and the room went uncomfortably quiet for several seconds.

Finally Johnson spoke, "Hi, Mrs. Miller, I just dropped by to see Jack and Dave about taking the kids fishing again tomorrow."

"What does Mr. Miller have to do with those kids and your taking them fishing?"

Dave was still holding her and he gave her a little squeeze as he said, "All this is my idea, Myra. I've been watching Jack and Virgil take the kids out for over a month, and they seem to have so much fun, I thought I would get a kick out of it too."

Sam Fields piped up, "Why sure, Myra, it sounds like so much fun, I think I'll go along."

Myra couldn't tell for sure, but she thought she hid her feelings well. That damn sheriff seemed to be around all the time and now he was in her home and making social plans to do things with Dave. She was so angry she could feel her neck get hot.

The four men seemed to be in some sort of rapture about the upcoming trip, and Myra could only think how silly the whole thing was. Letting her lower lip stick out a little, she said, " What do you expect Dora and me to do while you men are all gone?"

She expected Dave to answer but quite unexpectedly Dora said, "Now, Myra, don't give the men a hard time, it's all for a good cause and I can't tell you how much enjoyment Jack has gotten out of these trips over the years. This is how we first met Virgil and he has been almost like a son to us."

Myra could see that further words on this subject would only make her look bad and decided to shut up. Her mind partly shut out the ongoing plans for morning, but there was no question that she would have to put out some effort to get Virgil Johnson out of her life.

Chapter 46

Tate stepped onto the street from his doctor's office and headed across the little park at the courthouse towards the side door marked "Coroner". His stride was firm and he walked with more purpose in his step than he had in many weeks. The doctor had given him a clean bill of health. His blood pressure was way down and all the other tests were better than normal for a man his age. The doctor closed the appointment with a word of caution, pointing out that he had had a severe heart attack and even though he seemed to have fully recovered, he should heed the warning and continue taking care of himself.

Entering the coroner's office he made his way to the little office in the rear and entered without knocking.

"Hey, Wayne, how about lunch?"

His old friend was reading a paper-backed cowboy story and laid the book aside with a smile.

"Sure thing. Let's go out to that new place on the highway. It's Friday and I hear they have great seafood."

Tate asked for a table in the back corner and after ordering lunch and a drink, sat in silence. After a few minutes, Russell asked. "What's on your mind, old buddy?"

"Nothin' much, Wayne, I'm still preoccupied with the Myra Dillon case, and everyone else seems to have forgotten that it ever happened. I think I've made a pest of myself with all the people that should be working on the case. I guess I'm too persistent for my own good. Darlene gets in a snit every time I mention anything at all about the department, and I feel bad because now I'm trying to hide things from her. She has Bob on her side and between the two of them they make me feel like I'm cheating. I went to see the doctor this morning and he gives me a clean bill of health, if I don't overdo it. He wants me to keep my stress level down, but how the hell can I do that, if I'm sneaking around all the time? I'm feeling so darn good that I want to do something besides go fishing."

"What the hell is wrong with you, Ted? Did you turn into a wimp when you took off the badge? The Ted I have known all these years would sit his family down and tell them how he feels instead of sneaking around and crying on my shoulder. It's my bet they will see you in a different light when the old Ted that we all know and love comes out of hiding."

Tate's face was beaming. "Damn, if you're not the best friend a man ever had. I've been acting like a fool. Bob is coming over this weekend and it will be a good time to clear the air."

Tate stood on the curb and bid his old friend goodbye. When he drove out of the parking area, he saw Jewels Harts walking into the courthouse and thought, *Up yours, Jewels.*

Jewels kept his head down even though he could see Tate out of the corner of his eye. He had enough on his mind without putting up with that old fool of an ex-sheriff.

Things had not been going well with Lois for many weeks. He didn't know exactly what it was, but any contact with her left him cold and irritable. His work kept him occupied and any advances from her seemed to be a direct interference, which made him unreasonably angry. He had felt her pulling away from him more and more over the last month or so, but it didn't seem to matter. That was why he was so surprised that he felt so let down this morning when he got served with divorce papers. My God, they had only been married for a few months and it seemed odd that he felt nothing in the way of pain or regret. Was he that much of an unfeeling oaf? He closed the door to his office and sat staring out the window. He wondered if his old apartment was for rent.

Chapter 47

It was still dark when Myra realized that Dave was up and already in the shower. For a second she wondered why and then remembered the men were taking some children fishing. Anger welled up in her again. She didn't like the idea of Dave and that damn deputy being together. She wasn't sure if she would be able to keep her feelings hidden and then decided she didn't care. She would find some reason to intervene and put the skids under that high and mighty Johnson.

Dave came out of the shower and Myra thought he looked like an Adonis. She tried to figure out how she would start a conversation about the fishing trip and how she could turn the subject in the direction of it being somehow the wrong thing for Dave to do. Dave sat on the edge of the bed and throwing her a towel asked her to dry his back. As she dried him, she listened to him go on about how excited he was, and how much it would mean to the kids. After listening to several minutes of how these kids were underprivileged, and how he felt he was really making a difference in their lives, she decided to find another time to broach the subject. Dave finished dressing and then came to the bed and gave her a warm kiss. Then he said what seemed to Myra a very strange thing.

"You don't mind if I do this, do you?"

Myra answered, "Heavens no, why do you think I would?"

"Well, I don't really know. It's just that I feel some strange tension every time the subject comes up."

She kissed him and said, "This is no time to get into how I feel about things. You go along and have a good time with the kids and when the time ever comes that I feel neglected, or left out, I'll let you know."

With that he smiled and left the room. She could hear him meet Sam in the hallway and listened to their chatter all the way down the stairs. She rolled over in bed and tucking a pillow between her knees went sound asleep.

When she woke, she took a shower and dressed in jeans and a sweatshirt. Even though it was warm, she took her denim jacket and smiled as she felt the weight of her revolver. Taking the stairs two at a time, she bounded into the kitchen and found Dora hard at work cleaning the oven. Wiping her brow with the back of her arm, she told Myra there were some sweet rolls and coffee ready and if she wanted more she would be happy to fix it for her.

"I do declare, Dora, you are going to spoil us all if you don't watch out. I'm on my way to town and I think I'll do some shopping and have lunch. Don't bother to fix anything for lunch or dinner, as I'll probably stop by the club for dinner.

Dora's head went back into the oven and Myra skipped out to her pickup. The day was warm and rather than turning on the air conditioner, Myra rolled down all the windows and let the wind blow her hair.

It was 11:30 when she pulled up in back of the coin store and went into the mall through the rear entrance. Looking across from inside the mall, she could see there were two customers in Saul's store and that his son was there. She walked over and ordered a medium Orange Julius. Sipping on her drink, she walked the full length of the mall and back without going into a store, just looking through the windows. Looking across at the coin store again, it looked like the customers and Saul's sons were gone, so she crossed the end of the lot and pushed the bell. Saul buzzed her in and gave her his best brown-toothed smile.

"Long time no see, Mrs. Miller. How have you been?"

"Just fine, Mr. Feinstein, and you?"

"Never better. Business is good and the weather is fair. How could I not be fine? Oh, by the way, have you met my son David? He helps me in the store sometimes, as does his brother."

"Yes, I have, Saul. It's good to see you again, David."

David smiled politely and went on with what he was doing.

Saul said, "Is there something you had in mind?"

"Nothing special, Mr. Feinstein. It's just that the last time I was in, you mentioned you might be getting a collection that would be worth my while to look at."

"Yes, I did, Mrs. Miller, but the seller changed his mind about what was in the collection and we are still trying to work out a deal. I'll be seeing him again in about a week and I'll let you know. The entire collection is going to come to about $40,000 and I wasn't sure how much of it you wanted. When I first saw the collection, there were some pieces in it that were later changed and we have to get the original group back together, or negotiate a new price. What ever we do, the cost to you will be close to $40,000 and I could make a better deal if I was assured of a sale."

"Why don't we say this, Mr. Feinstein? If the collection is as good as you say, I will be very interested."

"My big concern, Mrs. Miller, is cash flow. At this time, the cost of the collection will leave me a little short of cash, and it would be a real help, if when we put a deal together, you could come up with a sizeable deposit."

"Don't worry, Mr. Feinstein, if the collection is what you say, there will be no problem giving you a check for the entire amount. When you firm up the purchase and know exactly what we are talking about, I'll be able to give you what ever it takes to solve the cash flow problem."

"Fine, I'll keep working on getting the best of the collection and let you know when I've settled it to the point where I can give you an inventory. We can work out the money at that time, okay?"

Myra turned to leave and when Saul buzzed the door to let her out she came face to face with the older son, Daniel. Like his brother, he was very handsome and Myra wondered again how he could possibly be an offspring of Saul. They passed without saying anything and in a moment Myra was out of sight around the end of the building.

Daniel gave a slow whistle and said, "Gees, Pop, is that the rich Mrs. Miller? She sure is a looker. If I was that Miller guy, I wouldn't let her out of my sight."

"You can keep your mind on business, Sonny Boy. Your old man has a plan in mind that will solve many problems. I'm going to lunch now and then to the bank. Do you think the two of you can make a buck while I'm gone?"

"You damn betcha, Daddio. Have a good lunch."

Saul stood while Daniel buzzed him out and went to the side door of the Mall and disappeared. When he was out of sight, David asked,

"What the hell do you suppose the old man is up to? He spent the last half-hour telling that dame about some collection he is working on buying."

"What's wrong with that?"

"Well, hell, Dan, you know as well as I do, that he's not buying anything. He's only trying to unload his entire gold stock 'cause he thinks the price is going down again."

"Again, what's wrong with that?"

"Nothing, except you weren't here when he was talking about some choice pieces and how he was going to struggle to keep the price of this collection under $40,000. Good God, Dan, you don't suppose he's going to unload the X inventory on her after all this time?"

"Careful, little brother, the old man will kick your ass if he hears you discussing the X file."

"I know, I know, but isn't it exciting, after all this time?"

"Remember when we were kids, Dave, and he first had his hands on those coins? He was a wreck. He knew if it ever became known that he had them, his ass would really be in a sling. Remember the old fart that gave them to him because he trusted him? The old boy must have been a hundred years old and was scared to death. He was sure the Nazi's were going to find him and kill him and then he dropped dead in the front yard. The funny part about it was that Pop believed every word of the story about the Nazis looking for the coins, and he was as scared as the old man. I guess Pop figures the people involved in the theft of the coins back in World War II must all be dead by this time and he can do what he does best, turn gold into money. Well, one thing for sure, he has zeroed in on a pigeon named Miller and he'll get every dime possible out of her."

"Before you came in, Pop was talking about giving her an inventory of a collection. I wonder if it's the same one as he had when we were kids? We never did see the coins on that inventory. You remember, it was pages long and had some real rare stuff on it. Pop only let us see parts of the collection. Also, there were a bunch of boxes he never showed us."

"The only thing I remember clearly was the parchment paper the list was on. It had a swastika water mark and the writing was like Pop's, so clear you could read it across the room. It was all in German, but pop could read it and that always struck me funny because I didn't think he knew any German at all. You know, little Davy, we'd better get this place squared away before Pop comes back, or he'll have our butts."

Chapter 48

Tate watched Bob pull into the driveway and get out of his car. He wondered how Bob was going to take what was going to be the topic of conversation today. Darlene came up from the basement with some canned fruit for lunch and went into her usual gleeful mode when she knew her son was around. The two men sat at the kitchen table. Darlene poured them all a cup of coffee and said, " So, honey, how has your week been?"

"Just fine, Mom. Everything at work is the same old grind. 9 to 5 with an hour for lunch. We spent part of one day working on a fraud case that is ready for trial, but that was as close to excitement as we got. How have you guys been? You okay, Dad?"

"Oh sure, Bob. I went to the doctor and he gave me a clean bill of health. He said I seem to be over the heart attack and that I should go on with my everyday things without worry. This talk about my health brings up something I want to talk about. For months now, the two of you have treated me like an invalid and I haven't felt like one. I'm feeling stronger than I have in a long time and want to get on with the joy of living. However, not wanting to hurt any one's feelings, I have been hiding the fact that I am still working on the John Martin murder. I know I'm not the sheriff any longer, but I have watched the law people involved in this case drift away from it and it has fallen through the cracks. Well, no more, I'm going to go back and dig out all the records and find this Myra dame. I hope you two can see it my way and understand that this is something I need to do. I would like to do it with your help and blessing, but one way or another, I'm going to do it."

The room went silent for several seconds and then both mother and son started to laugh. With a big smile on her face, Darlene went to Ted, gave him a big hug, and said, "You know somethin', cowboy, the reason Bob is here this weekend is to side with me in getting you going on something. You have spent far too much time sitting on your backside and we got worried."

"Yes, Dad. We think it's great that you are feeling well enough to want to get back in the saddle and start doing what you like to do. We decided we would urge you to do what you are going to do and give you what help we can. Mom can be your secretary and I will give you as much help from my office as I can."

Tate felt warm and cared for. He sat with his wife in his lap and his son at his elbow and his heart beat, slow, strong, and healthy.

Chapter 49

It was late afternoon when Myra pulled into the driveway. She could see the light on in the kitchen at Dora's and was glad to look forward to an evening alone. She went directly to the bedroom and changed into an old nightshirt that she wore when she just wanted to sit and read or something. She opened the safe and removed her coin collection. She was surprised at the weight of it. Spreading the books out on the bed she decided to take an inventory. The clock downstairs was striking 9:00 p.m. when she laid the last coin book aside and recapped her inventory sheets. Impressive, she thought, over ninety coins. It's time to figure out a way of telling and showing Dave without giving him a heart attack. She no longer worried about the money aspect of her stash since she had discovered their bank account continued to grow no matter what she did. Dave spent little money on anything and the running of the house was a drop in the bucket when she considered their income.

Well, no time to worry about that tonight. Tomorrow will be soon enough when Dave gets back from this trip with the boys and that damn Sheriff Johnson.

Instead of putting the collection away, she stacked the albums on the shelf above the safe showered quickly and thought I know it's late, but I think I'll go down stairs and call Mamma before I go to bed.

As she put down the phone, her mouth was dry and she felt a strange sort of loneliness. She sat on the big leather sofa in the den with her knees pulled up to her chest. She felt like crying, but her eyes were dry. Her mind went over and over Aunt Madge's words. "Your mother is dead." The room was dark, the house was quiet, and Myra looked without seeing into the darkness. She was now alone in the world. Her father had been gone now for over six years, and her sister had died of cancer while Myra was in the facility. Christopher was also gone, but she didn't want to think about him. She tried to get her thoughts back to her mother, but now that Christopher had come to mind, her memory of the horrible day when Christopher died blocked everything else out.

It was mid-summer and Myra was almost seventeen. She had been happy with school that year and could hardly wait until it started up again in the fall. Only one more year of high school and then she was going to college. Papa had promised that if there was any way at all, she would get to go. For over two years she had been working at the Hadlock store and babysitting every chance she got. All the money she earned had been saved, and with another year to go, she would have a sizable sum to get her started.

The day had been warm and Myra was on the back porch helping her mother prepare tomatoes for canning. It was mid-afternoon when Christopher drove into the back yard with two friends in a pickup she had never seen before. Daddy met them at the corner of the house and she heard Christopher announce that the pickup was his. Daddy wanted to know where he got the money to buy a car like that, and Christopher told him it was none of his business. Daddy raised his hand as though he was going to hit Christopher, but as usual, he just threatened and turned and went into the house. Christopher called to his friends and told them to ignore the old man, he would get the beer from his room and be right back. As he came on the porch, he saw Myra for the first time and got the strangest look on his face.

Daddy could never figure out the strange actions of his son, but Myra knew him well, and knew exactly where the money came from. Christopher brushed past his mother and went inside. Myra emptied her apron on the table and ran to the barn.

Climbing to the loft, she went to the large timber that supported the hay sling. Pulling away a bail of hay, she fell to knees and dug out a metal coffee can. Even before she got the lid off she knew the can would be empty and her heart felt heavy. The can came open and she started to cry when she saw her reflection in the bottom. Her crying was uncontrollable and she felt empty. All the money she saved for nearly three years was gone.

She just sat there crying and only turned when she felt someone standing beside her. Looking up, she saw Christopher standing there with a drunken grin on his face, "Darn you, Christopher, you took my money."

"So what, little sister, what are you going to do about it?"

"I'm going to tell Papa and have him make you give it back."

"Like hell you will, you little snitch."

Myra tried to get past him and reach the ladder from the loft. As she went by him, Christopher grabbed her by the hair and threw her backwards on the floor. She went a little crazy and started kicking him as hard as she could. Christopher fell on top of her and pinned her hands over her head. He was very strong and she ceased to struggle. She could smell the stale beer on his breath and the weight of his body made her feel like a rat in a trap.

"You ain't goin' to tell nobody nothin', you little bitch. You shut your trap or I'll fix you good."

Their noses were almost touching and Myra spit in his face.

She didn't even see it coming. His fist slammed into the side of her head and made her feel dizzy. The next punch hit her in the middle of her stomach and she felt sick. Through the pain and the confusion, it took a few seconds to realize what was happening, but she became aware that he was tearing at her clothes and had ripped off her blouse and panties. She struggled again and he punched her in the side of the head so hard she could taste blood running down her throat. She tried to scream but all that came out was a gurgling sound and he hit her again. It was like someone else was there and she was far away looking on. She could feel Christopher force his knees between her legs and spread them apart. The searing pain when he entered her pushed her into a rage. She no longer felt the pain in her stomach. All she could feel was anger. With a strength she had never known, she kicked and hit and fought like a crazy person. Suddenly he was standing over her saying,

"Okay, now you have something to really tell Daddy, little miss perfect. But if you tell, I'll say you egged me on and even if they don't believe me, you won't be little Miss Perfect anymore."

He turned to go and as he reached the ladder, Myra took the hayfork that was sticking in a hay bail next to her head and thrust it just as hard as she could, right into his middle. He made a grunting sound and spun to the side, as he fell from the ladder. Myra heard a cracking sound and a flop as Christopher fell to the barn floor. Myra knew she had only slightly wounded him and was not prepared for what she saw when she crawled to the edge of the loft and looked down. When Christopher fell, he turned and hit the floor as the pitchfork was in a vertical position. The weight of his body had driven the fork clear through him and broken the handle off just where it fit into the fork.

Myra's rage turned to terror and she started to scream. The first to hear her screams was one of the boys that had come with Christopher and when he came to the barn and saw Christopher's body, he yelled back to the house and told the other boy to call the folks. Chris had fallen and was hurt. The boy ran back to the house and before Daddy got to the barn Myra found her panties and stuffed them in her apron pocket. She pulled her blouse together and climbed down from the loft. She went to the back of the barn and stood out of sight next to the end stanchion. Daddy came into the barn and fell to his knees by Christopher's body. Taking his son's head in his arms, he started screaming to call an ambulance. Myra's mother came in and kneeling by her son, put her arms around her husband. Myra felt cold. Her father repeated over and over, "Oh, Mamma, he was our gift from God, our only son."

The next hour was just a blur: the police and ambulance people all over the place, her mother crying, and confusion everywhere. No one seemed to pay any attention to her. The sheriff came to the conclusion that it was an accident because he found where the pitch fork handle had made a deep groove in the barn floor when Christopher's weight came down on the tines. Then there was the broken handle. "How else would the handle be broken, if it had not been that Christopher fell on it?"

The ambulance pulled out of the yard and Myra was sure that no one noticed when she slipped quietly into the house and went to her room. She washed as well as she could in her room without going into the bathroom. She had blood on her thighs and on her dress. Her eye felt puffy and she knew her lip had swelled a little.

It was well after dark when Myra saw the last of the concerned neighbors finally go home. The house became suddenly very quiet, and Myra lay on her bed wondering why she didn't feel like crying when her father came into the room. Myra lay on her stomach and her father touched her on the shoulder as he sat beside her. His voice was soft as he said,

"There, there, Ardy, don't cry. It was a terrible accident, but we all have to go on. Come down with me and let's see if we can't comfort your mother."

As he spoke, he turned her over and pulled her into a sitting position. The moment he saw her face, he said, "What is it, Ardy, what is wrong? Do you know something about my son's death you should tell me?"

Myra went cold again. Why had he referred to Christopher as "my son" the way he did? Why not "your brother" or just by name? She was just about to tell her story when he started to shake her violently, and at the top of his voice, said, "Damn you, Ardith, you know something you're not telling me about my son. What is it?" He had shaken her so hard, that for the second time that day, she thought she would be sick.

She vaguely remembered her mother coming into the room and after what seemed to be an eternity, calming her father down. In a very soft voice, her mother said, "Do you know something we should know, Ardy?"

"No, Mamma, I don't. I feel as terrible about all this as you do." With much hesitation her mother led her father from the room and she was finally left alone. She felt empty.

Christopher was buried on a cloudy, rainy day. There were the usual neighbors and a few of Christopher's friends at the funeral, but the two boys he was with the day of his death were not there. Myra felt a sadness, but didn't understand why she was unable to cry. Daddy cried openly and repeated over and over, "My son, my son."

Daddy sold the pickup and purchased a huge headstone for Christopher's grave without so much as a word to Myra or Mamma. The inscription read, "In memory of our only son, Christopher."

All the happiness seemed to go out of Daddy after that and he only spoke to Myra when he wanted her to do something. He never spoke of college again, and the one time Myra brought it up, answered her by saying, " No, Ardith, not till you tell me what really happened to Christopher."

Chapter 50

Myra woke with the sun warm on the end of the bed. She missed Dave and her mind started churning about getting that damn Johnson out of her life. That's strange, she thought, he isn't really in my life; he's in Dave's. Logic, she told herself, would say that she really had nothing to get upset about, but that didn't matter. She didn't like the pushy bastard and he was going to go. Her mind went back to her coins and the deal she was making with Saul. There seemed to be something fishy with this new deal, but she didn't feel he had been dishonest. All she had to do was make sure he kept everything open and above board. Speaking of being above board, the time was coming when she was going to have to tell Dave what she was doing. She was sure he loved her and he had said many times that she could have anything she wanted. There shouldn't be any problem, so why was she this uptight about it? This worry about telling Dave was getting to be depressing. Next week, next week she would tell him.

Dressing in jeans and a sweater she went down the back stairway to the kitchen and was a little surprised to find it empty. There was fresh coffee in the maker but no other sign of activity. Pouring a cup, she went to the refrigerator to get some cream and found a note on the door. The note was from Dora explaining that since the men were all fishing, she was going over to see her daughter and would be home about 6:00. The men were not expected home until after 7:00 and this would give her time to fix dinner. There were things in the icebox to make lunch and some sweet rolls in the breadbox for breakfast.

Well, what do you know? She was alone in the house, and would be for the entire day. She got one of the huge sweet rolls that Dora was famous for and taking her coffee she went to the den and curled up on the leather chair.

On the stand next to her chair was a book she had started a week ago and she turned to the dog-eared page where she had left off. The story was about a family during the black plague in England. It was very well written and when she finished it, was surprised to find the day had passed.

Going to the kitchen, she rinsed her cup and was pleased to see Dora coming up the walk. It was just after seven o'clock when Dora entered the kitchen and the phone rang. It was Dave calling from the clubhouse. The men had dropped off the last of the boys and since it was getting late, decided to have dinner at the club. Myra could tell by his voice that Dave was having the time of his life and he was doing a "man" thing. When he asked if she and Dora wanted to join them for dinner, she begged off without even consulting Dora. Dave explained they would probably have a drink with dinner but would be home before too long.

The two women had some canned soup and a sandwich for dinner and after cleaning up the dishes Dora went home and left Myra alone again. Myra felt tired even though she had done very little that day and slowly climbed the stairs and went to bed.

Myra woke to the sound of Dave and Sam bidding a very drunken goodnight to each other. Myra could hear the clock downstairs strike two o'clock when Dave fell clumsily into bed. She could smell the liquor on him and after he went to sleep, vowed again that she would get that damn Johnson.

It was late when Myra woke and she was surprised that Dave was still asleep at ten. Slipping quietly out of bed she dressed quickly and went down stairs to find Dora just removing some sweet rolls from the oven.

"Well, there you are. I thought you two were going to sleep the day away. Jack is still in bed and I'm surprised that Mister Fields and Dave are not up yet. All of them seem to be early risers, but I guess yesterday was a bit much. I can't remember when Jack came in so late and so drunk."

Myra's voice was like ice when she answered, "Boy, you can say that again. I'm really upset that they would do such a thing. They had to drive home in that condition and I'm sure that's not the example a sheriff's deputy should be displaying. It's probably all Johnson's fault anyway. Dave never did anything like this before he took up with the likes of him."

"Oh my, Myra, you can't blame Virgil for that. He doesn't drink at all. He has some sort of a liver problem that makes him deathly ill with just a sip of any kind of liquor."

Myra saw red and thought that he would find some way to be beyond reproach.

"I'm going for a ride and perhaps do a little shopping. If those lazy bums ever get up, tell them I'll be home when I get ready."

Noting the look of surprise on Dora's face, she took determined strides out the door and into the garage. As she backed her little truck out of the drive, she could see Dora standing at he back door with her hands on her hips. Myra knew she had upset Dora, but she didn't care.

Parking in her usual area of the lot and taking note that the coin shop was still displaying a closed sign, she entered the side door of the mall. Going directly to the Orange Julius stand she got a small drink and started a leisurely window-shopping stroll. At the far end of the mall she noticed a bookstore. *Strange,* she thought, she had never been in this store, but then it was clear at the end of the mall and she usually didn't go beyond the dress shop.

The store was an odd shape because it was at the end of the building. It was wider at the rear than it was at the front, which made it a very large store. Having worked in a library as a girl, she was amazed at the extensive inventory. After nearly an hour of close examination of the entire stock of the store, she came upon a section that was marked, "Coin Collectors". This section was filled with all sorts of books and several racks filled with books on the history of coins and listing the value of thousands of coins, both domestic and foreign. After an hour of comparing, she selected two books that seemed to cover more information on gold coins. Purchasing the books she returned to her truck and headed home. She was just pulling out of the lot when she came practically bumper to bumper with Sheriff Virgil Johnson. He gave her the one-finger salute she had grown to hate and went his smiling way. She could feel the blood in her face and her heart beat in her ears, as she vowed, "I'm going to get that bastard, if it's the last thing I do."

When Myra pulled into the drive she could see the lights were on in the studio and she could see Dora at the kitchen window.

Dora was fixing dinner and said, "I'm sure glad to see you home. I've fixed enough food to feed an army. Mister Miller told me Mister Fields is going home tomorrow and wanted to have a special dinner for him. Mister Miller has invited Jack and me to join you and they have put in a call to Virgil Johnson. Mister Miller thought it would be nice if he was here too because of the wonderful time they all had on the outing with the boys."

"When Mister Miller comes in, would you tell him I have a dreadful headache and I'll not be joining you for dinner. I'm going directly to bed."

"Oh gee, honey, I'm sorry you don't feel well. Is there anyway I can help?"

"No, Dora, I'm going to take an aspirin and go to bed."

If that doesn't take the cake, Myra thought. *Not only do I have to sit home alone while they all run off to play with that son of a bitch, now he's being invited to dinner. Well, they'll all regret this.*

Throwing her books on the bed she took a quick shower and putting on a large flannel nightgown, opened her bedroom door so she could hear at least some of the activity in the house. It was getting dark out and she turned the light on and opened the history of coins book. She had no memory of when she went to sleep but woke when Dave sat on the edge of the bed.

"What's wrong, sweetheart? Dora says you're sick."

"No, not really, Dave, I've just got a rotten headache and I want to stay quiet for a while, take some aspirin and get rid of it."

"Well, everyone sends their best and we hope you get to feeling better soon. Dora has dinner ready and I think I'll go join our guests. I spent part of the day with Sam and he decided to go home tomorrow and get started putting another show together. He really likes some of my work and wants to display it in a new gallery that has just opened and is, as he called it, "real hot." Oh, and, by the way, Virg wasn't able to get away, so he's not going to be here. He says to give you his best and get well soon."

That dirty bastard, she thought, *he didn't come after all and now it's too late for me to change my mind and not look like a fool. I'm going to get him. I'm really going to get him.*

The history of coins book was just that. It was a history book that started way back in Egyptian times and was about early mathematics, as well as commerce and the need for man to develop a way of doing business that was better than the barter system. Because of their value, both silver and gold were used but were unstable until a standard was established. In later years, some paper money was used, but the true standard was gold and silver, with gold always worth more. Myra couldn't put it down. She read until she heard Dave and Sam coming up the stairs and pretended to be asleep. She listened to Dave shower and come to bed. It took a good half an hour before his breathing told her he was sleeping and several hours before she slept. She lay wide-awake, thinking about the Spanish nation and its quest for gold, which, at least for a time, made it the most powerful nation in the world. She envisioned all the different coins that were used in the world, from the Widow's Mite, of Biblical times, to the Spanish pieces of eight. They were really one eighth of a dollar, and how this one eighth had carried forward to the modern day stock market that still kept prices in eighths. *Fantastic,* she thought, *how all the nations and peoples of the world measure their wealth in gold.* Sleep finally came.

The next morning was cool and overcast. Dave had gotten up early and from what Myra could tell had met Sam in the kitchen and gone out to the studio several hours ago. Myra spent most of the time making an inventory of her coins. When the inventory was finished, she compared what she had paid for the coins as opposed to what her new book showed as a value. In the first few weeks of dealing with Saul, she learned that a lot of the coins she purchased were the value of the coin plus twenty dollars. Comparing these first few coins with her book, she found this to be true. However, starting with the third purchase, when she started buying collector's coins, the book showed a marked difference in value. Almost without exception the value of the coins was ten to twenty percent higher than the purchase price. The value of these coins changed in direct relation to their condition. In two cases she found that the coins were marked as extra fine and this placed the value over twice what they cost. She began to see that some of the conditions were somewhat arbitrary and the classification was in the eye of the appraiser. It was easy to see, however, that the coins marked extra fine, were in pristine condition, and were strikingly beautiful. She could feel a smile on her face when she came to the conclusion that Saul was treating her fairly and that her investment was increasing in value.

The clock in the hall was striking ten o'clock when she put the coins away and closed the safe. She placed the new books on the shelf next to the closet door and after a quick shower, dressed and went down stairs. Dave and Sam were in the kitchen and Dora was serving them breakfast.

"Well, there's our sleeping beauty," Dave said, " How are you feeling? You look beautiful."

Dora smiled and agreed, and then asked if she wanted something to eat or just coffee and a roll. Myra elected to have just a roll and bid good morning to Sam

"How's my favorite agent this morning?"

"Just fine, you gorgeous girl, you. My only problem is trying to get your smitten husband to take some time away from you and come with me to New York."

"Why in the world do you want to steal him away for a trip to New York?"

"Well, I spent a good part of yesterday afternoon on the phone with a friend that owns a gallery there and his clientele includes some of the most influential art people in the country. He has agreed to give us a showing if we can put it together in the next few days. He has a break in his schedule and would fit us in if we will guarantee to be ready on time. He will start the advertisement of the show now and be ready by the time we have the framing and matting done. This guy is no small potatoes and getting him to put on a showing with this short notice is almost a miracle. Some artists work years just to have him consider showing their work and we have a chance to be shown for an entire week with very short notice. He has seen some of your husband's work and feels it would be worth our while. After all this, Dave tells me he doesn't think you would like to go to New York and he doesn't want to go without you."

"Go to New York? Oh, Dave, could we? I've never been there and it sounds wonderful! Would we have time to see some of the sights and maybe even a show or two?"

"My God, Myra, I don't know why I figured you wouldn't like to go to New York, but if you want to, you bet we can. We can stay longer if you want to and see anything we can get tickets to."

"How much time do I have to get ready? A girl has to take lots of stuff with her when she's goin' to the Big Apple."

Sam came wide-awake. "Terrrriffic!" he cried. "We could have the artwork loaded and be ready to go in two hours. If we can get the 2:30 shuttle to Boise, we can be in New York by tomorrow morning."

Chapter 51

Dora answered the phone on the first ring and a whiny man's voice asked for Mrs. Miller.

"Sorry, sir, she's in the East and won't be home for another week or so. Would you like to leave a message?"

"Yes, ma'am, would you tell her that Saul Feinstein called and the information she requested is now ready."

Saul hung up the phone and slowly turned to face his younger son David, who had a look of wanting to ask a question.

"Well?" Saul said, "What are you lookin' at?"

"Just wondering, Dad, what the heck are you up to? You are working something out with this Miller woman, and Dan and I are a little worried."

"How so?"

"Well, we know about the coins you got from an old man back when we were kids and there is something about these coins that scared the hell out of both you and the old man. We think you are trying to unload these coins on Mrs. Miller and if there is something wrong with this deal, shouldn't you tell us?"

Dan came out of the back room and stood next to his brother without speaking. There was silence in the room for over a minute and then Saul spoke.

"Okay, boys, I guess it's time to tell you, and since you already know part of what went on, it's no longer a secret."

"Old man Grundbaum was a friend of your grandfather's and came to this country from Germany in the late 50's to see Grandpa because he felt he couldn't trust anyone else in the world. When he found out that grandpa was dead he about came unglued. Then he found that I had taken over Grandpa's business and really went nuts. He started crying and cursing and speaking

Yiddish so fast I couldn't make head or tails out of what he was saying. Finally I got him calmed down and he told me the story."

"Just after World War I, he and Grandpa were in the jewelry import business together and they made a lot of money. They lived in big homes like the one I was born in. You know, like in all those old pictures? They had lots of friends in the Jewish community they lived in and lots of banking and financial connections. In the mid 1930's the Hitler "Brown Shirts" started strong-arming everyone and taking over all the independent businesses, mostly ones that were owned by Jews. Grandpa tried to stop them, but they took over the police departments and since they were now the army, there was on one to defend us. Well, Grandpa saw what was coming, so he gathered all the money and valuables he could get in a hurry and came to the U.S.. I was just a small boy but I can remember what a time we had getting out of Germany. We came here through Brazil and then Mexico, all the time hiding the gold and jewelry Grandpa had brought with us. We finally got to the states and came to Boise where Grandpa had a friend from the old country.

"This friend helped us get settled and convert the jewels and things to American money. I got started in school and we all took English lessons at the YWCA two nights a week. By 1940, we were all naturalized and Grandpa had the coin shop going. World War II came along and Grandpa didn't have to go, since he was too old. In 1944 Grandma died and later in 1947 Grandpa died and this severed all the ties with the old country. It was years later, when this old Jew named Isaac Grundbaum showed up and after about a week, he told me what he had been up to."

Saul went on, "In the early years of World War II, there was a lot of confusion about who was or was not a Jew and at first old Grundbaum was able to convince the Nazis he was not a Jew. Then just at the end of the war it was discovered that the old man and his family were Jewish and they came to arrest them. Well, all the family except the old man was sent away to camp or were killed. The old man escaped and went into hiding with some kind of an underground group. This group did whatever they could to harass the Nazis and one of the things they did was to steal a bunch of art and things from the home of some famous general. Part of what they took was a very large coin collection. A small part of this collection was an American gold coin collection that contained some fifteen hundred coins. They were all twenty-dollar pieces in mint, or near mint, condition. In those days the value of the coins was about their denomination and since the U.S. was still on the gold standard, they were easy to dispose of. Old Grundbaum pulled a fast one on this underground group and hid the entire U.S. gold coin collection from them.

"The war ended and the old man went to France and Spain and several other places trying to stay ahead of the bunch he hid the coins from. He finally ended up in Palestine with the coin collection intact. He was afraid to trade or spend any of it, so he lived in near poverty for years. Finally some of the men from the underground group caught up with him again and it wasn't long until the word got out and the government got into the act. Now everyone was after the gold, but the old boy never gave an inch. After several years, some of the older men in the group died and the others finally gave up.

"Somewhere along the line he had seventy-five rosewood boxes made that held the entire collection. These boxes were all lined and were beautiful all by themselves. They had moisture seal to protect the coins, which were in mint or uncirculated condition, and were packed twenty coins to the box. These coins were all dated 1850 through 1865 and had a mixture of mintmarks. There was also a small box containing two twenty-dollar pieces struck in the Saint Gaudens die that were worth over $30,000.00 all by themselves. The value of the entire collection was well into the millions and the old man entrusted them to me. He was scared half to death that his theft would be discovered. For many years he thought he would outlive the story about the coins, but instead, there seemed to be more people looking for them each year. About a month before he came to me, two different groups approached him. One from a Nazi youth party, still active and protecting old-line party members all over the world. They were a rough bunch, but not nearly as determined as the next bunch a week later. They were a group of Jewish freedom fighters that were the remnants of the group that originally stole the collection from the Germans. This second bunch even got physical enough to put the old boy in a hospital for a week.

"There was no doubt in his mind, or mine, that either group would kill to get their hands on the collection. The old man and I came here to Twin Falls and rented a safety deposit boxes large enough to hold the collection and it's been here all this time. The week after we put the collection in the safe deposit box, the old man dropped dead on our front lawn of a heart attack.

"The next year we moved to Twin and opened this store. I've always been afraid to part with any of the collection, because most of the coins are rare enough to attract attention and if they came on the market, would cause enough of a stir to bring that bunch of ruffians directly to me. I've wanted to turn at least part of the collection over for several years, but until Mrs. Miller came on the scene, I couldn't figure a safe way to do it.

"There was one time when we were just starting the business when I had to have some money or give up the store. I took a chance and sold one of the Saint Gaudens to a dealer in Boise. He said he had a buyer who wanted it as a gift for his wife. The dealer would never tell me who he sold the coin to, and I've never heard of it since.

"Now along comes this dame. She is really loaded and is not buying coins for the investment. She's nuts about gold and is buying coins because they are pretty. I'm sure she will never part with anything she buys and this creates a perfect blind for me to unload some of the collection. I figure I can make her a deal she can't refuse and she will pay enough for your mother and me to retire. The rest of the collection will go to you boys when I die and that will probably let enough time pass for all the heat from these radical groups to be gone. I've been slowly raising the ante on the price of the collection I've been telling her about and I think if I work it right, we'll come up to price somewhere close to $100,000. I'm trying to stay vague enough to be able to add or subtract from the collection I'm offering, to get her to come up with the highest dollar she will part with."

Saul paused and the shop was so quiet you could hear the traffic on the street over a block away.

Finally Dan spoke, "Gees, Dad, isn't what you are doing dishonest? I've never known you to do anything like this. Couldn't you just give the coins back to their rightful owners?"

"Sure, I could, if I had any idea who the rightful owners are. As near as I can tell the legitimate owners were robbed of the collection over seventy years ago and since then it has gone from one thief to another. The way I see it the coins are now like buried treasure and its finder's keepers. Yes, I could turn the collection over to the authorities, but it would only be claimed by some nation as a national treasure and we wouldn't get a cent. We have an opportunity to set all of us up with security in our old age. If either of you bums ever get married, your families will be well cared for and your children, should you have any, will be guaranteed an education and a secure future. Dishonest? Well, maybe, but there is much room for debate and I guess every man has his price."

Again there was a long silence until Saul spoke again, "Well, that's my plan. You two think it over and we'll discuss it again later. But just so there is no misunderstanding, I'm determined to do this and if it's going to bother you to be a part of it, you sure don't have to be. Just speak up and it will be done without your complicity. You have a few days to think about it anyway, since

Mrs. Rich Bitch is back east and won't be home for another week or so. When she gets home and I give her an inventory of the coins I want to part with, don't either of you interfere if you don't agree. Understand?"

Chapter 52

Myra took a sip of her champagne and looked at Dave. Here they were, seated in first class on a jet airliner going to the Big Apple, a far cry from the bus seats where they had first met. *He's more beautiful now, than he was then*, she thought; *only now I think we're rich. We are headed for New York and his very own art show that Sam says will make us not only richer but famous too.* She finished her drink and laying her head on Dave's sleeping shoulder closed her eyes. The quiet hissing sound of the airplane soon lulled her into a peaceful nap.

The airline terminal was a madhouse and Myra was relieved when they were settled in their rooms at the hotel. She had never seen such a place. There were four large rooms in the suite. The bedroom was huge and the two baths were appointed with gold fixtures. The sitting room was large enough to play ball in and was furnished in a French provincial mode that took her breath away. "Wow! Dave, can we afford such a place? How much does this place cost?"

"Never you mind, darlin', us rich folks from Idaho can afford these little digs out of the butter and egg money."

Myra squealed with delight, "Oh, Dave, it's so neat to be rich."

"This is why we're here, baby. We're going to really do the town. I know the art show will probably take some of our time, but I still want to see some shows and all the sights. I want you to shop till you drop and not worry your head about one blessed thing."

The next six days were a whirlwind experience for Myra. There were times when she felt she just couldn't keep up. The show in the Gallery was a phenomenal success and Sam drove everyone to distraction.

After the second day Myra had to beg off and spent the third day in the hotel room resting.

CALL ME MYRA

The fourth day she spent alone and it was her intent to spend the day shopping. She left the hotel at 10:30 in the morning expecting to walk to the shopping area of town, but much to her surprise the hotel was about thirty blocks from where most of the stores were. She hailed a cab and for the first time in her life was embarrassed by the rudeness of someone serving the public. The driver, for no reason at all, swore at her and called her every name in the book when she paid him and only included a dollar tip. Next she found he had let her off more than two blocks from where most of the stores were and she had to walk the last two blocks anyway. She was amazed at the filth of the place, having almost to play hopscotch to avoid the dog poop that covered the sidewalk. She finally made it to what looked to be a very nice department store and went in. Again she was amazed at the rudeness of the sales people and when she started to look at the prices she was really shocked. After an hour of dismay she left the store and tried to hail a cab. The first one to stop rolled down the passenger side window and demanded she tell him where she wanted to go before he would open the door. The third cab took her the thirty some blocks back to the hotel and demanded a fare of $17.50. When she offered no tip, the driver who looked like an ordinary family man called her a cheap bitch and almost ran over her when he pulled away from the curb.

She reentered the hotel just before noon and went to the restaurant on the main floor. She was seated next to the window at a quiet, beautifully appointed table and a pretty young girl named Carla took her order. She had the luncheon special, which consisted of Dover sole and a salad that was delicious. When she finished her lunch, she asked Carla if it would be all right if she ordered some tea and relaxed for a while. Carla said, " Certainly, madam, if there is anything at all I can do for you, all you have to do is ask." Then she added, "Are you all right? Don't you feel well?"

Myra told her of the ordeal of the last few hours. Carla was understanding and hoped Madam would not hold it against all New Yorkers for the ill manners of a few. After talking with Carla, Myra thought that she would give New York another chance but not without the company of Dave.

The fifth day she went to the gallery with Dave and after three hours asked him to take her back to the hotel. He seemed a little put out with her request, but Myra could see he was tired and let it go.

Saturday, the sixth and last day of the show, was followed by a champagne party and when they got home at 2:00 a.m. Sunday morning, they were exhausted.

They slept until noon and had breakfast served in their room. Sam came in a little after 2:30 and informed them the show would go down as the hit of the season. After two hours of back patting, Myra had her fill of all the congratulating and interrupted by asking Sam if he could get tickets to one of the big shows on Broadway. Sam said he was sure he could but it probably wouldn't be until later in the week if they wanted to see one of the real hits. In the meantime, there were many fine Off-Broadway shows that they could see without as much notice.

Myra wondered why in the world Sam would think she was putting up with all his crap if all she was going to see was a second rate show in some dumpy theater? She wanted some attention paid to her for a change. Damn it, she could have stayed home if she wanted to be alone.

Sam went to his room about 6:30 and Dave said he was very tired and went to bed. Myra sat up until after midnight watching television.

The next day was Monday and Dave didn't even get dressed all day. They took their meals in the room and he spent the day reading the reviews in the art section of the Sunday papers. Dave went to bed about 8:30 and Myra spent another evening watching television.

It rained all day Tuesday and Wednesday. No, it poured all Tuesday and Wednesday. It was a real cloudburst. The streets were flooded and even the taxis had problems getting around. Wednesday night they had dinner in the hotel restaurant and tried a couple of times to dance to a little orchestra that played slightly out of sync. They gave up about nine-thirty and went to their room and to bed.

Thursday morning Dave announced that he was beat down to his shoes and wanted more than anything in the world to just go home. Myra never said a word She just packed their things while Dave made their plane reservations. They caught a 9:40 a.m. flight and were home by 9:15 that night.

Myra woke the next morning to the sound of Dave talking on the telephone. "Why sure, Virg. I would welcome the change. Why don't you pick me up about 4:00 and we can make a weekend of it." Myra sat up and asked, "What was that all about?"

"Nothin' much, honey. I just made arrangements with Virgil to help with the kids over the weekend. We are taking them up to Spirit Lake for an overnight campout. We'll be home by Sunday noon."

"Well, I'll be go to hell," Myra hissed. "Just what the hell do you think I'm supposed to do while you and that damn fool sheriff play baby sitter? You drag me off on some sort of a trip of terror with a promise of a big time in the big city and then you strand me in a stupid hotel for a week while you play big shot with a bunch of art nuts. And now that we are home, you're going to run off with Virgil Johnson. What is it with you and that no-good bastard anyway? You got a thing for Virg?"

"Now, Myra, don't get all worked up over nothing. I'm going to take a shower and when you've cooled down a bit, we'll talk, okay?" Dave stood and started for the shower and Myra exploded from the bed, grabbing him by the arm, spun him around and screaming like a Banshee said, "Damn you, Dave Miller, don't you turn your back on me. I'm not some little nothing for you to wipe your boots on and you'd better not forget it."

Dave caught her right arm with his left hand in the middle of a real haymaker, aimed directly at his left jaw. With his hand placed on her upper chest he slammed her backwards onto the bed and fell beside her.

"Now stop it, Myra, calm down and let's talk."

"Go to hell, you son of a bitch. Let me go or you'll be sorry."

"Damn it, Myra, I love you, but you have to quit this before one of us gets hurt."

She relaxed a little and he let her go. In a flash she was after him again. He held both of her wrists and rolled over on top of her. Myra had experienced some strong-arm tactics three other times in her life, once with her brother, once with old John Martin, and again with Jerry Jones, but never had she experienced the power she now felt. Dave was so much stronger than she thought anyone could be that it took her by surprise. She held still.

"Now then, you little wild cat. I want you to know that I love you more than I can say and it really bothers me to have to do this, this way, but I've got to tell you what I feel. I was just as unhappy in New York as you. I didn't want to be there at all. The only reason we went was because if it worked out the way Sam said, we would be set for life. Our fortunes would be made and we could pretty much write our own ticket from then on. Sure, I would still work, but it would be at my own pace with no deadlines or quotas to meet. I hated every moment we were there after the first day, but I stayed because I thought you wanted to. When I found you were dissatisfied too, I brought us home."

Myra went limp. He released his hold on her and when she didn't move, he sat up. "Lord, Myra, we have to start talking to each other more. It seems we live together and sleep together and make love together, but we don't talk. You, for instance, have never told me a thing about yourself and I didn't really mind. I told myself your past didn't matter. I was in love with you so much that I didn't care if you were a murderer or a thief or whatever. I knew that you were not as educated and sweet as you let on. You had the Timmons' fooled, but I could see you were not as erudite as you pretended. I know you are a good secretary and a super bookkeeper and somehow you are buying gold coins with money that I can't completely account for. I have the feeling, Myra, that part of what is wrong here, is that you have some sort of a guilt complex that you are using anger to satisfy. Hell, Myra, you don't have to hide anything from me. Everything I have is yours too."

"How long have you known about the coins?"

"Oh, I don't know, a month or so. It doesn't really matter."

"Yes, it does Dave. This has been killing me for months and I didn't know how to tell you. At first, I was spending some money I had when we met and then later it was like being a gambler. I took it from wherever I could, just to buy them. I wanted to tell you, I just didn't know how. How did you find out and why didn't you say anything?"

"Well, one day you left the coins on the shelf in your closet and I went in there to borrow one of your big old wool scarves to take on the first camping trip we took the kids on. I found the book of coins and an inventory slip for many more. I also found a book the other day about U.S. coins that priced some of the coins in your inventory. I went through some of the listed prices in the book and I found you might have even made a small profit on them. From then on I figured I'd just let you do your thing and let you tell me when you got ready. Now, what about Virgil Johnson? What's he done to get you so angry at him?"

"You make me almost ashamed to tell you now, but it's about when he came here after that deal with Jerry. He said some things that I felt were uncalled for and I got mad at him. I didn't want him around me at all and suddenly I couldn't get rid of him. You were spending time with him and I hated it."

"Well, Myra, you don't have to worry about Virgil. I think he's a dud anyway. I only went with him because he was the way to be with the kids. I really enjoyed the boys and being with him was part of the deal. Other than that, he means nothing to me. There is one of the boys that I really like. His name is Anthony Blevins and I'm thinking about applying for membership in the Big Brothers of America and being his big brother."

Dave looked at her and she was crying. Taking her in his arms, he said, "Just remember, I love you no matter what, and nothing you do will ever change that. Now dry your tears and lets take a shower and have some breakfast."

Myra fixed French toast and coffee and they ate without saying much. When they had finished, Myra said, "Now that you know about the coins, I want to tell you everything."

"You mean there's more?"

"You bet there is, and I can hardly stand it until I tell you the whole story. It's bothered me for so long, and now I can tell you everything – it's gonna knock your socks off."

Chapter 53

It was just before eleven o'clock when Myra seated Dave on the bed and starting from when she discovered the safe combination on the bed slats, told the story in detail up to where she and Tim Timmons made their compact. At this point, Dave, who had long been silent, interrupted and wanted to see the documents, especially the ones pertaining to his family. Myra opened the safe and removed all the items and placed them on the bed. The one item she did not remove was the box of bullets. The decision not to show them to Dave was a knee jerk reaction. Without any consideration at all, she elected to keep the bullets and the gun to herself. She handed him the white envelope and when Dave finished going through the letters and documents, he laid them aside, and Myra could tell he was on the verge of tears. After a few moments he placed the papers back in the envelope and picking up the phone called Virgil Johnson.

"Hey, Virg. I've had a change of plans and I don't think I'll go with you today. It's my first day home in over a week and there are some things I want to attend to. We'll make it another time, okay?"

Myra thought, *finally I've got the skids under that son of a bitch.*

Dave turned back to the pile of things on the bed and with a smile on his face said, "Damn, Myra, look at the size of your collection. I had no idea it was this large. You're really serious about this coin collection, aren't you?"

"Well, I never looked at it like that, Dave. I mean I have never looked at it like a stamp collection. I just felt the coins had a value that was here to stay, and it was a good place to keep money. Along with that and probably even more important, they are so beautiful. There is a quality about gold that just holding it in my hand gives me a feeling of security. As you have guessed, parts of my life have been very unsettled and just knowing the gold is there, has given me a feeling of safety I really need. On the other hand if you want to see some real security, let's look in these brown envelopes and I'll show what security looks like."

Taking the contents of each envelope and spreading them on the bed, they went over each page, item by item. When they set aside the last of the documents, Dave gave a long whistle and said, "Boy, you are a sneaky broad, aren't you? Do you know what these bearer bonds are worth today?"

"No, not exactly, Timmons was supposed to find out, and then we were all going to sit down together and decide what would be the best way to dispose of them and turn them into cash. He has a friend that is an accountant and he will have an answer for us. I think Tim figures they are worth close to a million. My slowness in telling you about all this has old Tim climbing the wall. He's been after me almost every week to bring you up to date. As your attorney he felt he was not doing the right thing and was soon going to tell you, if I didn't. The fact you were not told sooner was all my doing. I wanted to do it when I felt the time was just right. Number one, I didn't know how you would take all the information about your family, and two, I thought you would be upset about my spending money on the coins. Now I find I was wrong and I should have told you right away. I know I was sneaky and I promise I won't do it again. From now on, I'll tell you everything." In the back of her mind she thought about her gun.

Dave again picked up the phone and dialed Tim Timmons' number. "Hello, Tim, this is Dave Miller. Yes, how are you? Say Tim, we just got home from a trip to the East Coast, and Myra has been telling me some pretty remarkable things she has uncovered that belonged to my Aunt Alma. She tells me she has discussed these documents with you and that you have been working on a proper way to handle some bearer bonds. Have you come up with a recommendation? You have? Well, that's good. I would like to get together with you as soon as possible and talk this whole situation over."

"Oh, I don't care, Tim, any time you say; today would be fine for me. Yes, I understand. Well, if you're busy the rest of the afternoon, why not this evening? You and Betty could come over tonight. We could have dinner and let our hair down while we discuss this good news. Good. See you about sevenish? Wonderful, see you then."

Turning to Myra, Dave said, "Let's put all these things back in their place and find out if Dora is free to help with dinner or if we have to send out for pizza."

Myra's head was spinning. She thought, *boy, when old Davy gets involved, things really start to move. I sure had this figured all wrong. I should have had him in the loop from the start.*

"Before we get everything put back there is one last thing you should see. Have a look at this coin. It's a collectors piece and I'm told could be worth close to twelve thousand dollars. I found it in the safe and it was evidently a treasure of Alma's. I thought it was the most beautiful thing I had ever seen and when I went to find out about it, was when I got interested in the other coins."

Dave gave a low whistle and said, "I can see why; it's breathtaking. Now let's find Dora and see about dinner."

Chapter 54

Darlene Tate came into the kitchen just as it was getting light. She wanted to clean up a bit before everyone got up and wanted breakfast. The kitchen was in a mess, left over from the night before when Ted's brother Terry and his wife Vicki had dinner with them and played cards until the wee hours. She had gone to bed without even putting the dishes in the sink. She had just started when Vicki came in and offered to help. Darlene asked if she would put on the coffee while she started the dishes. Vicki agreed and when the coffee was done, the kitchen was back to looking like home. The two women sat with their steaming brew and Vicki asked, "How is Ted doing? He seems to be laid back in comparison to the way he was a month or so ago."

"Huh, you can say that again. After his heart attack he wouldn't let go of the job even though the doctor told him to and we found him sneaking around looking for that Myra Dillon dame. Well, one day a few weeks ago he came to Bob and me and told us to get off his back. He was feeling good and he was going to keep his hand in no matter what we thought. He seemed so happy when we agreed with him, and I thought he was going to turn into a real Sherlock Holmes. But instead of that, he backed off and hasn't even mentioned old Myra in days. He's been going fishing when he gets a chance and has even taken me on some short camping trips to places I want to go. I guess the old war-horse only wanted us to know he still had enough kick in him to whip the world and when we agreed, he was satisfied."

"Isn't that wonderful, Darlene? Terry and I were so worried about him and now he seems to have completely recovered from his heart problem. Terry feels especially good except for one thing."

"Oh, what's that?"

"Ted hasn't let him win a single game of chess or catch the biggest fish in weeks."

Lois Harts entered her boss's office and laid the eight inch thick file of Myra Dillon / John Martin on the corner of his desk. "Sir, what do you want me to do with this file? It's been inactive for over six months now and it's so large that it takes up most of my active file storage. I know you wanted to keep it on top of the pile at first, but it's now seriously in my way."

"I tell you what, Lois, why don't you put it on that end shelf of my bookcase? It will be out of the way there but not in the inactive file. When I get a chance I would like to go through it and see if I can find any loose ends. The police seem to feel it's a hopeless case unless a lead comes in from outside. Anyway, let's not call it inactive just yet."

Lois placed the file on the shelf and retreated to her desk in the front office thinking, *Since Sheriff Tate left, no one seems to give a damn about anything that requires a little work. The whole bunch is a lot of talk and no action. Jerks, that's what they are, jerks, especially Jewels.*

Darlene Tate answered the phone on the first ring and was pleased to hear her son's voice, " Hi, Mom, is Dad around?"

"He sure is, Bob, he's just poring his first cup of coffee and wiping the sleep out of his eyes."

Turning to her husband she said, "Here's the phone, Ted. Your number one son wants to speak to you."

"Hi, Bob, what's up?"

"Hi Dad, how you feelin'?"

"I'm feeling good, better than I've felt in a long time. What's on your mind?"

"Well, the guys in my office are planning a fishing trip. One of them has a brother-in-law who owns a charter boat up in Puget Sound. We have been invited to a three-day trip salmon fishing. The trip is scheduled for two weeks from Thursday and the boat will handle four. There are only three of us and I thought you would get a kick out of making it four."

"You bet I would, I've never been saltwater fishing and I've always wanted to try it. Are any of the wives going, or is it stag? Your Mom just slugged me in the arm and says she wants to go too."

"No, Dad, it's the just four of us. You'll have to leave Mom at home."

"Well, she will probably make my life miserable for leaving her behind but okay. How are we going to get together?"

"Since the trip is on me, I'll send you a ticket to Portland and we'll drive up from here. It's a little early in the morning but there is a flight that will get you in Portland at 11:45 a.m. and that will put us in Port Townsend by about 6:00 p.m. We'll get a good night's sleep and be on the water by first light. You won't have to bring any gear since the charter will supply everything. You will have to bring warm clothes and you'll need your rain gear. I under stand you'll need the rain gear even if it doesn't rain, because of the heavy dew in the morning. I can't think of anything else just now, Pop, but if I've forgotten anything, I'll get back to you. We have plenty of time. I've got to go now, Dad. Give my best to Mom and tell her better luck next time."

Chapter 55

Dora served a sweet and sour Sparerib over rice dish with stir-fried veggies and an apple and cabbage salad. The meal was delicious and the atmosphere was warm and cordial. They consumed two bottles of a good California wine and by eight-thirty were almost in a party mood. Dave invited their guests to join him in the living room for a brandy and when they were settled Dave was the first to speak.

"Tim, I invited you here tonight to clear the air between you and Betty, and Myra and me. I first want to say in behalf of Myra that she is my wife and anything she did in the way keeping certain facts from me was done to protect me from any sort of pain or anxiety. We have discussed the situation in detail and I want you to know I understand any action she has taken with respect to this long overdue revelation. Myra tells me you have no desire to be involved in the proceeds of the bearer bonds, and that your only concern is to keep private any involvement you may have had in the Jamore Corporation. Well, rest assured my friend that we will never speak of this to a living soul outside of the four of us. Now, with all this having been said, I think I'll pour us another brandy and let you give us the news about the bonds."

When Dave returned to his seat, Tim started to go over the details of his conversation with his accountant friend. He spoke at length about the way the dividends were paid in the form of coupons and how these coupons were never redeemed and on and on.

Myra's thoughts drifted back to the early part of the day and her amazement of the way Dave had handled all the confusing situations she had heaped on him. *In all her life, no one had ever treated her with true consideration. Here was Dave protecting and defending her in spite of anything she did or might have done. She thought about her coins and wondered if old man Feinstein had finished the list of coins in the collection that she wanted. If he did, what was she going to have to pay for them? She remembered the feeling she had when they last spoke, that he was not being completely open about what was in the collection. Well, no matter, if the collection was as good as he had convinced her it was; she wouldn't have a problem paying for it now.*

Dave had cleaned the slate between them and had told her in so many words that she could have anything she wanted. In spite of her anger early in the day, things had worked out better than she could have wished for. There was no problem with her gold, she had put the burden of the bonds onto Timmons, and she had put the skids under that bastard Johnson.

Just before midnight, Tim announced he was going home before he got to the point where Betty would demand the car keys.

Dave stood in the open door and watched them pull out of the driveway. When they were out of sight, he closed the door and watched Myra pick up the drink glasses and put the room in order. He followed her to the kitchen and when she had rinsed the dishes, followed her up the back stairs to their room. They undressed for bed and in the dimly lit room, he took her in his arms.

"Damn, Myra, what a day! In some ways I'm glad it's over, but I'm also thankful we have opened the lines of communication between us. All this secret stuff is no good. We have to tell each other what we think and feel or we will remain forever strangers. In keeping with that, I want to say again that I don't care about my past or your past. I love you in spite of anything. It doesn't matter why or what for, I just do." Myra felt her spring wind so tight she could hardly stand it.

Betty Timmons had driven home and as they pulled into their driveway she said, "Don't you think Dave took this whole thing well? And that Myra, what a wonder she is."

"Yeah, you can say that again. She's a wonder. And to think he picked her up in a damn bus station."

"Do you think the problem over the bonds is settled?"

"Yes, Dave will meet with the accountants next week and their conversion should be complete right away. From what I can gather, including the uncollected coupons, there will be about one and a quarter million to reestablish in a choice of several investment funds. I'm told that depending on what other income they have, almost all of the money will be tax-free until it's withdrawn. By the time they retire and they start to use some of the funds, the tax burden will be practically nothing. However it works out, those kids are well fixed and with Dave's art doing as well as it is, they are easily set for life."

It had been a hot windy day up until two-thirty and then the wind stopped and the sky clouded over. Myra was driving past the golf course and thought it felt like a summer storm was coming. The air was muggy and even the air conditioning in the car didn't take away the sticky feeling on her skin. Yesterday had been a real doozy and she hoped there would never be another like it. Even feeling this way, things had turned out better than she could have dreamed. Dave had shown in every way that he could, that he truly wanted to share everything with her and that he would do anything to see there were no secrets between them. He had even given his approval for her to spend any thing she wanted on her gold collection as long as she let him know in advance so there would be no surprises. She entered the backside of the mall and parked in the rear on Saul's store. As she approached the door, Saul saw her coming and with a wave of his hand welcomed her into the shop.

"Hello, hello, Mrs. Miller, how was your trip to the big city? Did all go well?"

"I guess so, Mr. Feinstein, but I'm very happy to be home. I got your message that you have worked out a deal with your seller and that you have the inventory you promised."

"Yes, ma'am, I sure do. I spent a lot of time working this deal and I think I have come up with the buy of the century. The biggest problem is deciding on just what part of the collection was up for sale. I have worked out a deal where the entire collection will be offered. Instead of the original thirty-six coins we are now looking at one hundred and twenty and some of them are real collector's items. Here is a list of the coins."

Saul laid a sheet of paper on the counter. The writing was in his very unusual hand that looked like it had been done on a typewriter. Each of the one hundred and twenty coins was listed by type, date, and mintmark, condition and price. The total price made Myra take a deep breath, $82,000.00.

"My God, Mr. Feinstein, this price is more than twice what we talked about."

"Yes, I know, Mrs. Miller, but there are over three times as many coins in the collection and you can pretty much have your choice of the number of coins and how much you want to pay. I made such a good deal that I can sell them at this price to you or any one. This price is what I would like if they are sold as a collection and they will command an even higher price if they are sold individually."

"Well, Mr. Feinstein, there is no way I could commit to anywhere near this much money without consulting my husband. I know you told me you were short of cash to complete this deal and I indicated I would come up with a portion of the price as a down payment, but this is way out of line. I came prepared to advance you as much as $20,000, but that's all I can do without my husband's approval."

"At the time we first spoke about this collection there were so many problems with whether the coins would even be available. But the deal is pretty firm now and we no longer have the problem of a down payment. We are a little pressed for time though and I will need an answer in the next few days. Let's say by Monday. Why don't you take the list home and talk it over with Mr. Miller? On Monday we can arrange a deposit amount in the form of an earnest money agreement. If we close the sale, I can have the collection in your hands by Thursday."

As she left the store, David and Daniel Feinstein passed her in the doorway. They exchanged pleasant greetings and Myra continued towards her pickup.

The two boys stood at the end of the counter for several seconds before Dan spoke.

"Well, Dad, did you give Mrs. Gotrocks the list?"

"Yes, I did, and I don't have a clue as to whether she will get her husband to agree to my figure."

" Well, hell, Dad, we got a chance to look at that list and if they have the money like you say, I can't see any reason for them to turn the deal down."

"When did you see the list?"

"Last Friday when you came back from making copies, you left one of them on the desk and we looked it over while you were out to lunch. Anyway, we went over the list and if there ever was a good deal this is it. We looked at the coins and the list, and checked out the conditions of each coin. Most, if not all of them are at least one grade above what you have them listed for and this drives the price much higher than you are asking. Dave and I figured the collection is worth well over $100,000."

"Yes, I know that, but I came up with this $100,000 figure because it's the amount I want to have in reserve when your Mom and I go south. I told you I'm still very wary of selling any part of the collection and having the word get out that we have it. I don't think this dame will ever part with a single piece and I think she is a hard customer to find, considering. Besides, these coins are the dregs of the collection. I'm offering her less than ten percent of the collection and most all the other coins are in almost perfect condition. There are at least three duplicates of each coin I'm offering her, and they are all in equal or better condition. I figure the balance of the collection is worth nearly two and a half million and in years to come, when the threat of getting your heads bashed in is less, both of you will have your retirements secured."

Both boys went to their father and gave him a three-way hug. Dave said, "We don't mean to question you, Pop, and we know you are trying to work out this very worrisome situation so that it works out the best for everyone – and we love you for it."

When Myra got home, Dora was fixing a steak and salad for dinner. Dora and Jack joined them and wanted to know all about their trip to New York. Dave told them all about his show and how pleased he was about the exposure of his work. Not much was said about the rest of the trip except that they were sure glad to be home. After they finished dinner, Dora started the dishes and Myra excused herself and Dave, claiming she was tired and wanted to turn in early.

Once in their room as they dressed for bed, Myra got her coin guidebook and the list of coins in the collection Saul was offering. They sat on the bed and one at a time went through the list of coins. When they finished they added up the total and it came to over $97,000.

"Gees, Myra, I can't see where we could go wrong with buying this group of coins. Over time, I think they will increase in value and this could be a great hedge against inflation as well as giving you the joy and pride you seem to get just having them. You know, you could be hung up on buying an expensive sports car and in a very short time there would be nothing left but the memory. Why don't you firm up the deal next week and if all is as advertised, go ahead?"

Myra felt a little dizzy and wondered how she could be so lucky as to have everything going her way. She felt the spring winding tight in her stomach.

Chapter 56

Dave was not sure of the time, but he thought it must be close to 5:00 a.m. It was Monday and he couldn't sleep with all that had happened since Friday on his mind. He was wearing his bathrobe and sitting next to the window where he could look slightly to his right and watch the sun come up or to his left and watch Myra sleeping. In the gray light of dawn, he could just make out her features and he thought how beautiful; she looked like a child.

Damn, what a weekend he thought. All the tension of going through the documents Myra had sprung on him and her upsetting actions over their trip to New York. He felt he had been successful in calming her down, but the fury of her attack scared him a little and this was a worry to him. The attack on Jerry Jones had revealed that she had a real temper, but this was the first time she had shown it in front of him. The first rays of sunshine caught his eye and the sky was turning from black to blue. He moved his chair and the movement slightly disturbed Myra; she turned over on her side and faced him. The sheet fell away and her breasts were exposed. He watched as her breathing made her breasts rise and fall in a slow even tempo. He was surprised how much watching her stirred him. After all these months just the sight of her made him almost giddy. He guessed he would just have to give up and admit he was hopelessly and completely in love with her. No matter what came, he knew he would never feel any different. A thought of his parents crossed his mind and he wondered if his dad had felt this way about his mom when they were younger. He guessed so and smiled.

He heard a noise from downstairs and realized Dora had come into the kitchen. He rose from his chair and saw Myra watching him. She smiled and said, "Hi, sweetheart, isn't it a beautiful day? What would you like to do today?"

"Well, I thought I would go with you to see Feinstein, but I figured I'd better check with you and see if you wanted me to. You have worked out a deal with him that we both agree on and I thought you just might want to complete it yourself."

"I don't think it matters much, Dave, but maybe it would be good to go alone. That way he won't get the idea that he can't deal with me unless you're along. I don't think I'll be long getting things wrapped up, since we seem to have things pretty well settled. Why don't I make it a point to have that business settled by noon and we can meet at the club for lunch?"

"Sounds good to me, why don't you get up and we'll shower and see if Dora will make us a super breakfast."

"Man-O-Man," Myra trooped, "sounds good to me."

Dan Feinstein was seated at a desk in the back room of the store reading the morning paper when he heard the buzzer and his father say, "Good morning, Mrs. Miller." He thought the old man sounded a little condescending since just a few hours ago he had referred to her as "Mrs. Rich Bitch".

"Just fine, Saul, Have you gotten my coin collection together?"

"Well, not quite Mrs. Miller. Are you ready to firm up the agreement?"

"Yes, I am, Saul. I've gone over this with my husband and we feel the collection you've offered is acceptable to us and we want to go ahead. I've come prepared to give you a check for $41,000 which is half the price of the collection and the other half when we take possession."

"That will be just fine, Mrs. Miller. I'll have the collection completed by Thursday, okay?"

Myra wrote the check and felt so nervous she could hardly remember leaving the store.

When she had gone, Dan came out of the back room and said, "Gees, Dad I can't figure you out. You just took a fifty- percent deposit of $41,000 on a deal that's worth well over $100,000. How come?"

"Never you mind, Sonny Boy, it'll all work out."

Chapter 57

Lunch at the club was, as usual, a pleasant time. The weather was bright and partly sunny but the wind had come up and it was blowing hard enough to bring most of the members inside. After the lunch hour, many members retired to the bar. Myra and Dave took a table in the corner and spent the afternoon people watching and drinking wine coolers. About 4:30 the crowd began to thin out and Myra found she had gotten a little tipsy. On a whim she suggested a swim and Dave responded with an enthusiastic yes. They changed in their respective locker rooms and Dave was the first in the pool. They were alone in the pool until nearly 6:00 and Myra suggested they stay for dinner. Only a handful of the usual Monday night crowd were there and by 8:00 the place was nearly empty. Myra again found herself a bit on the tipsy side and when Dave suggested they go home, she only smiled and started for the door.

The house was dark when they parked the car and went inside. They went directly to their room and while Myra got ready for bed Dave built a fire. The room had a warm cozy feeling and Myra dressed only in the tops of Dave's pajamas, stretched out on top of the bed. She lay there listening to Dave wash and brush his teeth and thought *how strange it was that she had spent $41,000 today and agreed to pay another $41,000 on Thursday and neither one of them had even mentioned it.* Dave came to bed wearing the bottoms of the pajama set and lay beside her, she rolled over and put her head on his shoulder.

She smiled and said, "Are you as smashed as I am?"

Dave laughed and said he was not sure if he was smashed, but he was surly feeling no pain. He put both arms around her and kissed her gently on her eyes. Myra kissed him back and felt her spring wind instantly to the breaking point. Their lovemaking was so passionate it was almost fierce, and left them so exhausted that neither of them could remember going to sleep.

The next day was hot and a little muggy and Dave spent the early part of the day in the studio. Myra had one of her fits of house cleaning and almost, as Dora put it, wore Dora to a frazzle. About noon Dave announced he had submitted his application for membership in the Big Brothers organization and that he had called the foster parents of Anthony Blevins requesting they let Tony spend the day with him. John and Olive Baxter were long time foster parents and the money the state paid them was their way of supplementing their income. John Baxter had suffered from emphysema for many years and was in no condition to offer Tony some of the things the boy and Dave did together.

Tony was just over eleven but was so well mannered that he seemed much older. Myra could see why Dave was taken with the boy; he was beautiful. He was slim, but not skinny, and he had dark hair and blue eyes. He had a face like an angel and the longest eyelashes Myra had ever seen. His movements were graceful and he spoke with the low confident voice of one who was at least in his late teens. They spent the day exploring the mansion and talking about Tony. It seemed a little strange to Myra that the boy should be so open with his thoughts, but his manner was so genuine that it soon ceased to bother her. Tony spoke freely of what he knew about his family and how happy he was with the Baxter's. He had been through a long series of unhappy relationships with several other foster homes, but strangely he placed no blame on the foster parents. Tony was a good student and wanted to go to college at the University of Washington. He told Myra that he wanted to take flying lessons and become an airline pilot. In the evening they drove to town for tacos and when they dropped Tony off about dark, Myra could see what Dave saw in the lad.

They drove home in a very pleasant silence and went to their room. This night was almost a carbon copy of the night before, except that their lovemaking was far less frantic. None the less, neither of them could remember going to sleep.

Chapter 58

Thursday morning came and Myra was glad they lived in the country. The air was filled with the smell of new mown hay and the sky was clear and blue. Dave had made arrangements with Tony to go fishing and was up and gone by 5:30. Dora made her famous cinnamon rolls for breakfast and when Myra got ready to go to town scolded her for wearing that big old denim jacket on a beautiful day like this. The mall was not yet open when Myra pulled into the parking lot, but she could see Saul was there and parked in the rear of the store in her usual place. The buzzer sounded just as she put her hand on the door and she entered. Since the store was on the shady side of the building, she came into an almost darkened room. Saul had only turned on the lights in the back room and just the small light over the safe lit the store. Saul was holding a copy of the collection inventory, and on the counter next to him were six beautiful little boxes that Myra assumed contained her coins.

She felt very uneasy and she was reminded of the feeling she had had as a child at Christmas time. Saul laid the inventory down and opened one of the boxes. Myra had to catch her breath. The absolute beauty of the coins made her tingle all over and she could feel herself start to perspire. She had worn her gloves thinking that Saul would want to shake hands and she didn't want to feel his sweaty palms. She was a little surprised that Saul was also wearing gloves. He was wearing a pair of white cotton gloves that she supposed was to protect the condition of the gorgeous boxes and their contents. After a few moments of silence, Saul said,

"What do you think, Mrs. Miller, aren't they the most beautiful things you've ever seen?"

Myra felt so nervous she couldn't speak and instead of answering, she took the check she had prewritten at home from her pocket and laid it on the counter.

"Here's the balance of what I owe you."

As she spoke the words, she saw the strangest look come over Saul's face.

"What's wrong with you?"

"Well, you see, Mrs. Miller, I've been going over the list and I find the collection is worth far more than we discussed. I have decided that there is no way I can let the entire collection go for so little. I'm afraid you're going to have to come up with another $20,000, or we'll have to reduce the size of the collection."

As he spoke he removed one of the boxes and placed it at arm's length down the counter.

Myra exploded, "No you don't you thievin' old bastard! We had a deal and you, by God, are going to stick to it."

"Now look, Mrs. Miller, I'm just trying to work out a deal that's fair, but fair or not, you can't speak to me that way. I'm calling the whole deal off until you can be more rational."

"Like hell you are, you old son of a bitch! A deal is a deal and you will hold up your end, or you'll wish you had."

Saul turned and opened the unlocked door of the safe and produced the first check Myra had given him. He literally threw the check at her and said,

"Not by a damn sight, Mrs. Moneybags, the deal's off!"

Myra and Saul reached for the stack of five boxes of coins at the same time and Saul jerked them out her grasp so hard it nearly pulled her off balance. She was not sure how, but the 357 Magnum was suddenly in her hand and aimed directly at Saul's head. Just as she pulled the trigger, she saw a look of disbelief on the old man's face. The bullet entered just to the left of Saul's nose and threw him on his back, almost into the opening to the back room. Myra stepped around the end of the counter and stood at his feet. Suddenly, she raised the gun and fired five more rounds into Saul's head. There was blood everywhere. After a moment she laid her gun on the counter and whispered, "There now. You won't ever try to cheat me again."

On the top of the safe was a stack of small plastic shopping bags. Myra took one and placed the six coin boxes inside. She gathered up the two checks and placed them in the safe. As she did, she noticed the Saint Gaudens coin that Saul had shown her when they first met and put it in her pocket. She closed and locked the safe, picked up her gun and placing it back in her jacket, pushed the buzzer and left the shop.

The parking lot was still empty and there didn't seem to be anyone around.

She sat in her pickup for several minutes trying to collect her thoughts and trying to figure out if she had been seen. In the next quarter of an hour, several cars came into the far end of the lot, but parked out of sight on the front side of the mall. Finally she started the engine and eased the little pickup onto the street and turning left headed for home.

When she pulled into the driveway, she noticed that Jack and Dora's car was not in their yard and when she entered the kitchen, she found a note from Dora saying she and Jack had gone over to their daughter's house and would be back before two o'clock. She went directly to her room and opened the safe. She inspected each box as she placed her prize inside and the beauty of the coins made her heart pound. She took six rounds of ammunition from the box to reload her gun and put the empty cases in their place. She removed her Saint Gaudens coin from the safe and compared it to the one she had taken from Saul. They were identical in every respect. She placed them back in the safe and locked the door. She closed the mirrored panels and, making sure her gun was in its proper pocket, hung her jacket in the far end of the closet. She took a very hot shower and lay down on the bed. In a very few moments she was in a deep exhausted sleep

Chapter 59

The radio in Virgil Johnson's patrol car was turned down and he missed the first call from central dispatch. He turned up the volume and heard; "Central calling Patrol one, come in."

"Patrol one, Central, go ahead."

"Hi, Virg, we just got a frantic call from Dan Feinstein, you know, the son of the guy who has that coin shop at the end of the mall? I think they have been robbed again. I think you better get over there and see what's going on. The kid was pretty upset and it was hard to get a clear picture of what happened, but I think the old man has been shot. The city boys are on their way, but I think we had better get in on this too. What's your 10-20?"

"10-4 Central, I'll be there in less than five minutes." He looked at his watch and it was 12:57p.m.

When he pulled up to the coin shop, the city officer was just getting out of his car. They met at the front door and were buzzed in by a very upset young man that they both recognized as Daniel Feinstein, the owner's son. He was almost screaming and was out of control. Virgil, being the much senior officer just naturally took over and instructed the city patrolman to get Dan under control. Virgil stepped behind the counter and what he saw almost made him sick. The body of Saul Feinstein lay in a pool of blood about one third of the way through the archway into the back room. He had been shot several times in the head and most of it was gone. The blood pool had been stepped in and there were bloody footprints all over the place behind the counter. Using his portable radio he called in.

"Central, this is Patrol One."

"Central to Patrol One, go ahead, Virgil."

"We have a robbery murder scene here. I want the crime lab and about three more for back up. I think you had better notify the deputy chief and maybe the state police. We need to secure this scene as soon as possible."

CALL ME MYRA

"10-4, Virg, I've got everybody notified and they are on their way."

Virgil went outside and found that the city boy had Dan Feinstein in his car and pretty much calmed down. There was a crowd starting to form and he was glad to see two other patrol cars pulling up. He gave instructions to the new arrivals to secure the area and get the crowd dispersed. He stepped back into the store and noted that there seemed to be only one set of bloody footprints and he was sure they belonged to Dan. Nothing else in the shop seemed out of place. The safe was closed and there was nothing on the counter. All the trays that held the coins for the display case were gone and he figured that they were still in the safe or they had been taken as part of a robbery. The blood pool had started to dry around the edges, and as a rough calculation he figured it had been at least three hours since the shooting. He noted the time again and it was just 1:22 p.m. Walking outside he found the crime scene people arriving and the gathering spectators were well back from the storefront. The news media was just arriving and he gave orders that they were to be kept back and outside of the yellow crime scene ribbons that were already in place. By 4:00 the crime scene crew was completing their work, and the body was being removed. The fingerprint team was still at work and said the only thing left was the safe. They felt the inside of the safe should be printed before they wrapped it up. Virgil noted that David Feinstein had shown up about an hour before and the two brothers were sitting in a car that had been driven inside the ribbon barrier. He walked over to the car and asked if one of them knew the combination of the safe and Dan said he did. The two brothers went into the store with Virgil and were joined by the deputy chief of the city police. The chief's name was Oscar Mundt. Oscar had been a police officer for over fifteen years and seemed to be a good man. A little laid back, Virgil thought, but quite thorough. So far, it had been Mundt that had overseen all the procedures and Virgil was pleased to step back and watch. When the safe was opened, Mundt instructed the print crew to go in first and then he wanted a compete inventory of the contents, disturbing the position of things as little as possible.

Chief Mundt was a man in his mid-fifties who spoke in a very deep but soft voice. He gave the impression that he was slow and easy going but Virgil suspected that he was anything but. Mundt asked the two brothers to come outside and join him in his city car. The car was a new full-size Buick that had plenty of room for the four men. Virgil wondered what kind of pull he had to have to have a city car like that. The Chief sat in the front with Dan and Virgil sat in the back with David. The chief told the boys how sorry he was that this terrible thing had happened and he would make this interview as short as he could.

The first question was: "When did you see your father last?" Both boys said they were all together when they closed the store on Wednesday night. They expected their father to open the store on Thursday because he had an appointment with a client to close the sale on a fairly large gold coin collection. They were to come in later and run the store until closing. Mundt asked if Dan knew who the client was. Dan said that it was Mrs. Myra Miller.

Virgil felt as though he had received an electric shock. *Good God,* he thought, *how could she be involved? Well, one way was the violence of the crime. His mind went back to the club tennis pro and the savage nature of the beating she had given him.* His mind came back to the present as Dan said there were no other people expected that day and he was not sure what time she was to have been there. The only way they would be able to tell without asking her, would be to see if the collection she was buying was still in the safe. She had paid their father a $41,000 deposit and was to pay another $41,000 on delivery. Their father had made a special deal with her and they were not sure of all the details, but they were sure the collection contained one hundred and twenty coins and the amount agreed on was at the very least $82,000.

"Well, boys, we want to thank you for your time and consideration in this very sad time. I know you want to get home and be with your mother, so you can go now and if there is any thing more that comes to mind, let me know. Just call the station and ask for Chief Mundt. I'll be available around the clock. Oh, by the way, boys, if the coin collection is in the safe, is there anyway we would recognize it?"

Dan answered, "Yes, there is, chief, the collection is in six small rosewood boxes containing twenty coins each."

After thanking them again, the two officers sat while the two brothers walked to their cars and left the lot.

Finally Chief Mundt spoke, " What the hell gives with you, Virgil? You looked like someone had kicked you in the ass when that kid mentioned Mrs. Miller. Do you know this gal or something?"

"You bet I do, Oscar. She was involved in a very savage beating less than a year ago. It was a county beef so you probably didn't pay any attention to it, but she beat a guy named Jones so badly even his mother didn't recognize him. It was a real mess. Nobody could tell at the time, but she was pregnant and the stress of the encounter caused her to lose the baby. Anyway, she beat the living crap out of the guy. It was the same level of overkill as we see here. It just seemed strange to me that the same woman would be involved in two unreasonably violent crimes in less than a year. What do you think?"

"Can't say yet, Virgil. Let's go look at that safe. Maybe we'll find some answers there."

The safe was an older model with lots of room for the display trays that were put away each night. There was a section of the safe that had a key locked metal door and it contained several bookkeeping type ledgers. There was another heavier locking door that probably held cash. There were twenty-four display trays but no small rosewood boxes and on top of the cash lockbox they found two $41,000 checks written by Myra Miller.

"Well, what do you think now, Virg? Nothing out of place here as far as I can tell. The coin collection is gone and the money we were told should be here, is. It looks to me, as though Mrs. Miller completed her business and that the murder took place afterwards. The safe was locked and there was nothing else in the store worth stealing. I think we are going to have to cross our fingers and hope the crime scene and forensic people can come up with some hard evidence that we can hang our hat on."

"You're probably right Chief, but the only suspect we have is Mrs. Miller and she gets my vote just because of the violence connected with things she was involved in, in less than six months."

"Huh! I think a hunch is one of the best tools a cop can have, but in this case a little evidence wouldn't hurt. It's my understanding that this woman is one of the richest in town and is in a position to give us a bad time if we're wrong. Let's go by the book and see what the lab people have to tell us before we go off half-cocked."

Chapter 60

Myra was looking out the window when she saw Dave pull into the driveway. It was just 4:30 and Myra felt rested and at ease. She wondered if Dave would be anxious to see the collection. He unloaded his fishing things in the garage and went into the house carrying a plastic bag. She pulled on a pair of jeans and a sweater, ran her fingers through her hair, and went down the back stairs two at a time. Stepping into the kitchen she heard, Dora say,

"My, aren't those nice trout, so big! We can have them for dinner if you'd like. I'll make some corn bread and fry some potatoes. Well have a good old-fashioned fish fry."

"Sounds great to me, why don't you and Jack join us? Where's Myra?"

"I'm right here, nature boy. It looks like you and Tony had a great time."

"We sure did. I remember you said you liked to fish, so Tony and I have decided you should go with us next time."

"Okay with me, sweetheart, only don't you two men get your feelings hurt when I out fish you."

"That'll be the day. By the way, Dora, when do you think dinner will be ready? Myra has been starting a coin collection and today she picked up a sizable addition. I'm sure she's just dying to show it to me, so we'll be upstairs until you ring the dinner bell."

"You two run along and I'll ring the bell when it's ready."

They went to their room and while Dave took a shower, Myra opened the safe and removed the six boxes and the inventory sheet and spread them on the bed. Dave came in dressed in jeans and a sweatshirt and sat on the other side of the bed. Myra was all smiles and displayed a feeling of pride as she opened each box and placed it so Dave could see the contents.

"My God, Myra, no wonder you were so anxious to have them. They are beautiful! How many are there?"

"One hundred and twenty. Twenty coins to the box. I saw when Saul made up this inventory, he broke the list into six groups of twenty, and now I see why. Let's go through them a coin at time and check each one against the list."

"Gees, Myra, you don't think we got cheated, do you?"

"Oh, no, Dave, I just want to see how he graded them. You know we decided that there is a lot of room for opinion when it comes to grading coins and I'd just like to see where we stand in relationship to Saul."

They went through the coins one at a time and had just completed the task when Dora called and announced dinner. Based on their opinion of the condition of each coin, they came up with a value of $135,000.

"You know, Myra, that we are amateurs at this coin grading business, but amateur or not, I think we made ourselves an outstanding buy."

Myra beamed!

Dinner was delicious and when they finished, Dave suggested they have some wine to cap off such a delicious meal. Everyone agreed and while Dave went to get the wine, Dora cleared away the dishes. Myra and Jack were left at the table and Jack said, "I understand, Myra, that you have started a coin collection. I've collected coins on a small scale for fifty years. When I was a kid, Dad bought me a set of coin books, and over the years I've filled all the ones he gave me, and several more besides. The pride of my collection is a Liberty Head nickel that has been appraised at six hundred dollars. Are there any coins that you are particularly interested in?"

"No, not really Jack. I started buying the coins as an investment and I decided to stick with one denomination. I felt that we would be smart to invest in something that would be a hedge against inflation, so I decided on United States twenty-dollar gold pieces. Partly because of their consistent value as gold and also because I think they are beautiful. We added a sizable number to our collection today and I think my collecting is going to be put on hold for a while."

"I'd like to see them some day when you have the time."

"Sure thing, Jack. I would have shown them to you today if you had been home when I got back from town."

"Darn, it's too bad we left when we did. We just missed you this morning. We passed you on the road as we were leaving and we wondered where you had been so early. It wasn't even ten o'clock."

Dave came in with the wine and they spent the rest of the evening talking about their daughter and their grandkids. It was a little after ten when Myra announced that she was tired and would Dora mind cleaning up in the morning so she would feel good about sneaking off to bed. Dora laughed and promised there would be no hard feelings no matter what.

They were in bed and asleep in less than twenty minutes.

Chapter 61

Chief Mundt drummed his fingers on his desk while he waited for the phone to answer.

"May I speak to Deputy Johnson, please?"

A female voice asked him to stand by and again he drummed his fingers. It took what seemed forever for Johnson to answer and Mundt wondered if people calling his office felt strung out the way that he was feeling now.

"Hello, Chief, what's going on?"

"Man, what a morning! I walked into my office at 7:30 and the report from the coroner was in my in-box. I barely had time to read it when Daniel Feinstein and his mother barged in. They wanted the immediate release of Mr. Feinstein so that he could be buried before sundown today. I told them that I wouldn't be able to do any thing from my office and they would have to wait until the coroner completed his examination and issued a death certificate. Daniel blew his stack. He said it was my doing that his father was sent to the butcher shop and that it was me that had better get on the ball and release his body. He claimed his religion required his father be buried immediately, and if I didn't arrange it within the next hour, he was going to do some very serious things to my body. As we speak, the crime scene report has been handed me, and I would like to meet with you and go over the information. Can you come to my office now?"

"Sure thing, Chief, I'll be there in fifteen minutes."

It was 10:05 when Virgil Johnson seated himself in Chief Mundt's office. The chief looked like he had been pulled through a wringer.

"You know, Virgil, I don't know that I have ever seen anyone so upset over a funeral not taking place in a matter of twenty four hours of the death. This Dan character says its part of his religious duty to see that his father is in the ground as soon as possible after death. Any delay in placing the deceased in the ground is a dishonor to the departed. You know, I've seen people who wanted the funeral as soon as possible in an act of closure. But this guy says his father's spirit won't be free until he's in the ground, and it's his moral and religious duty to see that it takes place."

"Well, as I see it Chief, there is no real reason to not release the body if all the work has been done. Let's go over the reports, and see if we have left anything out that would screw things up if we have to go to court at some future date. Do you think it would be wise to get someone from the district attorney's office in on this now?"

"Huh, well, I'm finally ahead of the game. I spoke to a Donna White. She's a deputy D. A. and should be here in a few minutes."

"Good, until she gets here, let me have a look at what we have."

The coroner's report stated that death was caused by multiple gunshot wounds to the head. There were no contributing causes. The gunshot wounds were six in number and were inflicted by a .38 caliber or a 357 Magnum pistol, more likely a 357 Magnum due to the extent of the tissue damage. The pistol was fired at close range as determined by the powder burns. None of the projectiles were found in the body and individual exit wounds were not evident due to the extreme cranial damage. Death was instantaneous and took place between the hours of 9:00a.m. and 11:30 a.m. on Thursday the 17th of August.

The crime scene report didn't add a great deal, except that what was being presented was a preliminary report and when the balance of the fingerprints were investigated, there would be a final report. There were five bullets found in the floor beneath the victim's head and a sixth in the wall fifty-eight inches from the floor above the safe. All six of the rounds were fired from the same gun but due to the extensive damage to each bullet it was hard to determine with any certainty what make of gun fired the shots, most likely a Ruger Revolver. There were multiple fingerprints in the store that seemed to be mostly members of the family and the remaining sixteen sets were being run through the files. There was no other forensic evidence except for the footprints found at the scene where someone had walked through the blood pool at the victim's head. It was determined that all the prints were made by the shoes of the victim's son, Daniel Feinstein, and that they had been made at least one hour after the victim's death."

Donna White arrived and both men sat silently while she went over the two reports. When she finished, she laid the papers neatly on the corner of Chief Mundt's desk and said,

"You men seem to have very little to go on and I see no need to involve my office in this investigation until you have a valid suspect."

Mundt said, "With respect to a valid suspect, Ms. White, the only person involved that we know about is a Myra Miller. She was in the store that morning and closed a deal on a coin collection worth some $82,000. The coins were known to be in the possession of the deceased prior to that morning and are now missing. There are, however, two checks from Mrs. Miller to the deceased, totaling $82,000, that were found in the locked safe. Sheriff Johnson feels strongly that she might be involved due to a prior violent episode she was party to a little less than a year ago. All this is a hunch as far as Sheriff Johnson is concerned and in no way represents grounds for a search warrant or a demand for her to submit her finger prints as part of our investigation."

"You are one hundred percent correct, Chief. You have, at this point, no grounds for anything. Your only avenue of investigation at this time is to speak with her as a potential witness and nothing more. When, and if, you come up with any firm evidence, give me a call. Good day, Gentlemen."

"Well, there you have it, Virgil. Since Mrs. miller lives in the county and since the hunch is yours, perhaps you should do the questioning of Mrs. Miller as a potential witness, and I'll complete the fingerprint research."

"Okay, Chief, if I come up with anything, I'll let you know."

Mundt picked up the phone and asked for the coroner's office, leaving word that the body of Saul Feinstein was to be immediately released to his family.

Virgil Johnson was not one to skip a meal, and he was acutely aware that he had missed his lunch. He drove to the lower side of town to his favorite diner and ordered a deluxe burger and onion rings, a glass of milk and a slice of peach pie. He sat alone in the rear of the diner and went over the events of the day as he ate. Even though he felt sure there was some connection with Myra Miller and the death of Saul Feinstein, the only thing he was going on was a hunch and the fact that she was in the store at the approximate time of the murder.

On the wall at the end of the diner was a TV that played all the hours of the day and he was pulled back to reality by a local news story about the shooting and perhaps the robbery of a local merchant in the Country Mall. Now the news was out and he felt there would be very few people that would not be aware of the shooting. This, he thought, could work to his advantage. There would be nothing wrong with asking questions of Myra now. Surely there would be no effort on Myra's part to cover the fact that she was in the store that morning and she would be, or could be, a witness.

For now, he thought, I'll go back to the office and get started on a report while my notes are still fresh. Then tomorrow I'll go out and visit the Millers.

Chapter 62

Dora was in the kitchen starting dinner when Dave and Myra came in from the back yard and were really carrying on about the way the area by the stream looked now that Jack had it cleared.

Myra asked what she was up to and Dora said she thought she would make a salmon loaf for dinner.

Then Dora asked, "Have you heard about the shooting in town? It's been on TV all afternoon. There was what seemed to be a robbery in the mall and a merchant had been killed. I think you two know the man that was killed. He was the man that ran the little coin shop and I think he's the man that called while you were in New York. Was his name Feinstein'?"

"My God, Dora, when did they say this happened? I was there just yesterday morning and picked up a coin collection he ordered for me. We have been working on gathering a collection for several weeks now. Yes, he is the man that called while we were in New York. He wanted to let me know that he had the collection together and for me to come in and complete the deal. When did they say he was killed?"

"I think the TV said he was killed before noon yesterday."

"Oh, Dave, what should I do?" Myra's voice was shrill and excited. I was in the store until about 9:00 and he was all right then. It must have happened soon after I was there. What should I do? I think I should let someone know, shouldn't I?"

"Gees, Myra, I don't know. Who would we talk to?"

Dora spoke, "The television said that Virgil was involved in the investigation. Why don't you call him?"

Dave saw a look on Myra's face that was, he thought, one of pure horror.

"Don't worry, sweetheart, I'll be with you all the way. I know you would like to avoid any involvement with Virgil, but I think going to him is the best thing to do. I think we should call him right away. Do you want me to call him?"

"No, I think I should."

Dave handed her the phone and gave her the number to dial. It took several minutes to get through to his office and when she did, another officer answered. The officer informed her that Deputy Johnson was out of the office but was expected in momentarily. Could he have Deputy Johnson return her call, or could he help?

"Would you please have him call Myra Miller? My number is—"

Before she could finish, the officer interrupted and announced that Deputy Johnson had just returned and would she hold a moment.

"Hello, Mrs. Miller, this is Virgil Johnson. May I help you?"

"Yes, please, Virgil, we have just learned about the terrible thing that has happened to Mr. Feinstein. Are you involved in the investigation?"

"Yes, I am, Myra, and I was planning to speak with you about the case. We have learned that you were possibly the last person to see him alive and we were hoping you might be able to shed some light on what took place in the store yesterday."

"Well, I was in the store yesterday morning, but he was alright when I left. We had just completed the sale of a collection of coins and he was alone in the store."

"Myra, I wonder if you would come to my office and give us a statement about what you just told me. I know this is a great inconvenience, but since you are possibly one of the last persons to see him alive, it would be a great help in our investigation."

"Certainly, Virgil, when would be best for you?"

"The sooner the better, Myra. The sooner we get to the facts, the fresher they will be in your mind, and the more helpful they will be. Could you make it this afternoon, say in an hour?"

"Okay Virgil, we'll leave right away."

"Dave, I think the only thing we need to take with us is the inventory of the coins Saul sold us. It lists all the coins and their prices. Our checks will show we paid for everything and will help show we were not part of a robbery, if there was one."

"What the hell. Myra, you don't think they suspect us do you?"

"Who knows what anybody thinks at a time like this? Let's go."

Virgil sat for several minutes pondering the situation and then flipped on the intercom to the desk of his secretary. "Georgia, would you come in for a minute, please?"

Georgia came in and seated herself in front of his desk, asking if he wanted to write a letter.

"No, not now, Georgia, but I would like you to do me a favor. When Myra Miller arrives in a few minutes to give us a statement on the Feinstein killing, I'm going to offer her a drink of water. When I do, I will ask you on the intercom to bring her a drink. When you bring the water, I would like you to use a tray to serve the drink and use a sterile glass so there are no fingerprints on it. As soon as Mrs. Miller has finished her drink, I want you to remove the glass and take it directly to the lab and have it fingerprinted. Got that?"

"Yes, I sure do, sir, I'll go get the things ready now."

It was just after 4:00 when Myra and Dave arrived at the sheriff's office and sat down with Deputy Johnson and a police recorder. The recording officer had a tape recorder and after a brief introduction on the tape, Myra was asked to account in detail her activities of the previous morning. Her statements were simple and straightforward. She met with the victim shortly before 9:00a.m. and completed their transaction. Since they had come to a firm agreement on the sale, very little time was spent closing the deal. She had checked the time when she left the store and it was 9:20a.m. by her watch. She arrived home at about 10:00a.m. and was home the rest of the day. She knew nothing of this catastrophe until this afternoon, when her friend and housekeeper, Dora Potts, told her about it. She saw no one else in the store or around the store while she was there. Dave handed her the inventory list and she explained it was the list of coins she had purchased. Virgil thanked her and gave it to the recorder to make copies. The interview ended and the recorder gathered his recording things and left the room.

"I'm sorry to have to put you through all this, Mrs. Miller, but police work is a very demanding thing when it comes to records and it's a very necessary part of my job.

"You look like you could use a drink, let me get you one." He turned and asked someone on the intercom to bring Mrs. Miller a glass of water. In a moment a policewoman appeared and set a tray with a glass of water on it in front of her. The water was cold and refreshing and Myra emptied the glass.

The recorder returned with the inventory list and Virgil thanked Myra and Dave sincerely for taking the time to come in and for being such good citizens. Myra and Dave left the sheriff's office at 4:35 and stopped for a taco on their way home. Myra wondered what Dora was going to do with the salmon loaf she was fixing.

David and Daniel Feinstein had returned from their father's funeral and were finally alone. Both of then were in a state of shock and remorse about the death of their father and were doubly upset over the grief of their mother.

"What should we do now, Dan? I think the sheriff suspects Mrs. Miller and since there is no one else involved that we know of, she could be responsible."

"Nonsense, Dave, there is no reason at all to suspect her. She made a deal with Dad and she paid for the coins as she agreed. I'm not sure of all the details of the sale because Dad wouldn't tell us, but she paid him exactly what he had on the inventory list and how can you argue that? Dad wasn't robbed because he had over three thousand dollars in his pocket and we both know that was normal. There was nothing missing from the store either."

"What about the St. Gaudens? That used to be in the safe and it's gone."

"You know as well as I do that we haven't seen that coin for ages, and Dad could have done something with it and not told us. The thing that has me concerned now is that if the police keep digging and find out about the rest of the collection, the whole world will find out where it came from. If this happens, we could lose the whole works, and have those people Dad was afraid of, coming after us. I just can't picture that Miller woman killing dad, and I think the best thing we can do is go deaf and dumb about the whole thing. We should just go on running the store as if dad were still here. There's not a fancy living to be made here, but we will make enough to take care of our needs and see that mom doesn't have to go without. We can live our iives just as we would have if dad was still alive and things will work out for us the way he planned. With the rest of the coin collection to fall back on, our financial situation is pretty well taken care of, just the way Dad wanted. I'm for going dumb about the whole deal and let the police do their thing. If they can find dad's killer, all well and good, but I vote we stay out of it as much as we can and let the chips fall where they may. And besides all that, we have the $82,000 to use as a nest egg just in case."

"Okay, big brother, okay!"

Chapter 63

Bob Tate was feeling on top of the world as he dialed the phone. Things had all worked out and the fishing trip he was looking forward to was all coming together.

"Hello, Dad, just calling to let you know we have finally got our act together and we will be fishing in Puget Sound next Wednesday at dawn. I've had my travel agent order your ticket to Portland and you are booked on the 7:40a.m. flight. We will pick you up at the Portland airport at 11:45 and be on our way."

"Are you sure I don't have to bring anything but warm clothing and rain gear?"

"No, dad, that's all. The charter people are all equipped to take care of even those things if need be."

"Okay, son, I'll see you in Portland on Tuesday. Oh, your mother says hello and she wants me to tell you she's still mad at you for leaving her home."

"You give her a big hug and tell her I love her. Bye for now and I'll see you Tuesday."

Theodore Tate was a meticulous man and because of this had never been late for a bus, train, or plane, and today was no different. He was a good thirty minutes early for his flight to Portland. He had left Darlene at the main entrance to avoid having her park the car. Once inside, he checked his single bag and settled himself near the gate with a newspaper he had found on the seat. Just as he started to read, Sheriff Charles Harrison appeared in front of him and seemed almost overjoyed at their meeting.

"By God, Tate, you're looking fit, you must be taking care of yourself. What's been going on with you?"

"Hello, Chuck, what brings you to the airport this time of day?"

"Oh, I'm off to Santa Fe to pick up a prisoner that skipped bail and got picked up by the Santa Fe cops. Nothing serious, just a young kid that got busted for dealing. I also wanted to get together with the sheriff there and talk about some upcoming legislation that we want to make sure gets passed. Where are you headed?"

"I'm going to meet my son in Portland and then join him and several friends for a fishing trip on Puget Sound."

"Say, Tate, what do you think about Jewels Harts quitting?"

"What? What the hell are you talking about?"

"Cripes, haven't you heard? Chief Denny gave notice of his intent to retire and instead of giving the job to Jewels, the city fathers gave notice that they would be advertising for a chief out side of the department. This really pissed ol' Jewels off and he just quit. They got Chief Denny to stay on a little longer until they hired someone, but they accepted Jewels resignation and didn't even bat an eye. I guess he had made more enemies than any of us knew."

"Man if that isn't the darnedest thing I've ever heard! I thought Harts would be there forever and would definitely be chief someday. How do you feel about his leaving?"

"Makes little difference to me. When I worked for him, we got along okay, but most of the force thought he was a pompous ass."

The public address system announced their flight and they started towards the gate. Harrison asked if Tate had his seat assignment and Tate said he did.

"Too bad we didn't have some idea we were on the same flight and we could have gotten seats together."

Ted was happy that they were seated apart but said nothing and they boarded the plane.

In Santa Fe they got separated in the crowd and Tate was pleased. His connecting flight was in twenty minutes and he set a brisk pace to the departure gate, so as not to be late.

Chapter 64

Saturday started off about as quiet as a Saturday can be and both Dave and Myra were silent about the events of last Thursday. About noon Tim Timmons called and said he was coming over to cheer them up. He had heard about the murder and that Myra had given a statement to the police as the last known person to see the victim alive. As an attorney he was somewhat familiar with the ways of police investigations and he was sure the episode was depressing.

Tim and Betty arrived and changed the entire somber scene to one of gayety. Within minutes Tim had Dora and Jack going full steam in the direction of a backyard barbecue that, as he put it, would blow them away. Dora was instructed to prepare enough food for an army and Jack was to get the fatted calf out of the freezer and light the grill. He then proceeded to get on the phone and invite half the membership of the country club to a hoe-down at the Miller Mansion. By 2:00 the place was a sea of people and their children. Jack and Dora's daughter and her children were among the first to arrive, and this caused Dave to think about Anthony Blevins. He called Tony's foster parents, they agreed to bring Tony over and be three more at the party. In all, over fifty people showed up and there was food and music and dancing for everyone.

The festivities lasted until nearly midnight. Then as if by a prearranged signal, everyone but good ol' Tim and Betty thanked their hosts and bid them goodnight.

Tim, as usual, had played his drunk act, but as soon as the last guest had departed, he again became stone sober.

"What a wonderful day! I'm so happy things turned out the way they did and that Betty and I were able, with the help of a few of your friends, to get your minds off the tribulations of the past few days. Having the police interview you, even as a witness, is a very stressful thing and I want to encourage you to turn to me at any time if their inquiries become unduly so. With that, we bid you goodnight and God bless you."

Dave and Myra stood and watched the Timmons car drive away and turned with exhausted steps to their room at the top of the stairs. They showered and went eagerly to bed. Dave was asleep in a matter of moments, but, even though tired, Myra lay awake and wondered why the old faker Tim had made such a fuss. Did he suspect things that she was sure hadn't even entered Dave's mind? She finally drifted away into a dreamless sleep.

It was late Monday afternoon when the fingerprint report came to Chief Mundt's desk. He was surprised when he noticed that the sheriff's office had added a set of Myra Miller's prints to the comparison list and that they had shown up as a match to prints found at the scene. Her prints, however, were over laid by at least two other sets of as yet unidentified prints, indicating that several people were there after her prints were left. This seemed to shoot down at least some of the suspicion, that Myra was involved in any part of the crime. He had read the witness statement from Myra and was more convinced than ever that they had absolutely nothing to go on as far as suspecting her of the crime was concerned. He called Sheriff Johnson and conveyed his thoughts about the reports. Johnson agreed that there was nothing to go on other than the fact Mrs. Miller was in the store about the time of the murder and that she had previously been involved in a very violent situation. Since both of these things amounted to almost nothing, there was nothing left but Johnson's hunch and in Mundt's mind it was crap.

"I don't know where we can go from here, Virgil, but to me chasing Mrs. Miller around is not it."

"As much as I hate to admit it, chief, I guess you're right. I am, however, going to submit Mrs. Miller's prints to the FBI for comparison and finish checking her story about the time she was at the crime scene."

"Okay, good enough, Virgil, if you come up with anything new that can be seen as real evidence let me know."

Chapter 65

Bob met his Dad as he left the plane and after picking up his bag they went out to the parking area and met Bob's two friends. They were both about Bob's age and seemed to be friendly and easy going. Tate was sure they were going to have a great time.

The taller of the two men was Stewart Barnes, the more outspoken of the two. The shorter man was Lyle Cunningham. He was a very quiet man with a broad southern accent.

Leaving the airport they were soon on a freeway, heading north. Tate was taken with the green of everything and couldn't get over that there seemed to be water everywhere. Along the way there was a series of rivers and lakes and tidelands, and Tate was spellbound by the beauty of the passing scene. Stew Barnes did the driving and kept up a steady commentary about the area they were passing through. Names like Hood Canal, Duckabush, Dosewallips, and Quilcene were strange to Tate's ears, but they seemed to match this beautiful land.

They arrived in Port Townsend and checked into a small old-fashioned motel located between a busy street and a body of water that Stew said was Puget Sound. A seafood restaurant on an old wooden pier was chosen for dinner, and the view and the food were excellent. Tate slept surprisingly well in the strange bed and was rested and ready to go when the alarm went off at 3:45a.m.

After a ham and egg breakfast, the men went to a small marina and were welcomed aboard a spotlessly clean and well kept vessel that Tate was told was a forty-five footer, but to him looked much larger. As they pulled out of the marina, Tate was glad he had on warm clothes and his raingear. There was dew on everything and a cold wind blew off the water that, even though he was protected from the elements, seemed to chill him to the bone. They cruised for about an hour to a place called Protection Island. When they slowed down, the skipper, who was a relation of Stew's, came back and helped with the rigging of the gear. Most of the equipment was strange to Ted, but once the lines were in the water and the poles in their holders, it became the old fisherman's game; wait patiently for a bite. They had fished for less than an hour when the rocking of the boat caused Tate to be violently ill. He had never thought about being seasick, but there it was and it stayed all day. By noon he was sure he was going to die and by three he was wishing he would. By three-thirty, they had landed twelve beautiful salmon and having reached the legal limit for the group, headed for home. Tate was the first one off the boat and was surprised that the feeling of sickness left him almost instantly. It took a little longer before the unsteadiness in the legs left him, but in less than ten minutes he could hardly remember that he had spent the day throwing up his toenails. All he felt then was hunger.

    That evening before they went to bed Tate announced that he was not going to spend another day being seasick. He would stay ashore and take in some of the local sights instead. Every one seemed to understand and Stew offered to let him use his car so he wouldn't be motel bound.

    At four o'clock the next morning, Tate wished them good luck and went back to bed until after nine. After a shower and shave, he was ready for breakfast and drove the few blocks to a small cafe in the center of town. While he ate, he scanned a large hand-painted map on the wall, and there, just a short distance from Port Townsend, was the town of Chimacum.

    This was the town Sandy Longtree had spoken of when she gave him the information on Myra Dillon's credit card bad debt. At the time it had seemed a very slim lead and the location so far away. Now, here he was less than fifteen miles from Chimacum with a car at his disposal and an entire day on his hands.

    The drive to Chimacum took less than thirty minutes and on arrival he found the community to be exactly the way Sandy had said it would be – just a wide spot in the road. At the crossroad of the town there was a country store, a small restaurant and a few other tumbledown structures. One of them still had an old sign that said "Blacksmith." On the perimeter of the town were perhaps twenty homes, all in need of paint and repair. Everything had a weather-beaten look, almost like the town was abandoned. About a half a mile before he came into the town, he had passed a rather modern looking school building and even though it was summer vacation time, there were several cars parked in the lot. Tate returned to the school and found the front door was open. He went to the office and was met by a smiling woman wearing a nametag that read Doris Stroud.

"Yes, sir, how may I help you?"

"Well, ma'am, I'm not quite sure you can, but what I'm looking for is rather important to me and I'd like you to try."

"Why don't you tell me your problem, and we'll see, okay?"

"My name is Theodore Tate and I'm a retired sheriff from another state. I'm trying to locate a missing person who might have lived in this area. The woman I'm looking for went by the name of Myra Dillon and she is about twenty-eight years old."

"Well, sir, I've lived in this town all my life and I don't remember anyone by that name. I'm sure there has never been a family named Dillon with a daughter named Myra. I was a teacher here before I retired, and I would have known any one by that name, especially as a student."

"The name Dillon was more than likely her married name and I think it's possible she grew up here. I think I would recognize her if I could find her picture. Perhaps in an annual from about ten years ago?"

"My gracious, you are looking for a needle in a hay stack aren't you? Well, if you can spend the time, I have copies of all our annuals since we started. They are all in this bookcase over here. I have some work to do, but I can let you go through them if you'd like. Just come around the counter here and you can use that desk in the corner. I'm going to lunch at one o'clock and you may have 'til then."

Tate selected annuals that were eight, nine, and ten years old and seated himself at the assigned desk. Most of the pictures were group photographs and were quite small. These pictures were of the non-senior students and only the photographs of the graduating class were large enough to make any kind of identification. It was 12:30 when he was going through the ten-year-old yearbook that he spotted a picture that was, without a doubt, Myra. The name on the Photograph was Ardith Carter. "Girl most likely to go to college."

"Mrs. Stroud. I've found her picture."

"Mercy sakes! Isn't that wonderful?"

"She's shown here with the name of Ardith Carter. Do you remember her?"

"Oh my, yes, she was one of my favorite students. Her brother was also a student of mine, but he was always up to no good and finally came to a bad end when Ardith was a senior. Christopher was his name and he died in a horrible accident that almost tore the family apart. Ardith left town almost the same day she graduated, and her father died soon after. Her mother still lives in town with her sister Madge Pike. Well, they don't really live in Chimacum; they live in Irondale. You can get to their house by turning left at the Jackson's store and going clear to the end of the road. They live in a little house right on the bluff, on the right hand side."

The house was small and almost completely covered by wild roses. There was a picket fence that was barely visible beneath wild roses and philodendron plants. There was a porch with a sagging roof that went the full width of the house and it gave the place a tumbled-down look. The porch was only two inches above the ground and the floor of the house was level with the porch. There was no sign that the house had ever been painted and the cedar siding was gray and weather-beaten.

The woman who answered the door was short and round, with a pink shiny face that made her look like Mrs. Santa Claus. With a smile that warmed Ted's heart, she said, "Whatever you're selling, mister, you didn't come very well prepared. You forgot your sample case."

It was all Tate could do to keep a straight face. "Are you Mrs. Carter?"

"No, sir, I'm Miss. Pike, Madge Pike. You must be looking for my sister, but I'm sorry to say she has passed away. Is there any way I can help you?"

"Well, perhaps there is. I'm trying to locate a young woman by the name of Ardith Carter."

"Oh, do you know Ardy?"

"No, I've never met her, but I spoke to one of her old teachers, a Mrs. Stroud, and she thought you might be able to help me."

"So Doris Stroud sent you. Well, any friend of Doris' is a friend of mine. I guess you know that Ardy's married now and she lives in Idaho. Why don't you come in? I'm just fixing some tea and cake for lunch and you can join me while I look for her address. You will join me, won't you?"

Tate smiled and thanked her. Entering the house, he thought, isn't it strange how open people are when they have nothing to hide?

"You just have a seat at the table there and I'll get the tea on. I'm sorry, sir, I didn't get your name. You might have told me but I can't remember."

"My name is Tate, Theodore Tate. My friends all call me Ted."

"Okay, Ted, I hope you like ginger cake. It's my own recipe and I'm pretty proud of it."

She served a slice of cake about three inches thick and tea in a mug that easily held a pint. The cake was moist and filled with raisins and the tea was stout and hot.

"Your recipe is fantastic and your hospitality overwhelms me. You had better be careful, Madge, because I might decide to become a steady customer."

She smiled and said, "Most men do like my ginger cake."

When they finished their cake, Madge excused herself to find Ardy's address. While she was gone, Tate occupied the time by looking around the house. It was filled to overflowing with all sorts of logging and fishing memorabilia. There were pictures of gigantic trees with loggers standing around, and saws with hand paintings on them. There were fishing nets and poles and large glass balls in fishnets hanging from every corner. Tate thought the kitchen was almost unusable due to the number of old cooking utensils hanging everywhere and dozens of African violets in every nook and corner. Madge returned, seated herself with a big sigh, and laid an address book in front of him, saying.

"I'm sorry but I can't locate my glasses and you'll have to find it for yourself. This was my sister's book, and I think you'll find Ardy under the name of Miller."

Finally there it was. David and Ardith M. Miller (Myra). He had found the elusive Myra A. Dillon. Strange he thought. Her initials were MAD. He wrote the address and phone number in his note pad and after thanking Madge for her hospitality, went hurriedly to his car. It was 3:30 and he wanted to get back to Port Townsend before the fishermen returned.

The fishermen had had a wonderful day and all were excited about the forty-six pound fish caught by Lyle. It had taken over an hour to "boat" the fish, and Tate thought it was the most beautiful fish he had ever seen. They had an early dinner and a few drinks, and when they got back to the motel, everyone but Tate took showers and went to bed early. Tate found a quiet corner in the lobby overlooking the water and spent until well after midnight getting his notes of the day in his evidence book.

Chapter 66

The next morning Tate had breakfast with his three companions and they had made arrangements for him to check out of the motel and meet them at the marina at about 2:20. This would get them on their way home by about 3:00 and they would be back in Portland before dark. All except Tate had cleared their things out of their rooms and put them in the car. They had made arraignments with the Charter Company to take all of their fish except two and have them canned. Lyle and Stewart wanted the two fish that were not to be canned, iced down and packed to take home. They were both married men and wanted to take a fresh fish to their families. The canned salmon was to be shipped to Lyle's place in Portland and they would divide it up amongst the four of them later.

After taking the fishermen to the marina, Tate returned to the motel and lying on top of the bed slept until ten o'clock. He showered and had an early lunch at the little cafe in the center of town. After lunch he took a drive through town and looked at the many Victorian homes that were a major tourist attraction. At noon he went back to the motel and spent the next two hours using a borrowed typewriter to transcribe his notes to a more readable format.

The boat pulled into the marina right on time and since all the arrangements for taking care of the fish had previously been made, they were on their way home in a matter of minutes. The ride home was very quiet. Except for a gas stop and changing drivers twice, there were no delays. The first stop in Portland was at Bob's. Tate was scheduled to spend the night there and fly home in the morning. In parting all three men expressed their regret that things had not gone better for Ted and that he had not caught a fish. He assured them that all in all, it was one of the best trips of his life. Besides that, he thought, I caught the biggest fish of all, Myra.

Chapter 67

In the morning Bob took him to the airport and with an hour to spare he made his way to the ticket counter and asked if there was any way he could trade his ticket in for one to Twin Falls, Idaho. After a few minutes with the agent, he decided to exchange the ticket he had, for one that took him to Twin Falls first and then on to his original destination, with an undetermined layover in Twin Falls. He paid an additional sum and had to hurry to catch his flight.

When his plane landed at 4:05p.m., he rented a car and checked into a down town motel. The room was large with two beds and a big screen TV. He had dinner in the motel restaurant, and then he purchased a city map at a gas station and drove out of town to the address of Myra Miller on Country Club Road.

He was a bit taken back when he saw the mansion and wondered what kind of a deal Myra had, living in a place like that. A little more than a year ago she had been in a prison mental institution for murder and now here she was, living in what was obviously the lap of luxury. He drove back to the motel and spent the rest of the evening watching television.

He slept late the next morning and didn't get started until after nine o'clock. He showered and shaved and had breakfast in the restaurant next to the motel. Back in his room he found the housekeeping people had cleaned and he didn't have to be concerned about being bothered the rest of the day. He picked up the phone and called home, collect. Darlene answered on the first ring and accepted the charges.

"Ted, where are you? I've been so worried. Bob called last night to see if you were home okay and when he found you were not home yet he got in a panic. He thought there might be a problem because of how sea sick you got and after that, you didn't seem to be communicating very well. Are you alright?"

"I'm just fine. I'm in Twin Falls, Idaho."

"What in the world are you doing there?"

"I'm bringing the Myra Dillon case to a close. Do you remember I told you about the slim lead that Sandy Longtree gave me about Myra having a family connection in a little town in Washington? Well, on the second day, when I made up my mind that I didn't want to be sick again, I stayed behind and discovered we were only about fifteen miles from the little town Sandy told me about. So on Thursday, I drove to this little town of Chimacum and found that Myra was from there, and that she was now living in Twin Falls. I traded my ticket in for one to Twin Falls and since yesterday afternoon, I have pretty much verified that she's here. I'm going to stay over until tomorrow and check in with the local cops. From the looks of things, I'm sure the locals don't have any idea who she is or that she's wanted. I have no idea how long all this is going to take, but I'm going to try and be home by Wednesday at the latest."

"Oh, Teddy, this is so exciting! All of your tenacity has finally paid off. I'm so proud of you."

"I'm kind of proud of me too. I guess I showed that bunch of doubting Thomas's that I'm not the old has-been they thought, especially that smug bastard, Harts. Enough of this chatter, it's costing a fortune for me to do all of this sleuthing on my own and spending an hour on the phone isn't making it any cheaper. Will you call Bob and tell him where I am? I'm at the Holiday Inn, room 226. If he wants to know more than you can tell him, he can call me on his nickel. I'm going to hang up now, but before I do, I want you to know how much it means to me that you stuck by me through all these months of tribulation. Solving this mystery has meant more to me than any one outside of you and Bob will ever know. I love you, Darlene, I love you, Love you."

"Me too, Teddy, Me too."

Tate woke with a start. The television was on and it was dark outside. The knock on his door was firm and insistent and he realized who ever it was had been knocking for some time. He swung his feet off the bed and looked at his watch. It was 10:15pm. The knock came again even more insistent than before. He half stumbled to the door and asked, "Who's there?"

"It's me, Dad, Bob."

He opened the door and exclaimed, "How the hell did you get here?"

"Mom called me this morning and told me where you were and what you were up to. There was no flight to here until tomorrow that I could take, so I got a flight to Boise and rented a car and drove from there."

"Well, come in, come in. I don't understand why you would go to so much trouble to run me down but I'm glad you did. How will you account for being away from your job and how long can you stay?"

"The job's no problem, Dad. I'm still on vacation for a week. I took two weeks when we planned the fishing trip and I still have a week coming. My plan was to spend the rest of my vacation just goofing off, but it seems you have come up with something far more interesting."

The two men talked until after midnight. Tate went over all the aspects of the case and even though it was from memory left no detail unexplained. Finally they collapsed exhausted in their beds.

Chapter 68

Dora entered the kitchen at 7:30 on Tuesday morning, thinking things used to be easier than they seemed today. The party on Saturday was a real mixer and she couldn't remember a better time. But since then there had been nothing but hard work cleaning up after a crowd of fifty or more people. It had taken Jack two full days to get the grounds in order and she was still a good half day away from setting things right in the house. Even with Myra's help it was a big job. This morning Myra was off to meet June McKay at the club for tennis, a swim, and lunch. Dave was planning to work most of the day in the studio on some kind of a rush job for an auto-racing magazine and Jack was going to replace a sprinkler head that somehow got broken during Saturday's free-for-all. Really, she thought, there wasn't all that much to do except for the three upstairs bathrooms and that wouldn't be so bad, since Myra and her demanding ways wouldn't be involved. She had used a great many of the pantry items to feed so many people on Saturday and spent the next hour and a half making out a shopping list to restock.

Dave came down at a little after nine, and she fixed some toast and fruit for his breakfast. As soon as he finished, he headed for the studio saying he didn't want to be disturbed unless it was something very important. At ten, Myra came down and after tea and toast, went singing out the door on her way to the club. Now Dora was alone in the house and she knew she could finish her tasks in less than an hour. When Dave came in for a coffee break, she informed him that she would be away at the market replacing the pantry items. She would be gone for the next several hours and would not be there to answer the phone.

This was all right with Dave since he hadn't read the mail in several days and there was a huge stack to go through. Besides he needed a break. Dora left and he was about half way through the stack of mail when the phone rang. It was Tim Timmons wanting to come over and pick up the bearer bonds. He would be bringing the accountant Todd Stone with him. Stone was to start the conversion of the bonds and would also need Dave to sign a power of attorney so he could act in his behalf with respect to the bonds.

Without thinking Dave told him to come on over, but after he hung up, he realized that he had spoken too soon. Myra was not there and he had no way of getting to the bonds. Just on a hunch he went upstairs to see if by some chance she had left the safe open and when he swung the mirror open, he saw what he had seen so many times, but had forgotten – the safe combination taped to the back of the mirror. After two tries the safe came open and he removed the folder holding the bonds. Before closing the safe he noticed a box of what looked to be bullets. It was a box of fifty 357 Magnum bullets with six empty cases and six bullets missing. Dave was stunned. What could this mean? He remembered that Virgil had told them that Saul had been shot with a 357. He went through the safe quickly but found no gun. Why the bullets and no gun? Taking the bonds he went downstairs and within ten minutes Tim and Todd were there. Tim explained they didn't have a lot of time since Todd had to catch the afternoon flight to Boise and was happy that Dave had been home to handle the paper work. Their job took less than twenty minutes and the two men hurried on their way.

Dave went back up to the bedroom and went through the safe again to see what else he could find that he didn't know about. The safe was about half full of albums and boxes of coins, but there was nothing there he had not seen before. It wasn't until he opened the inner lock box that he got another shock. In the back of the lock box were two small plastic boxes, each containing a St Gaudens coin. As far as he knew there were only two of these coins in existence, one had belonged to Alma and the other to Saul Feinstein. He felt sick.

Myra returned at four and went yoo-hooing all through the house calling for Dave or Dora. She finally came to the bedroom and found Dave sitting on the bed with the box of bullets beside him and holding in his hand the two plastic boxes containing the very valuable St. Gaudens coins. Myra stood looking wide eyed at him for several moments and then said, "What's wrong, Dave?"

"My God, Myra, what have you done?"

She didn't answer, she just stood there weaving back and forth and crying silently.

Dave went to her and putting his arms around her, held her close and said, "Oh, my sweet, sweet, sweetheart, you've really got us in a peck of trouble,

247

haven't you?"

Again she didn't respond. He lifted her and gently laid her on the bed. She didn't make a sound; she just lay there and wept. He joined her on the bed and taking her in his arms held her close until they both went to sleep. They didn't hear Dora come in, or the clamber she and Jack made putting the groceries away. They slept through the night without even removing their clothes.

In the first light of dawn Myra woke and found Dave looking at her. Her eyes felt like they had sandpaper in them and without speaking she went into the bathroom. She was gone for nearly thirty minutes and when she came out, Dave was seated in his favorite chair next to the window. She stood behind him and placing her hands on his shoulders she said, "What can I say?"

"I don't know if anything needs to be said. I'm sure that his trying to cheat you, or hurt you in some fashion, caused the action you took against Saul. I've known for some time that any attempt to attack you in this way causes you to fight back with a sometimes-unreasonable response. It seems to me that what took place doesn't need discussing. It's what are we going to do now? I've been going over all that the police seem to have as evidence and even though I'm far from an expert about these things, I'm sure they don't have a single thing to go on that would connect you with the actual death of Saul Feinstein. When we were in Virgil's office the other day, he was pussyfooting all over the place because he has nothing concrete in the way of evidence. He was trying to get you to say something that he could turn against you and from what I remember, you said nothing that could place the slightest hint of any wrong doing onto you. As things stand now, the only thing that could turn things against you is the discovery of the gun and bullets. I don't think they have cause to get a warrant to search our house, but just in case I'm wrong, I think we should get rid if those things as soon as possible."

Knowing she was lying when the truth would have been better, Myra said, "I've already gotten rid of the gun." She just couldn't tell him yet. "Maybe you could help me get rid of the bullets."

"Are you sure that you disposed of the gun so it will never show up again? I don't want to know where or how you disposed of it. I just want you to assure me that it will never reappear."

"Don't worry, It is gone for good."

"Good. I don't see any reason to think that there is a single thing that the police could make a case on. What we need to do is keep a clear head and not let things fluster us. If we just go on like we had nothing to hide, but still say as little as possible, they will have no alternative but to forget about us and look elsewhere for a suspect. Now let's get dressed and go about things as usual."

In the shower Myra hugged him as hard as she could and said, "I don't ever want to be apart from you, Dave. I love you more than I have ever loved anything or anybody in my whole life. You have made me feel more loved and protected than I have ever felt before, even in my sweetest dreams. I'm sure that you are being foolish by standing behind me through this horribly wrong and stupid thing I've done, but I will try to never ever let you down and I promise to love you until the day I die."

Chapter 69

Deputy Chief Mundt sat at his desk looking at the completed fingerprint report and concluded that there was nothing there of any value. Johnson still was convinced Myra Miller was involved but he'd be damned if he could find a thing that could give any sort of credence to his theory. Six days had passed since the murder and in his mind all they had accomplished was to eliminate their only possible suspect. Where could he look now, there were no clues or physical evidence. What should he do now? – Shit!

It was late Thursday afternoon. Dora had just sent Dave, Myra, and Tony Blevins on their way to Crystal Lake for a couple of days of camping and fishing. She had spent most of the day getting them ready to go and was feeling a little tired. Jack had gone over to their daughter's to fix a leaky faucet, and she was thinking of taking a nap. She crossed the road and was just entering her kitchen door when Virgil Johnson pulled into her driveway in his patrol car.

"Hi, Dora, what are you up to?"

"I just sent the Millers on their way to Crystal Lake for a couple of days camping. Both of them are still upset about that Mr. Feinstein being killed and they need a few days away from things."

"Mr. Feinstein's murder is why I came by. Do you remember last week when Mrs. Miller came home after buying the coin collection? What was her mood?"

"Gosh, I don't know Virgil. We were just leaving when she got home from town that morning. It was about nine-thirty and we were on our way over to see Ruthy. We were just passing the clubhouse when she drove by on her way home. We didn't see her again until later that afternoon but she seemed in very good spirits at that time. Dave had gone fishing with that Blevins Boy and she could hardly wait for him to get home. We found out later that she was excited about showing him her coin collection. Why do you ask? You don't suspect Myra of anything, do you?"

"Oh, you know us cops. We have to question everything and everybody. Well, thanks, Dora, got to run along now. See you later. By the way, Dora, I would appreciate it if you wouldn't mention this conversation to the Miller's, okay?"

Dora watched him drive away and thought. Sure is funny, him asking all those questions about Myra. He should know there was no way she could have anything to do with a terrible thing like murder. Well, at any rate, she hadn't promised to not tell Myra and that was a good thing because that's the first thing she intended to do when they got home. No wonder Myra didn't seem to care much for Virgil. He could sure be funny sometimes.

Early Sunday afternoon, Dave, Myra, and Tony returned from their camping trip and after dropping Tony off, spent time putting things away and taking care of the fish they caught. Dora saw them return and came across the street to lend a hand. Dave and Myra were in exceptionally good spirits and talked at length about their enjoyment of Tony. Dora was pleased at Myra's attitude about Tony and was only mildly surprised when the subject of adoption came up. There didn't seem to be a firm commitment to such a thing, but she could tell they were considering it. Dave had taken several rolls of film on the outing and wanted to, "get them in the soup", as he called it, so he could have them printed by Wednesday when they planned to have dinner with Tony. After Dave went to the studio, Dora spoke to Myra,

"You know, Myra, after you left the other day, Virgil Johnson came by and started to ask a bunch of questions about the day that Mr. Feinstein was killed. He wanted to know what I saw and what time it was when you got home. He wanted to know what kind of a mood you were in and were you acting normal. He asked me not to tell you about our conversation, but I didn't promise him, and there's no way I would not tell you about his strange attitude and the odd questions he was asking."

"Oh, Dora, dear, don't worry about things like that. It's okay that he asked those kinds of questions. He is a police officer and his job requires him to question everything. I have nothing to hide and I had nothing to do with that horrible event. I have, as you know, not cared much for Virgil because of his attitude about things when I had that problem with Jerry Jones. But I've pretty much gotten over my hard feelings about that time. Again, Dora, don't give it another thought, okay?"

"Whatever you say, Myra, but I still don't care much for all of his strange attitudes. And as far the Jerry Jones thing is concerned, I think you had every reason to give him a good thrashing and all this junk about you overdoing it, is just that, junk. That little punk deserved everything he got and more."

Myra smiled and changed the subject. "I think when Dave gets the things put away in the garage that we will turn in early. We had a late lunch with Tony and we will not be wanting supper, so I won't be needing you the rest of the day. We are both tired and I know, at least for me, I need some rest for my aching body."

Dora smiled and patted her gently on the back, "Sure, honey, I'll get out of here and let you have some peace and quiet."

After Dora had gone, Dave came in and they went to their room. Myra told him in detail what Dora had told her about Virgil's visit and Dave listened without speaking. The rest of the afternoon and evening went by with hardly a word between them. They showered and went to bed before it was fully dark and slept a deep sleep that came from complete exhaustion.

Myra woke just as it was it was getting light and found Dave sitting by the window in his favorite chair. In a soft voice she said, "Are you okay?"

"I don't know, Myra. That visit from Virgil has me worried. I've been thinking it over and I've come to the conclusion that he truly feels you were involved in the death of Saul Feinstein. If I'm correct, we have to be very careful about what we say and do as far as the police investigation is concerned."

They went over the story that had been told to the authorities and Dave had to admit he found no loopholes in it. As far as he was concerned the only possible telltale evidence would have been the gun, but he had thrown the bullets into Crystal Lake and Myra had assured him she had disposed of the gun days ago. He concluded and Myra agreed, that all they needed to do was keep a low profile, and sticking with their story, say as little as possible.

Myra felt a cold chill run through her. She knew she was lying to this man that she loved, even at a time when he was placing everything on the line to protect her. Yes, she knew all this, but she just couldn't bring herself to admit it and she didn't know why.

Before breakfast, she thought, I'll tell him after breakfast. After all it was Monday and the start of a new week. I will tell him. Before lunch, I'll tell him.

Chapter 70

Both Ted and Bob were on edge as they drove to the sheriff's office in the center of town. They had started their day early and had even had a leisurely breakfast. Ted felt he was well prepared to speak with the local boys about Myra. He had gone over the details in his mind so many times just since Thursday, and with these last four days of preparation he was ready.

A very pleasant deputy met them at the front counter and Ted explained to her that he was a retired sheriff from New Mexico that had been following the trail of a suspected murderer by the name of Myra Dillon AKA Myra Miller. He felt there was reason to believe that she was in this community and he would like to speak with someone about her. There was no mistake. The young deputy was shocked about what she had just heard and very nervously told them to stay put. She would get Deputy Johnson. He would be the one to speak with.

In moments, a tall, clean-cut deputy appeared and introduced himself as Virgil Johnson. Ted in turn introduced himself and his son Robert, an FBI agent from the Portland, Oregon, office.

They shook hands all round and Johnson invited them into his office. Before closing the door he spoke to the deputy, "Carla, unless it's something that just can't wait, I don't want to be disturbed."

"Yes, sir!"

After they were seated, Ted told the story of Myra Dillon / Miller. The narration took nearly an hour and in all this time he spoke without interruption. When he was finished Sheriff Johnson spoke,

"Please call me Virgil, and I'll call you Ted and Bob if that's all right. To start with, I can't tell you how much your information is going to help me with a case I'm working on. This case is also one of murder and, like you, we have very little to go on. Even though we had nothing solid, it has been my gut feeling that Myra Miller, as we know her, was the perpetrator of a very vicious killing that took place a few days ago."

For the next twenty minutes, the Tates sat silently while Virgil told the tale of the murder of Saul Feinstein. Just as he finished the door opened and Deputy Carla Smith poked her head in and said, "Sorry to interrupt, sir, but we just got a communication from the FBI informing us of a perfect match on the prints we sent them on Myra Miller. They show her as AKA Myra Dillon. She is wanted for murder in New Mexico. There is a warrant for her arrest."

"Wow," Virgil said. "Talk about things coming together!"

By two o'clock they had informed Chief Mundt and the district attorney of the facts of the now fast-moving investigation and with the help of Assistant District Attorney Donna White, had attained an arrest warrant. They gathered two additional deputies to assist with the arrest and taking two cars headed for the Miller mansion, followed by Ted and Bob in Bob's car.

Myra was stretched out on the bed looking at the pictures Dave had taken on their camping trip and Dave was looking out the window. He was watching Jack and Dora in the front yard. Jack was cleaning out a flowerbed and Dora was obviously speaking to him about something. Suddenly, Dave said, "Myra, come look at this."

She joined him at the window and saw two sheriff's cars pull into their driveway so they were blocking both ends of the drive. Virgil and two other deputies were speaking with Dora and Jack. Virgil waved his hand and both Jack and Dora went scurrying across the street towards their home. Another car pulled up and two men in suits got out and stood by one of the patrol cars.

"I don't like the look of this, Myra. I think this bunch is here to give us a problem. I think you had better disappear until I can figure out what they are up to. I want you to go out the back way and follow the creek through the woods to the back of the country clubhouse. Go into the bar and wait for me. I'll sort out what these guys are after and meet you there later."

Without a word, Myra ran to the closet and grabbed her denim jacket and taking the steps two at a time, went down the stairs, through the kitchen and the sun room and out the back door.

After sending Jack and Dora out of harm's way, Virgil sent one of the deputies around the backside of the garage to cover the rear of the house and instructed the other man to cover the kitchen door while he went to the front. Just as they started to approach the house, they heard a shot that came from the back of the house and both men went on a dead run past the end of the garage. They entered the back yard and came up to the side of the gazebo where they could see Myra standing by the stream where she had come face to face with the third deputy. She had fired one shot and the third deputy was lying on the ground at her feet. She was about five feet from the downed man and raised her gun as though she intended to shoot the officer again. Virgil's action was almost instinctive and from a distance of about forty feet he fired one shot and Myra went down.

As they had been instructed, Ted and Bob had remained in the driveway not knowing what was taking place. They heard two widely separated shots from what sounded to Ted like two shots fired from different guns. Several seconds later, the deputy that had gone behind the garage with Johnson, came out from the back yard at a dead run. He went to the patrol car and practically screamed into the mike that they needed an ambulance and that an officer was down.

Ted and Bob hurried around the end of the garage and saw Johnson kneeling beside his fellow officer and not more than three feet away, half in the stream, lay the still body of Myra. They ran to the side of the fallen officer and found he was wounded in the fleshy part of his left arm. He was speaking clearly to Johnson and seemed to not be in a great deal of stress.

"Good God!" Bob said "What happened?"

Johnson replied that she had shot the deputy and was standing over him with the apparent intention of shooting him again, and he was forced to shoot her to stop her from killing the man.

At that moment from the direction of the house, Dave came running and before anyone could stop him, he was on his knees beside Myra, cradling her head in his arms. Tate knelt beside them and saw she was trying to speak.

In a voice that was no more than a whisper she said, "Oh, David, my love, much better than gold." Her body went limp and Tate knew the miracle of her life had ended.

Father and son backed away from the scene and stood watching as Johnson reassured his fellow officer that help was on its way and Dave Miller bent over the small figure in his arms and wept.

Tate was struck by the similarity of this scene and one he had observed nearly a year ago. A person who had died an hour or so before and the one in front of him now, that had passed away in front of his very eyes. They were both lying with their feet in a stream and clutching something in their left hand. In Myra's case it was a small plastic case that contained a bright shiny twenty-dollar gold piece.

Tate felt a sadness that almost brought him to tears. In his long years of police service, he had seen his share of this kind of human tragedy, but none seemed as sad as this. He could hear Dave's mourning cries and felt a deep sense of the man's loss.

He knew that time heals the pain of the passing of a loved one, but would the lost love that he saw here ever know a healing moment?

He wondered.

THE END

Printed in the United States
35961LVS00005B/205-222